check on your happy friends

Endorsements

"As a therapist who holds the sacred, hidden stories of high functioning and "happy" clients who have experienced unthinkable trauma, I found Kathryn's work to be accurate and familiar. I saw my clients, my past self, and my loved ones in Dani, Tommy, and Henry. The depiction of trauma, intrusive thoughts, and the weight of abandonment is written with haunting precision and compassion. Kathryn's storytelling honors the complexity of healing. It can be messy, confusing, nonlinear, and deeply human. This story broke and opened my heart, all at the same time. It also spoke to many of my unhealed and healed parts in the most beautiful way. I won't forget the characters and think about them often."

KARA CRUZ, LMFT, PMH-C
Psychotherapist

"Check on Your Happy Friends provides a unique voice that tackles mental health topics that are often taboo in today's society. The main character, Dani, is captivating as she spotlights a struggle many people face, simply getting up and getting through the day. I found myself reflecting on this book and its characters long after I read the final page. Check on Your Happy Friends is a powerful read for anyone touched by depression. Thank you, Kathryn Inman, for creating a story that reminds us that even in our darkest moments, we are never alone."

MORGAN ROSSITER
Educator

Endorsements

"Kathryn has an uncanny gift with words. Her stories reach deep into your soul, unlock the secrets within, and gently guide you on a transformational journey of hope and healing. "Check on Your Happy Friends" isn't merely a book to keep on your shelf—it's a message to carry in your heart."

NIKKI S. WHITE
Author, "Me, Mom, & Jesus"

"We don't know the struggles people don't share. This book offers an emotionally captivating depiction of what that can look like through the eyes of an abuse survivor, and though fictional, her story is all too real. Whether we're aware of it or not, we ALL know someone who is hurting. We're surrounded by trauma and pain, too often carried in silence and shrouded in shame, but it doesn't have to stay that way! When we truly ask, "How are you doing? How is your heart?", it's amazing what can come from that and how God can work. One person can make a difference. One person can save a life. Will you be that one for someone?"
"Check on Your Happy Friends is an inspiring call to action woven into a heart-wrenching journey through the darkness and isolation of suicidal despair, the power of true friendship, and the hope and healing found in Jesus."

MICHAEL JAMES EMBERGER
Author, and advocate for survivors of trauma and abuse

*even in our darkest moments, **hope** can **break through***

check on your happy friends

a novel by

kathryn mae inman

Bailey & Huhn Publishing, LLC

Check on Your **Happy** Friends

Library of Congress Control Number: 2025950749
ISBN: 979-8-9881060-1-2

Scripture quotations marked (NLT) are taken from the Holy Bible, New Living Translation, copyright ©1996, 2004, 2015 by Tyndale House Foundation. Used by permission of Tyndale House Publishers, Carol Stream, Illinois 60188. All rights reserved.

Scripture quotations marked (NIV) are taken from The Holy Bible, New International Version®, NIV®. Copyright © 1973, 1978, 1984, 2011 by Biblica, Inc. Used with permission of Zondervan. All rights reserved worldwide.
www.zondervan.com

Edited by Michael James Emberger

Cover Design* & Book Layout by Traci Huhn
*Inspired by a concept from Martha Copra

Printed in the United States of America
First Edition, First Printing

Bailey & Huhn Publishing, LLC
Spring, Texas 77380
www.baileyhuhnpublishing.com

Dedicated to Vivian,

You are the inspiration behind this story.

You were a light—bright, kind, and unforgettable.

No one knew the depth of your pain,

but everyone saw the beauty of your heart.

Love remembers. Always.

We only wish you could have stayed.

A Message to Martha

My sister, writing coach, and best friend

since the very beginning.

This book wouldn't exist without you.

It started as your idea—

and you never let me forget that I could do it.

You've cheered me on,

shaped every chapter with your brilliance,

and believed in this story

—and in me—

even on the days when I didn't.

God has woven our lives together for a purpose,

and this book is part of His beautiful plan.

This is ours.

WE DID IT!

I LOVE YOU!

Trigger and Content Warning

Check on Your Happy Friends contains sensitive themes of trauma, abuse, addiction, anxiety, depression, suicide, and human suffering. These topics are described in-depth—including details related to suicide and its aftermath—which may be distressing for some readers. Please know that while the details are included to serve the integrity of the narrative and to portray the subject matter honestly, they may be triggering. If you or someone you know might be affected by the content described, please use caution while reading. Take care of yourself, and seek support if needed. The depiction of suffering in this story is heart-wrenching, but our prayer is that it leads readers to hope, healing, and freedom found in Christ.

Acknowledgments

To Jesus Christ, my Lord and Savior—all I am is forever Yours.

To Darwin Anthony—My husband. My heart. My anchor. Thank you for your unwavering strength and for always believing in me. I could not have done this without you. I love you madly.

To our children and grandchildren—my oldest son Dillon, wife Jessica Ann, and sons Ledger McKnight and Leo DeWitt. My youngest son Justin Dean, wife Amanda Grace, daughters Everly Grace and Emersyn James, and sons Jeremiah Dean and Jeddison Dillon. And to Shaylin, Justin Anthony, Kayleigh and husband Lane. May the light of Christ shine on you all the days of your beautiful lives. I will love you forever with all I've got!

To Dorothy—my mother-in-law, dear friend, and sweetest encourager. Thank you for always being in my corner. I love you so much.

To all my people—family, friends, warrior brothers and sisters in Christ, beta-readers, and the writing community—there are too many of you to list, but y'all know who you are. You make me brave. I love you!

To Heritage Church in Escalon, California—you have truly changed my life. Thank you for boldly teaching truth, for leading with wisdom, and for being a church that lives out the love of Christ. Keep going—we need you more than ever.

To Blake and the Fitness Fanatics family in Modesto, California—thank you for strengthening me physically, emotionally, and spiritually. Your prayers, encouragement, love, and support through this journey mean more than words can say. May God bless you abundantly!

To Mom, Dad, my brother Randy, my father-in-law Don, and all my loved ones in heaven—I love you and will see you again on that glorious day.

To my dear friend, Michael Emberger—brother-in-Christ, kingdom word-weaver, and champion editor. Your love for Jesus, your devotion to your beautiful family, and your passion for survivors of trauma inspires me daily. You believed in this story from the beginning and helped shape it into its best form. A million thank-yous wouldn't be enough, but I offer you all the gratitude in my heart. God is using you in powerful ways, Michael. Keep going—His hand is on you.

To Kari and Traci at Bailey & Huhn Publishing—I prayed, "God send me who I need," and then you came. He faithfully walked us through this journey—and what a journey it has been! Thank you for your love for Jesus, your belief in me, and your steady support and encouragement. Can't wait to see what God has planned next! You have my heart.

Empathy came
and sat down beside me,
not to correct or convince,
but to show me
what I had not yet seen.

She asked me
to take a second look—
beyond the obvious,
beneath the surface,
where lives the unnamed
and unseen.

She invited me to linger,
to remain a while,
not preconceiving,
only present.

With patience, she stayed
just sitting with me,
not judging, not pushing,
simply being.

Quietly, Empathy drew back the veil,
revealing what we seldom explore—
what lives just beyond
what we believe we know.
And there,
Empathy showed me
a hidden door.

by *Traci Huhn*

A Note to Readers

This book was written with a heart surrendered to the Lord. Time and time again, I found myself on my knees in prayer, asking for clarity, direction, and the courage to share what God placed on my heart—and He answered. He faithfully led me through the journey of writing *Check on Your Happy Friends.*

This story moves through loss and tragedy and ultimately lands in hope, though tragically not every story does. Suicide rates remain staggering and continue to rise. According to provisional CDC data, in 2023 alone, over 49,000 lives were lost to suicide in the United States—echoing the heartbreaking, historically high rates of recent years. The need for awareness, support, and compassion has never been more urgent.

I've learned that every journey is different. What works for some may not work for others. If you're reading this book with a heavy heart, having walked through the loss or near loss of someone you love, I am so sorry. Trying to support someone who is struggling can feel impossible—like carrying the weight of the world.

I think it's important to remember that trying your best is enough. You can do everything in your power to help someone you love, but there's no perfect formula for supporting someone who's suffering. And sometimes, despite all our love and efforts, the outcome does not change.

There were times when I couldn't show up for people I loved, because doing so would have jeopardized my own well-being. And there were other times when I showed up again, and again, even when it cost me. Did my actions save anyone? No. Did they help—or possibly make things worse? Maybe.

This story doesn't offer easy answers—I don't believe there are any. But I pray it offers a reminder that kindness matters, showing up matters, and even in our darkest moments, hope can break through.

If you find bits of a loved one somewhere in these pages, or if you've struggled with suicidal thoughts or you're fighting that battle now, know this—there is hope. There is real, living hope that you can cling to. His name is Jesus.

I prayed over this book, and you, my friend, more times than I can count. My heart is with you as you turn the pages.

With love and hope,

Kathryn

Table of Contents

"The LORD is close to the brokenhearted; he rescues those whose spirits are crushed."

Psalm 34:18 (NLT)

1
Trying Hard

I wake up in a complete panic. Roaring assaults my ears. My chest is tight, and I can't breathe. Frantic, I leap out of bed, run to the window, and try to open it, but my hands are shaking so badly I can't get a grip.

A deep groan catches in my throat as I clutch my chest and shove against the sash with all my strength. It sticks—then finally jolts loose just enough for me to wedge it open, press my face into the gap, and gulp down as much fresh air as I can.

Inhale.

Exhale.

Deeper now.

Inhale.

Exhale.

Slower …

In…out…in…out…

Finally, my anxiety subsides, and the rhythm of my breathing slows. Relieved, I collapse onto my sweat-soaked sheets and lie there, staring at the ceiling and replaying my dream…

I'm a little girl with tangled hair and bare feet, sitting cross-legged in front of a broken television pretending to watch cartoons. Frosted Strawberry Pop-Tart® wrappers and crumbs litter the floor. I'm nervous, confused, and hungry. I walk into the kitchen and pull open the cupboard, but quickly slam it shut because it's full of screeching mice. My mother isn't home, and there's a strange man sleeping in her bed—suddenly he's awake and walking toward me—I'm terrified—I try to run but my legs won't move. Screaming screaming screaming but no sound comes out.

And then I wake up.

I've been having nightmares ever since I can remember, but lately, they're happening every night—sometimes multiple times a night. Even though I'm a grown woman and I haven't seen her in over a decade, my mother still manages to torment me just like she did when I was a little girl.

They say you should work through your trauma, but that's not possible for me—mine is attached. It's permanently seared into my skin like a gruesome tattoo. The voice in my head that tears me down is so constant, it feels normal—like background noise I've just learned to live with. Sometimes it screams relentlessly; other times it lies dormant in my brain for weeks. But it's always there ready to crush and belittle me.

I barely slept, but it's already 5:00, and since I have to open the shop in two hours, I might as well get going.

I head for the shower.

No, change of plans.

Coffee first.

I press the button on my coffee maker and stare at it, hoping it might brew faster.

Drip...

Drip...

Drip...

After an eternity, I pour a cup and slurp my first sip. It's a loud, annoying sound, but one of the benefits of living alone is that there's no one around to judge me, so I slurp away.

chapter 1: Trying Hard

The coffee does the trick. The fog lifts, the dull ache behind my eyes releases, and I feel almost human again. I make a conscious decision to let the nightmare go; I refuse to ruminate over a dream that means absolutely nothing.

Two cups later, I'm ready to officially start my day. I head for the shower again.

Before stepping in, I glance at the mirror. Dark circles hang under my eyes. Hopefully I have concealer in my makeup bag, because I'm definitely going to need it.

I study my reflection. My hair looks just like my mother's once did—dark brown, long, thick, and curly. Otherwise, I look like my dad, with olive skin, brown eyes, slender build, and average height. There is nothing special or memorable about my appearance, which is fine with me. I prefer to blend in.

Besides sleeping, showers are another area I struggle with, especially after nights like the one I just had. When memories of my early childhood surface, they make me feel dirty. Not the kind of dirty you can wash off with soap and water, but the shameful kind of filth that never washes away.

I was the weird girl in school who smelled bad and never fit in. The teasing and bullying I endured left a mark that's never really faded—I carry it with me every single day.

As soon as I turn the shower on, the inner voice begins its assault.

DO YOU REALLY THINK YOU'LL EVER BE CLEAN? YOU WON'T. THIS IS WHO YOU ARE, DANIELLE. YOU'RE DISGUSTING.

I turn the water on full blast, pour shampoo over my head, and scrub my scalp. I scrub and scrub, then shift my attention to my body, scrubbing harder. But no matter how much soap I lather on, or how red my skin turns, I still can't wash away the ugliness.

YOU'RE STILL DIRTY. YOU'RE FILTHY!

I yank the shower knob all the way to the left—hotter, hotter, until the water is steaming and scalds my skin. "Stop!" I plead, hating myself.

I'm shaking.

I can't.

I just...

I cry until fatigue washes over me and my manic frenzy ends. I lean against the tile, slide down to the floor of the tub, draw my knees in close to my chest, and wrap my arms tightly around my body, trying to make myself small.

Shivering, I let the cold water beat down on me until I can't take it any longer. I scramble out of the shower, dry off, and face the mirror. It's all fogged up with steam, hiding my reflection.

Good.

I hate my reflection. Always have.

Trying to stay focused, I brush my teeth, wrap my hair up in a towel, and head to my bedroom to get dressed.

An hour, a little makeup, positive affirmations, and a few tears later, I'm finally ready to go. I take one last look in the mirror to check my appearance before heading out, and I'm pleasantly surprised. I still look tired, but much better than I did earlier. I whisper, "thank you" to the brilliant soul who invented concealer.

I scan my apartment three times making sure everything is in order, and three times I conclude that it is in fact in perfect order.

Keys in hand, I pause at the door.

A dark wave is coming. I can sense it.

I squeeze my eyes shut, take a deep breath, grip the doorknob, and wait for this feeling of dread to pass.

Inhale.

Exhale.

Slower and deeper this time.

Inhale.

Exhale.

In.

Out.

/ ## chapter 1: Trying Hard

Steady now, I put on my best smile for no one at all, hop into my car, and venture out into the world.

Just before I merge onto the freeway, my phone rings. It's Mama Sharon. She's my dear friend who happens to be my boss, and she's the owner of Thrive, the plant shop where I work.

I clear my throat, trying to sound okay when I'm not okay at all. "Good morning, Mama Sharon. I'm almost at the shop. How are you?"

"Good, just running a bit late, sugar. How are you doing?"

I change lanes. "I'm great! What's up?"

"Can you manage the shop for me this morning? I have Sammie with me. We're going to get some breakfast before I drop him off, so it might be a few hours before I can make it in. Does that work for you?"

"Absolutely. I've got it, but only if you bring me a coffee!" I tease, trying to sound peppy. "I could definitely use a bit more caffeine, but only if you were planning on stopping at The Café to get some for yourself. Tell Sammie Auntie says hi!"

Mama Sharon laughs softly. "Oh wait, okay, let me put you on speakerphone. He has something to say to you."

Samson, who we call Sammie, is Mama Sharon's four-year-old bonus grandson. We're very close. I adore him!

"Titi?" Sammie says, his little voice sending joy straight to my heart.

"Yes, Sammie!" I respond, smiling from the inside out.

"Will I see you today?"

"Hope so, buddy! We'll see, okay? And if not today, soon!" I picture his sparkling blue eyes, long, golden-brown hair, and that huge smile that spreads wide across his beautiful little face.

"Woohoo!" Sammie shouts. "Soon!"

I chuckle and ask, "How much do I love you?" It's how we always end our chats. It started one day when I asked him that same question, and instead of stretching his arms wide and shouting, "This much!" he looked up at me, his eyes twinkling, and asked three questions in a row: "Every day? All the time? Everywhere?" And from then on, it became our thing. A sweet little ritual that says more than a thousand words ever could.

"You love me every day, all the time, everywhere!" Sammie says, his voice full of sunshine and butterflies.

"That's right, buddy! Every day, all the time, everywhere!"

Mama Sharon takes me off of speakerphone and we both can't help but laugh. Sammie has a way of making everything fun and easy. He is quite possibly the sweetest, funniest, most charming little boy in the world.

"Okay," Momma Sharon says. "I'll see you in a while." She promises to bring me my favorite hot latte—extra shot, with whole milk—and while I'm painfully aware that I drink too much coffee, my caffeine intake is the least of my worries today.

I continue my drive, feeling much more relaxed until something bright hits my eyes and I squint. The sun is peeking up from behind a big semi-truck that's approaching in the oncoming lane.

TURN THE STEERING WHEEL AND SMASH HEAD-ON INTO THE TRUCK.

My heart thumps at the thought. It's horrible!

END IT! YOU'RE NOTHING BUT A BURDEN!

What? I grip the steering wheel hard with both hands. The truck barrels by, and I do my best to focus and drive as cautiously as possible until my exit comes. By the time I finally pull off to the side of the road, I'm a bag of nerves.

What in the world was that? What just happened?

I breathe—in, and out—as terrifying images play like a movie in my mind...

My car smashing into the truck.

The crunch of metal.

Shattered glass.

The metallic smell of blood.

People driving by, watching in horror.

What in the world is happening to me?

chapter 1: Trying Hard

I take a few more deep breaths and finally calm down enough to get back on the road. As I drive toward the shop, I turn the music up loud hoping it will distract me from the horrific images flashing in my mind.

I'm safe. I'm okay. I'm in control.

I'm safe. I'm okay. I'm in control.

I'm safe. I'm okay. I'm in control.

I whisper the words over and over, trying to believe them.

check on your **happy** friends

2
My Happy Place

I'm exhausted. The morning passed quickly, but this afternoon is dragging. I made the mistake of looking at myself in the shop's bathroom mirror, and that's *never* a good idea. The concealer is worn off, and the bags under my eyes are getting deeper and darker by the minute. I'm positive customers are noticing. Sleep deprivation is a real monster. I'm going to lose my mind if I don't get some decent rest soon.

"Dani," Mama Sharon says, snapping me out of my thoughts, "I'm asking a lot of you today, but I need to leave early. Do you mind closing tonight?"

"Sammie again?" I ask, smiling because I know Mama Sharon can't say no to him. I can't either!

She shakes her head. "I wish it were Sammie! But no, I have an appointment. You sure it's okay?"

"Of course!" I say, dreading the idea of being on my feet any longer. "I'm happy to stay and close. I have a lot to do anyway." It's not true, but I don't want her to feel bad for asking.

"Thanks, sugar. Papa Reg will be by to pick up Daisy girl later. I will see you tomorrow."

I give her a little wave. "See you tomorrow. Have a good evening!"

She leaves, and I exhale, happy to finally be alone. I love Mama Sharon, but I'm glad to have some time to myself. There *are* things I can do, but before getting to work, I spend a few minutes with Daisy,

Mama Sharon and Papa Reg's sweet golden lab. She used to be a service dog for their neighbor, Mitch, a retired veteran who suffers from post-traumatic stress disorder. When he had to move in with his son back East, he left Daisy with them—grateful she would be with people who already loved her.

Daisy spends most of her days with us here at the shop. She's adored by everyone in the community, and spoiled by all who walk through our doors. In the rare case that we have a customer who isn't comfortable with dogs, we've got a sign outside that reads: *"Our shop dog, Daisy, is here. We think you'll love her. Not a dog person? No problem. Just let us know."*

Daisy stirs from sleep as I rub her belly, her tail thumping in delight. Her graying muzzle and cloudy eyes show her nine years, but she's still a healthy, happy bundle of energy.

I stand. "Okay, Daisy, here's a treat because you're the best girl!"

She sits, patiently waiting to gobble up one of her Blue Buffalo Health Bars for seniors. Mama Sharon is *very* selective about what Daisy eats.

Daisy devours her treat in less than two seconds, stretches her front legs in a long, easy motion, pauses, and then breaks into a full-body shake that sends loose hairs and dust spraying everywhere. Satisfied, she wags her tail gently and heads to her bed in the back of the shop, where she settles in. That's my cue to get to work!

I start by unboxing our latest delivery of the most fabulous looking sundews. Knowing carnivorous plants are my favorite, Lyle, the owner of the nursery in Half Moon Bay, handpicked these beauties just for us. I make a mental note to bring him a box of cookies as a thank you next time I pick up plants.

As I'm working, my mind drifts to when I first met Mama Sharon and how our relationship has grown over the years. She's always treated me like a daughter, not just an employee, and I'm truly thankful for that. Other than my grandmother, may she rest-in-peace, Mama

chapter 2: My Happy Place

Sharon is the only parental figure who makes me feel genuinely loved. She treats me like family—she *is* my family.

Thrive opened four years ago, and has been a shining treasure in our town ever since. I started following the shop on social media because of my love for plants, and I was excited to visit in person. Mama Sharon greeted me when I first walked in, and I froze for a second. There was something about the way she carried herself that got my attention—tall, poised, and confident. She was dressed in a flowing, colorful print, and had her black and silver hair pulled up in a high bun, away from her face. Her high cheekbones and smooth, deep brown skin made her appear much younger than her 65 years. Mama Sharon's laugh came easy, and her smile seemed genuine. I felt warm and comfortable standing next to her that day, as if we'd known each other for a long time.

We connected instantly, and one thing led to another. I mentioned I was looking for work, she asked me to tell her everything I knew about plants, and before I could even finish, she offered me a job. She didn't bother to look at my resume or check references; she just offered me a decent wage and a consistent work schedule. It sounded perfect, so I said yes on the spot, and started working that same day. I've been working full-time at Thrive ever since.

Business is booming. During the week we get a steady stream of our regulars, and on Saturday mornings it's not unusual to have a line of plant-loving customers waiting at the door. Valentine's Day, Mother's Day, Lunar New Year, Christmas, Small Business Saturday, and springtime are particularly busy. I've suggested we hire more staff, but Mama Sharon is very particular about who is representing her shop, so for now, it's just me, her, and two trusted volunteers. My best friend, Tommy, has a full-time job but manages to help us out with special projects whenever we need him. Our team is small, and it can be hectic at times, but we make it work.

The shop is not large square footage wise, but the high ceiling and giant front windows make it feel open and spacious. The walls are painted a warm white, giving the interior a fresh, clean look. Natural light pouring in and music playing softly in the background create a welcoming atmosphere. Customers often mention that they leave feeling better than when they arrived, and I feel the same. There is something uniquely special about this little plant shop.

I walk the aisles packed with familiar goods. We carry wind chimes, note cards, decorative pots, and a few fantastic smelling soy candles that we keep in the display case, but mostly the shop is filled with happy, healthy plants. We have a large selection of house plants, rare plants, succulents, air plants, and more. Our inventory changes weekly, and we take a lot of special orders from our customers.

Thrive is an amazing place, and it has become my sanctuary. When I started working here, I had recently quit a high-stress, fast-paced job in marketing, and I'd just ended a relationship with a controlling boyfriend. I couldn't take it anymore—the controlling boyfriend *and* the high-pressure job. I was heading for a mental breakdown, so when I received my grandmother's generous inheritance, I was able to take a pause and make some desperately needed changes. Plants are my passion, and I needed to work, so this job was perfect for me.

When I'm here, my breath comes easier. The dark, intrusive thoughts that typically run wild in my head tend to quiet down a bit. In some ways, this job has saved me, because if I didn't have a place to go every morning, I'm not sure what I would do with myself. Isolation is not good for me, and sometimes my apartment feels more like a prison than a home.

I need to lock up for the night, but not before spending a few minutes with Daisy, breathing in her fur that smells like pine trees and sunshine. I love her scent. I love everything about Daisy girl. Sometimes I wish I could take her home with me, but they don't allow pets where I live, so I just treasure the time I have with her at the shop. Even on my worst days—when I'm messy, broken, and empty—

Daisy greets me with tail wags and slobbery kisses. She loves me no matter what.

I stand in the middle of the shop, enjoying the quiet company of these beautiful plants that have become such a joy to me. There's something about the process of tending to them and watching them grow that calms my nerves and helps me focus on something other than my own misery.

The clock reads 9:15, which is late. I have no idea where the time has gone, but I need to get home and catch up on my sleep. I'm wrung out and I long for rest, but I'm not looking forward to another night. I feel sick just thinking about it.

As soon as I sit in my car, my stomach twists into knots, and driving only makes it worse. I stop at a red light and sense a dark cloud of dread hovering over me—it feels like a warning that something terrible is going to happen. So, instead of going home, I head to the gym. I know I won't be able to sleep, so I might as well get in a workout.

check on your **happy** friends

3
Sunshine in December

I'm glad Christmas is over. The weeks leading up to it felt like a whirlwind—traffic was heavy, we had big sales at the shop, and it seemed like there was always something to wrap, clean, or cook, and now, finally, I have a day off.

I didn't bother to get a tree or decorate my apartment. Christmas morning, I ended up at Tommy's. We ordered Chinese food and watched movies all day, and it was fine, but I'm glad to put the holiday behind me so I can get back into some kind of a normal routine.

My phone rings, shattering the quiet. I was trying to enjoy a slow morning, but oh-my-gosh-here-we-go-again. This phone is a constant battle for me. I turn the ringer up high because I'm afraid I'll miss a call or sleep through my alarm, but the truth is I don't *ever* miss calls, and I *never* oversleep because I barely sleep at all! Every time my phone blares it reminds me how my twisted brain turns small, simple things into a big deal. It's ridiculous. I need to turn the volume down, pick a pleasant ring tone, and be done with this nonsense. I'll change it right after this call.

I answer quickly before it rings again. "Hi Tommy."

"What's up?" he asks, sounding extra chipper.

"Nothing much, just enjoying my first cup of coffee. Why are you calling so early on my day off?"

"Were you sleeping?"

"No, I've been awake for hours." I smile. I'm Tommy's person. Early in the morning or late at night, it doesn't matter to him. If he wants to talk, he calls me no matter what time it is.

"Okay, good," he says. "Besides, 8:30 is *not* early. I've basically had a whole day already, and I forgot you were off today. Sorry. Anyway, do you want to go hiking with a group of us? We're shooting for the first Saturday in March if it works for everyone, and I'm checking with you first. You in?"

"March?" I mentally flip the calendar pages. "That's too far in advance for me to give you an answer," I say, honestly. "I'm just trying to get through today."

Tommy is quiet. "What do you mean, *'just trying to get through today?'* Is something wrong?"

IDIOT! The voice inside chastises me. *WHY DID YOU SAY THAT? YOU SOUND DESPERATE.*

"No!" I nearly shout back, then try to play it off like I'm kidding. "I mean, no, everything is fine. It's just that sometimes I have a hard time planning things because it takes all my energy just to get through each day. You know what I mean?"

"Um," Tommy says, sounding confused, "no, I don't. I love planning things! That way I always have something fun to look forward to. You sound down. Want me to come over? Or can we meet somewhere for lunch in a bit?"

HE'S JUST SAYING THAT TO BE NICE. HE DOESN'T WANT TO SEE YOU. WHY WOULD HE?

I take a deep breath and push away the thoughts. "I'm fine, just tired. And no, but thanks anyway. I have to get going and figure out my day."

"Oh!" Tommy exclaims. "That's right. You're not working. If you're tired, why don't you do nothing?"

"I can't waste my entire day off doing nothing."

"Umm, yes you can," he snaps back. "I do it all the time."

chapter 3: Sunshine in December

"I don't think that's allowed, Tommy," I say, sounding ridiculous.

He laughs. "Not allowed by WHO? Do you think someone is going to pound on your door and catch you in the act of doing nothing? You're a grown woman, Dani, who cares?"

I giggle despite myself. He has a point.

"Danielle Vivian, my dear confused best friend, you're always going, going, going. Maybe you need a day of rest. It's easy. You just turn off your phone, stay in comfy clothes—preferably pajamas, relax, eat, and maybe watch a movie or read a book. Then tomorrow will come and you'll feel refreshed. Trust me. It works."

I consider his idea. "Literally, just do nothing? As in not one single thing?"

He laughs again. "Yep. Not a thing. Do it. Please! And then maybe you can commit to going hiking with us. Listen, I'm going to let you go so you can get to your first well-deserved-do-nothing-day. I promise not to bug you until tomorrow. And if you don't have anything good to eat at your place, just have food delivered, because going to the store *definitely* counts as something. Have fun. Love you."

Tommy hangs up before I can respond, leaving me to figure this out on my own.

I know it shouldn't be a big deal, but I've always believed that a "good day" is measured by how much I accomplish. There's a force inside of me—a relentless push toward perfection. I crave control, I must have order, and I constantly measure my worth by how productive I am and how well I perform. I can't rest. I can't let go. Not until everything is done, and it's done right. So, for me, doing nothing just proves that I'm a failure. I'm aware this is not a healthy, rational way of thinking, so maybe I'll give this a try. It might be good for me.

"Okay," I say to an empty room. "If doing nothing is the goal, then that's what I'll do. A whole lotta nothing!"

My mood lightens as soon as I commit. The idea of a day to myself with no expectations or tasks to complete has literally never occurred to me, and for some reason, because it was Tommy's idea, it feels easier to justify.

Out of habit, I start to make my bed, but then stop. It's a do-nothing day. I need to follow the rules. It can stay a mess.

Still in my pajamas and with no intention of changing, I brush my teeth, wash my face, pull the band out of my hair—letting it fall loosely, and then look around my apartment. What's next?

The heater has been on most of the week, but the sun is shining brightly today, so I think I'll venture out onto my little balcony.

Trying my best to channel Tommy, who eats more than anyone I've ever met, I head to the kitchen for snacks. I refresh my jug of lemon water, then check my options in the refrigerator. Since preparing food counts as doing something, I grab what's easy and load my tray with a cheese stick, an apple, three tangerines, and two of Mama Sharon's delicious homemade oatmeal raisin cookies. They're Tommy and Sammie's favorites, so Mama Sharon makes sure we all have an endless supply of them.

Maybe Tommy is on to something, because I feel excited as I grab one of my fleece throw blankets, a small pillow, my headphones, and the latest Vogue magazine and haul them all out to the balcony. It's nice being on the second floor, because I have complete privacy.

It's the last days of December, but it doesn't feel like winter here in sunny California. Living in the Bay Area, we don't experience harsh winters. One moment it might be dull and overcast, but then the sun breaks through the clouds into a beautiful day, like today. It's cold in the shade, but in the sun it feels golden and warm like the tail end of summer. I'm grateful for the sun and what it provides—not just vitamin D, I've learned it also helps your circadian rhythm, immune system, and can be a natural mood booster. I need *all* of it. As much as I can get!

I have privacy, but even so, I double check and make sure there's no one around as I step out of my pajama bottoms, pull off my top, and settle onto my blanket in just my underwear.

A blissful feeling washes over me. There's something freeing about lying out here in the quiet with my hair down, a freshly washed face, and my bare skin exposed to the cool air and sunshine. This is actually lovely, and easier than I thought it would be.

I plow through most of my snacks, sip on my lemon water, flip through the pages of Vogue, and surprise myself by dozing off. When I wake up, billowy white clouds have filled the sky, but it's still warm enough, so there's no hurry to go inside.

As I peel the last tangerine, something about it sparks a memory of a day when I was in first grade:

It was picture day, and I remember waking up extra early—too excited to stay in bed. I remember standing over the bathroom sink pouring water on my hands and using it to slick down my poofy hair as best I could. I can see myself digging through piles and piles of dirty clothes until I find my favorite purple dress with yellow roses. I didn't have any socks that fit, so I slid my bare feet into my worn-out tennis shoes. The scratchy insides rubbed against my skin. When I looked in the mirror, I smiled at my reflection. I remember feeling proud of myself, and thinking I looked pretty.

As usual, my parents didn't pay the fee or complete the forms, but my teacher, Mrs. Wallace, who was always kind to me, allowed me to have my photo taken anyway. When the photographer told me to say "cheese," I was ready. I tilted my chin up proudly and smiled my biggest smile.

After the pictures, and right before we were dismissed for the day, Mrs. Wallace brought out snack bowls like she always did on Friday afternoons. Sometimes they were filled with mini packages of graham crackers, and sometimes my favorite cheese sticks, but on this particular day she gave us tangerines. I remember my mouth watering because I hadn't eaten, and I was hungry.

I grabbed two and quickly peeled them with my teeth. As fast as I could, I bit off pieces of the bitter peel, spitting them out onto the table as I went. I was in my own world—happy about my pictures, and excited to get to the juicy fruit inside my tangerines.

I didn't peel them with my fingers like everyone else—I didn't know any better. The kids sitting at my table noticed how I was eating and began to tease me. They said I was eating like a pig. They called me dirty and weird. I remember my eyes dropping down to the floor in humiliation. I sat there frozen in my chair, wanting to disappear.

When I looked down, I saw stains on my dress that I hadn't noticed before. I remember seeing dirt under my chewed up fingernails and quickly stuffing my hands into the pockets of my red sweater so no one else would see.

I remember how it felt when I realized, for the first time, that I was different from the other kids. I was dirty, and I was NOT pretty. Even though my mother called me awful names, my dad always told me I was a pretty girl, and I believed him. My vulnerable heart shattered that day. I felt betrayed, and I didn't understand why my dad would lie to me. The shame was crushing.

Tears fall as I do my best to shake off the memory. It still hurts to think about it. I had a horrible early childhood, but I can't allow those thoughts to ruin this perfectly beautiful day.

Clouds have filled the sky and there's a chill in the air, so I pop the last tangerine slice in my mouth, throw my pajamas on, and haul everything back into my apartment. The kitchen clock reads a little after four. How has the day gone so fast?

I open the refrigerator and rummage for something more substantial to eat. What can I have that doesn't require effort to prepare?

My phone dings. It's a text from Tommy: "Hi. It's me, not bothering you on your do-nothing day. Open your front door right this second. I had to because I knew you wouldn't."

He *had* to? Curious, I rush to the door and find a brown bag sitting on the mat. It's warm and the smell makes my mouth water. He brought me food! I swear, it seems like Tommy has access to my brain

chapter 3: Sunshine in December

and can read my thoughts.

I plop down on the couch and rip the wrappings off a loaded veggie burger and large order of sweet potato fries—extra crispy. I pop a few fries in my mouth and dig a little deeper into the bag, hoping Tommy remembered, and he did! A container of ranch dip and three packets of yellow mustard make this a perfect meal. He knows me so well.

As I'm devouring my food, thoroughly enjoying every bite, I think back to younger me staring at a mess of tangerine peels and taking a lashing from my schoolmates. Those hateful words deflated me like a pin to a balloon. My soul withered and withdrew into the shadows that day, and I hated school after that. I absolutely *hated* it.

Without thinking, I rip off a thick shred of skin next to my thumbnail, causing it to bleed, and immediately regret it. I need to stop picking and shredding my cuticles. It's a horrible habit. I hold my hands out and inspect them. Hideous. I'm disgusted.

I dump the burger and fries on the coffee table. My appetite is gone.

Why didn't my parents provide for me? Why didn't they teach me proper manners so I didn't eat like a scavenger? The more I think about it, the more vivid the memory becomes, and it rattles me. My stomach churns and nausea grabs me by my throat. The smell of food is too much, so I quickly wrap up my leftovers and put them in the refrigerator. Maybe I'll have them tomorrow, but right now I need to settle my stomach.

I boil water, fill a mug, and drop in two lemon ginger tea bags, letting them steep while I lie down on the couch.

I close my eyes.

THEY DIDN'T PROVIDE BECAUSE YOU WEREN'T WORTH THE EFFORT.

My throat constricts at the accusation, and I have to swallow, trying not to vomit.

WHY WOULD THEY BOTHER WITH SUCH A HORRID LITTLE GIRL?

"No!" I curl up against the pain. I tell myself over and over to stop thinking about it. It's in the past. I'm okay. I'm okay. I'm okay.

I sip the tea, repeating my affirmations, and after 20 minutes I feel better. Thank goodness.

Needing a reset, I get up and tell myself to focus on a task. "Just do something, Dani. Anything! Get back on track!"

I remember my phone and grab it, lower the volume, and listen to several ringtones, considering my options. I decide on "Island Pulse – a tropical, laid-back melody with smooth rhythms." It sounds like peace and sunshine. Perfect.

While I'm thinking about it, I send Tommy a quick text: "This is me not messaging you on my do-nothing day. Thank you! I'm still in my pajamas. Not kidding! It was a great day, and the food hit the spot. You are the best!"

Tommy gives my message a heart emoji. I'm sure he'll call tomorrow morning wanting to hear all the details. I'm excited to tell him because I really did enjoy myself, but I'll leave out the part about my tangerine fiasco. Why would I ever share that with *anyone?* It's a humiliating memory that's been floating around me all afternoon as if I'm supposed to do something with it. I need to let it go. Just let it go.

Despite it all, it was actually a good day. I might have to do this again.

Apparently "doing nothing" is exhausting, because it's only 8:30 and I'm ready to turn in for the night. I can't remember the last time I crawled into an unmade bed, and have to fight off the sudden urge to make it.

It's time to loosen up a bit!

I glance in the mirror as I'm brushing my teeth. A soft blush of pink is spread across my face and chest. Looking closer at my reflection, I don't hate what I see. I might even like it. The sunshine and nap were good for me. I look more rested, and my skin looks pretty and refreshed.

chapter 3: Sunshine in December

YOU'RE UGLY, DANIELLE. YOU'RE A SLOPPY MESS, the scolding inner voice hisses back.

All the air whooshes out of me. I'm so sick of this! My heart is racing, so I take a second to gather myself and get back in control.

"I'm okay. Everything is just fine," I say as I search my apartment, for what I have no idea.

"I'm okay. It's fine. I'm okay."

My eyes feel heavy as I trudge into my bedroom and crawl underneath the covers. I take deep breaths, inhaling and exhaling slowly until the panic subsides. I'm relieved, but I'm sensing my relief is temporary. Something is stirring, and it's not good. It's just a feeling, and it's probably nothing, but if it is something, whatever it is, I hope I survive.

check on your **happy** friends

4
You are Beautiful

After weeks of struggling with sleep, I decided to move my futon into the closet. It might sound strange, but sleeping under a bright fluorescent light in a small space works for me. Nights are always tough, but being in a smaller space makes me feel more protected from the darkness that presses in when I close my eyes. I want to sleep. I *need* to sleep. But it seems impossible, so I'm learning to function on very little.

Last night was particularly brutal. I slept fitfully for just a few hours and then the night terrors became so real and vivid that I was scared to even try to go back to sleep. I got up, turned every single light on in my apartment, and sat on the couch drinking coffee and scrolling through social media until sunrise. Not okay, I know. All it did was make me feel worse. They say comparison is a thief of joy, and last night's scroll through social media took every ounce of mine. For hours I watched reels of flawless bodies, glowing skin, happy couples, perfect houses, perfect smiles, perfect love, and perfect lives. I know it's a distorted view of reality, but it still hits hard and leaves me feeling empty—like I don't belong in this world.

Nights are a literal nightmare, but mornings are getting increasingly difficult for me. I hate myself for allowing painful rituals to take over my life. I can never just leave my apartment; I have to check everything three times before I can even open the door and step outside. And I don't just take a shower; I scrub my skin raw because I feel dirty. And it's not just that my place is tidy, it's impossible for me to do *anything* until everything is clean and orderly. People think I'm easy-going, happy, and full of life, but that's not who I am.

I'm a complete mess.

I'm a fake, and my nightmare life is getting worse and worse.

I often wish I were dead, but I try to counter those thoughts by doing things that make me feel better. I've tried it all—early-morning walks, gratitude journaling, grounding, meditation, cold plunging, and more. Sometimes those things work for a little while. Other times they don't, and I'm left trapped in the chaos of my mind, which is the last place I want to be.

But even though I'm quietly falling apart, I still show up every day and drag myself through it—smiling when I should smile, laughing at all the right moments, and acting like I'm fine. I'm exhausted from pretending, but I don't really have a choice.

"Okay, Dani. It's time to get going. You got this!" I say, cheering myself on for the day.

It rained most of the night, so the air feels fresh and earthy this morning as I'm walking to my car. On the drive to work, I put my windows down and listen to one of my favorite playlists—a mix of Hamilton, The White Stripes, and Red Hot Chili Peppers. The music and fresh air seem to do the trick because by the time I arrive at the shop, my mood has lightened, and I'm ready to get to work. With the specials we're running, I expect it will be a busy day. I hope it's busy because I want to be distracted. I *need* to be distracted.

It's still early when I arrive at the shop, so I run across the street to The Café to get coffee for me and Mama Sharon. Henry, The Café manager, greets me with a brilliant smile.

"Your regular?" he asks.

"Yes, and a tall Americano for Mama Sharon. Thank you!"

Henry has our coffee ready in minutes, then puts a few muffins and pastries into a bag and hands it to me. "This is for whoever is working at the shop today, on me," he says with that smile again. Wow, this guy.

With coffee and goodies in hand, I walk back across the street to Thrive and notice the parking lot is empty, which means Mama Sharon hasn't arrived yet. I prefer being the first one here. It gives me a chance to take a breath and get my head straight before we open.

I hear a tap on the front window just as I'm starting to organize the shelves. I glance at the clock. We still have 30 minutes. Then I look to see who's tapping. It's a man. He's tall, with a muscular build, dark hair, and an impressive beard. I wave at him, smile, and point to the clock.

Impressive beard guy looks at it, then back at me, and then puts both hands together as if he's pleading with me to let him in. He seems harmless, and the shop is pretty much ready, so I do what anyone would do when a customer needs something. I bounce up and unlock the door.

"Good morning!" I say in my brightest I-am-not-sleep-deprived voice, then instantly wonder if I put enough concealer under my eyes.

Impressive beard guy faces me. Does he notice?

"I'm hoping to impress my new girlfriend," he says.

"Oh?" I didn't expect him to get to the point so abruptly.

"With a plant," he adds. "I want to buy her a plant."

The "new girlfriend" part relaxes me a bit. Not that he would be interested in me, and I'm certainly not looking, but he is *definitely* my type.

"Okay, well you've come to the right place! My name is Danielle, and I can help you find the perfect plant for your new gal." I try to smile confidently, but I'm certain it comes off as awkward.

YOU ARE AWKWARD, the inner voice says, waking up. *YOU'RE DISGUSTING.*

Beard guy smiles. "Cool. I appreciate this so much, Dani. My name is Gabe."

Impressive beard guy has a strong name—it suits him. Interesting that he jumps right to calling me Dani. Do I like that? I think I do.

HE FEELS SORRY FOR YOU. YOU'RE PATHETIC.

"Nice to meet you, Gabe. Now, tell me about her," I say, trying to shake off the ugly whispers in my mind.

Gabe follows me into the shop. "She's interested in environmental issues, animal rights, and all that stuff. She has a garden, and she grows her own vegetables. Definitely into health and fitness. Um, let me think of what else. Oh, for plants—she has a small house with huge windows, so lots of natural light. Does that help?"

My response is genuine. "Yes, it does help. What's your price range?"

He shrugs. "I'm not worried about what it costs. I just want her to love it."

My breathing comes a little easier—he seems like a nice guy. I just need to help him find a plant and not think about anything else!

We mosey around the shop together, considering options for his girlfriend. This guy is not what I had in mind when I was hoping to be distracted today, but I'm not complaining. The inner voice is quiet as I focus on the plants, and I'm grateful for it.

I point at a stool. "Okay, I have a few ideas. Take a seat here, Gabe, and let me show you what I'm thinking."

Gabe perches on the stool, which makes us eye level. His are green—a detail I didn't notice when he walked in. I show him a few options and save the best for last.

"This staghorn fern is one of my favorites. The cool thing about it is that it's an epiphyte plant. In nature, you'll find it growing on trees. The price is $59.00. I recently saw one at a botanical garden up north that weighed over 100 pounds! They're pet-friendly, fairly easy to care for, and quite extraordinary."

Gabe smiles. "Did I hear you say it's one of your favorites?"

I smile too. "You *did* hear me say that."

I avoid eye contact and keep my gaze on the plant. I can feel him looking at me, and I'm embarrassed. I must look pathetic to him.

"Then I'll take it!" Gabe says. He seems excited, and I'm happy about that.

"Great! I hope she loves it. I'm going to wrap her up for you, so give me a few minutes. We have blank cards over there if you want to include a note."

Gabe selects a card and takes it over to the counter. I prep and wrap the plant, and notice he hasn't written a single word.

He seems at a loss, so I offer, "I would keep it simple, something short and sweet."

Gabe nods, but his pen still isn't moving.

I walk over to where he's sitting. "Tell me what you're thinking of saying and I'll help if I can."

He looks relieved. "I was thinking something clever. Maybe 'I hope our relationship grows just like this plant.' What do you think? Does that sound okay?"

I look at him with my head cocked to the side, one eyebrow raised, trying to keep from laughing. He's got to be joking!

He's not, judging by the genuine confusion on his face.

I clear my throat and regain my composure. "Oh boy, you're serious? Okay, sorry. Maybe something a bit more subtle? How about, 'A beautiful plant for my favorite girl!'"

Once again, Gabe looks relieved. He writes the exact message I suggested, word for word. "That's perfect. Thank you!" he says, looking pleased.

I ring him up, and he's all set to go when Mama Sharon strolls in with Daisy by her side. Mama Sharon glances at our customer, looks back at me, and raises her eyebrows.

I shrug. I know what she's thinking. He's handsome and I'm single, which is true, but he has a girlfriend and I'm a disaster, so none of it matters.

Mama Sharon smiles brightly at Gabe. "Good morning to our first customer of the day. Are you finding everything you need?"

"Yes, ma'am," he says. "Absolutely. Dani's been a life saver."

"Wonderful!" Mama Sharon says. "Come back and see us again!" She gives me a knowing look, then disappears into the back room, but Daisy doesn't follow. She's too busy bouncing around Gabe's feet.

Gabe crouches down, letting Daisy sniff and slobber all over him. "Oh hey," he says in that talking-to-dogs voice, "who are *you*? Hi! Oh, did you want to say hi to me? Okay, come here girl, aren't you sweet!"

"I'm so sorry," I say, trying to pull Daisy back. "She doesn't usually pounce on new customers like that!"

But Daisy is not having it. Her entire body wiggles in delight as Gabe ruffles his hands through her fur.

Mama Sharon comes from the back room. "Daisy, come."

Daisy does as she's told, her tongue hanging out in a sloppy grin as if she's pleased with herself.

"There's a coffee on your desk!" I yell to Mama Sharon.

"You're an angel!" she yells back, leading Daisy away.

I turn back to Gabe. "Sorry about that. Daisy doesn't usually get so excited."

But Gabe seems just as pleased as Daisy did. He laughs. "Oh, no worries. She's great! I love dogs, especially labs. I have a black lab at home."

He's smiling proudly—no doubt, this man is a dog person.

We make our way to the door. "All right," I say. "Thank you, and please don't hesitate to reach out if your girlfriend has any questions. Tell her to call or message me, and I'll be happy to help however I can."

Gabe starts to walk out, but then stops and looks at me. "Dani," he says, "may I tell you something personal?"

I cross my arms. "Okay..."

His expression seems sincere. "I hope this doesn't come across the wrong way, but there's something about you, Dani. You're beautiful.

I mean, I'm sure you've been told that a million times, but there's more than that. It's your kindness, your voice, the way you light up the room. I don't know what it is exactly, but it's special. And I just felt like I should tell you."

My cheeks burn, and I'm suddenly embarrassed. Why would he be saying this to me? I feel like a fool standing here.

"Aww, so kind of you. Thank you, Gabe," I say, trying to steady my voice so I don't look like a total idiot.

He seems to sense something, and gently steps back, giving me space. Our eyes meet, and I can feel heat rising in my chest.

YOU'RE PATHETIC. HE FEELS SORRY FOR YOU. HE'S JUST SAYING THAT TO BE NICE.

My eyes blur with tears, and I'm mortified. Am I that hungry for scraps that I need a stranger with a girlfriend to tell me I'm beautiful?

I'm the first to break eye contact, then take a step back. "Okay, charming first customer of the day, thanks so much for coming in. I hope she loves it!"

I hold the door open for him. He hesitates for just a second and then smiles, softly this time.

"Have a good day, Dani," he says. "I'm sure she'll love it. Thanks for everything."

My gaze falls to the floor, but as soon as he leaves, I turn to watch him walk away, releasing the breath I didn't realize I was holding.

Mama Sharon must have heard the door shut, because she rushes in beside me, watching him too. "Well," she says, "who's that handsome guy that looked more interested in you than the plants!" She's all smiles, and I can tell she's quite amused.

I'm smiling, despite myself. "Stop. He was shopping for his new girlfriend. But he *was* kind of cute."

We both giggle, but inside I'm reeling—I need a minute.

"Hey, Mama Sharon, I'm going to take a quick bathroom break before we get busy. Is that okay?"

She nods. "Take your time."

I head to the bathroom in the back and lock the door behind me. Hesitantly, I stand in front of the mirror, trying not to pick myself apart for once. When Gabe told me I was beautiful, I know he didn't mean it, but I want to try to see myself through his eyes. I take my time looking at my hair, my face, my neck, and my shoulders. I turn to the side and check my profile. I smile, frown, and look at myself from all angles, trying to imagine what people think of me.

I whisper to my reflection, "Not bad. You're not hideous. Everything is okay. Right here, right now, everything is fine." I close my eyes, hoping to hang on to this feeling.

HE DOESN'T THINK YOU'RE BEAUTIFUL, the inner voice whispers. *NOBODY DOES. DON'T KID YOURSELF.*

I do my best to shake off the ugly thought and get back to work.

The hours fly by and Thrive is hopping! I hand out cake pops, crayons, and plant-themed coloring books to six cutie-pie kids who come in with their parents. I adore little ones—seeing their faces light up fills my heart.

Two elderly women come to pick out plants for their women's BINGO group. They're so delighted with the succulents and with how I help them that they both give me a hug.

A rare plant collector stops in and is thrilled to see our Monstera Deliciosa 'Mint.' She buys it on the spot and leaves her number so I can call her when we get more.

Dozens of customers come through the shop and buy a ton of plants, and we have one of our best sales days ever. We don't even get to take a lunch break, but that's fine by me, and Mama Sharon is ecstatic.

After Gabe left, I managed to stay present for the rest of the day and didn't ruminate on anything negative. I'm beyond exhausted, but it's been the best day I've had in quite a while.

We clean up the shop and prep for tomorrow, then sit together for a few minutes giving our feet a rest before heading home.

chapter 4: You are Beautiful

Mama Sharon looks at me thoughtfully. "You're wonderful, do you know that? I've never met anyone like you, Dani. You know how to make people feel special. Those kids left here feeling like they had a new best friend, and the two ladies from the BINGO group were delighted with you. And my Samson? He thinks you hung the moon—your relationship with him is so special! You have a gift with people. I mean that sincerely. You were radiant today as you were busy helping our customers. You're a beautiful young woman, Danielle, inside and out!"

I look at Mama Sharon and say the first thing that comes to mind. "You're the second person who's told me that today."

"Told you what?"

"That I'm beautiful."

A knowing smile spreads wide across her face as she gets up to leave. "Oh, he'll be back, sugar. You mark my words—he may have a girlfriend, darlin,' but he ain't married yet!"

Her laugh is deep and booming, and it catches me off guard. A snort escapes me, and soon we're both laughing so hard we're in tears. I haven't laughed like this in months!

Mama Sharon wipes her eyes with a pretty floral handkerchief she always keeps in her pocket, rolls her shoulders, takes a deep breath, and then reaches out and hugs me tightly. "Okay, now, that's enough excitement for one day. Let's go home and get some rest. I love you, sugar. I'll see you tomorrow. Come on, Daisy girl. It's time to go."

I rub Daisy's ears and plant a kiss between her eyes. "See you later, pretty girl. Love you, Mama Sharon. Thank you for a wonderful day. I'll see you tomorrow."

Happiness bubbles inside of me as I walk to my car, and it makes me feel insane. What in the world is wrong with me? One minute my anxiety is raging, the next I'm laughing like a lunatic. I'm filled with hope, and then I'm filled with dread. I catch myself enjoying life, but then I want to disappear. Everything takes effort, even breathing, and I'm just so tired of it. I need to sleep, but I don't want to go home and face another night alone. I'm terrified of dying, I'm terrified of living, and I'm terrified that I'll never have another good day like this one again.

5
The Café

Tommy's late and I'm crunched for time, so I send him a text: "Hey, are you close? Message me what you want, and I'll order our food so it's ready when you get here. I have to be back at the shop by 1:00."

His reply comes within seconds. "Yep, on my way. Sorry, I got held up. French dip with extra aww juice, fries, and a coke please."

I burst out laughing as I type my response. "Umm, it's au jus. LOL."

"Not to me, it's not! #awwjuiceforever."

"What's so funny?" Henry asks, startling me. I didn't hear him walk up.

"Oh, hey, I was just laughing at my friend, Tommy, who is ridiculous. Busy today, huh?" I look around The Café, which is humming with activity.

Henry nods. "Yep! Business has been great lately and our new cook is phenomenal. Just you for lunch?"

"No, I'm waiting for Tommy. But I'm ready to order for both of us. I have to be back at the shop by one."

"Okay, no problem. I'll let the cooks know. What can I get for you and your friend?" Henry's charming smile spreads wide across his face.

"French dip and fries for Tommy, with a coke, and he'd like extra au jus, please. And for me a Caesar salad with salmon, and an iced tea. Thanks for putting a rush on it."

"Of course! Hey, I wanted to let you know that I won't be here early tomorrow just in case you were planning on hanging out before we open. I don't want you sitting in the parking lot alone. Oh, and you left this when you were here this morning." He pulls my pen out of the pocket of his apron.

"Hey!" I respond, as I take it from him. "There it is. This is my favorite pen! I've been looking all over for it. Thank you, and thanks for letting me know about tomorrow. I really appreciate your kindness. It's been nice to be able to have my coffee here in the peace and quiet before work." I say, grateful for his friendship and for this place that always feels so warm and comfortable

"It's my pleasure. You're good company," he says, then turns and heads toward the kitchen.

Finally, Tommy walks in the door. Our eyes meet, and I wave him over. Tommy is handsome in his own way. He's medium height, on the lean side, and has great taste in clothes. He has a prominent long nose, a fabulous smile, and a slightly crooked front tooth which only adds to his charm. His eyes are always a bit puffy as if he just woke up, and his eyebrows are raised high, like he's in a constant state of surprise.

"Sorry I'm late," he says. "I'm starving! Please tell me you ordered for us."

I notice the dark shadows under his eyes. He looks tired. "I did. It should be ready soon. Are you okay?"

"Cool. Yep, I'm good. So, what's up? My life is boring, so please tell me something exciting happening in yours."

"Well, not much exciting going on with me. Just work, the gym, my usual stuff. Oh, but I do have something kind of fun to tell you. Yesterday, a ruggedly handsome guy came into the shop and told me I was beautiful, so THAT made my day."

Tommy's expression brightens. "You *are* beautiful, Dani. You're the only one who doesn't see it. Did he ask for your number?"

"No, he didn't, and even if he did, I wouldn't have given it to him. He's a complete stranger. Besides, he's taken. He was shopping for a plant for his girlfriend." I smile as I think of Gabe and wonder if she was happy with the plant.

"Okay. Well, tell me when you're ready to *actually* start dating again, because I have a whole list of dudes who would LOVE to go out with you." I watch him scan the room. He seems fidgety.

If he only knew what I go through—dating is the last thing on my mind.

YOU'RE A MESS. The inner voice tears into me. *NO ONE WANTS TO DATE YOU.*

Henry walks up to the table with plates full of delicious food. With eyebrows raised, he looks at me and points a finger toward Tommy. "Ridiculous friend?"

"Yep! That's the one," I say, laughing. Something about Henry puts me at ease.

Tommy looks confused. "What did I miss?"

Henry ignores the question. "Hi, I'm Henry, the manager here. Any friend of Dani's is a friend of mine. It is a pleasure to meet you."

Tommy shakes his hand, friendly as ever. "Thanks, man. I've been here twice now so I'm happy to finally meet you too! Dani loves this place and the food is fantastic."

"Wonderful! Enjoy, you two. Let me know if you need anything else." He turns to me. "You have about 15 minutes to eat, my love, so get to it!"

"My love?" Tommy whispers, leaning over the table as Henry walks away. "That's kind of bold, isn't it?"

"I think he's just a tender-hearted guy. I know how it looks, but it's not like that. For months now, I've been coming here almost every morning before work. But yeah, sweet nickname, right?" I smile because it *is* sweet. Henry is a true gentleman.

"Hmmm, okay, if you say so," Tommy says, shoveling food in his mouth. "He seems like a good guy—I think you might have a crush on him."

"Stop..." I give him a don't-tease-me-like-that face. "He's just a friend and a lovely human. For real. Is your food good? Mine is."

We devour our food in just ten minutes. It's *that* tasty. Just as we're finishing, Henry stops by our table again, surveying our empty plates.

Tommy looks down at his, which is licked clean, and grins. "I didn't care for mine."

"Had to choke it down, eh?" Henry asks, playing along.

Tommy smiles. "Dude, it was so good! I'll be back for sure. Thanks, man. Everything was great."

"Brilliant! I'll let the cook know. He's new, so he'll appreciate it." Henry turns to me. "Be safe, and take good care, my love."

A flicker of something dark passes through Henry's eyes, but he walks away before I can place it.

Tommy pays the bill, I leave a generous tip, and we walk out of The Café together, arm in arm.

I whisper, "Did he seem okay to you? He's so charming, but he seemed different when he said goodbye. Sad or something."

"I have no idea," Tommy whispers back. "I don't even know the dude."

I dismiss the thought as we make our way across the street so I can go back to work and Tommy can get to his car.

He stops me. "I'm bummed you didn't notice my new kicks. They're Jimmy Choos. How could you NOT notice? They're sooooo clean!"

I swear, Tommy loves shoes more than most women I know. "Oh wow," I say. "Can't believe I didn't notice either. Love those on you!"

I mean it. They ARE cool.

Out of the corner of my eye I notice Tommy reach into his coat pocket, pull out a handful of white pills, pop them into his mouth, and start chewing.

"What were those?" I ask, hoping they were mints.

"Adderall," Tommy says, matter-of-factly.

"You're chewing Adderall, Tommy? Are you kidding me? I thought you gave that up?"

chapter 5: The Café

He shrugs. "They work faster when you chew them. I figured that out a long time ago. I have a ton of work today, and I need help focusing. And yes, I did give it up. But then I started again, and now I'm weaning back off. I'm trying. I'll be fine." He gives me a quick hug and takes off down the street.

No wonder he was fidgety and looks so tired. Tommy has battled drugs most of his life. He works hard and functions quite well, but he's always struggling with something, and now I guess it's Adderall. I hate it. I wish he would stop. I make a mental note to check in more often and see if he wants me to go with him to an AA or NA meeting. I can't believe he's popping Adderall like its candy. This is NOT good!

Pushing my worries about Tommy aside, I rush to the shop, eager to get back to work.

"I'm here Mama Sharon!" I shout as I walk in the door.

She looks up from her phone. "Okay, great! It's been slow since lunch. If it stays that way, will you do a once-over and take a quick look at all the plants I just shelved? I inspected each one, but some are bone dry, so please water them. And let's be sure to turn the humidifier on tonight, okay sugar?"

I nod. "You got it! Enjoy your afternoon with Papa Reg, and I'll see you in the morning."

Mama Sharon smiles and starts to leave, then stops. "One more thing. If you go to The Café later, will you ask Henry if we can use his back room for interviews next week? I have a few folks interested in volunteering, and I'd like to meet with them there if he has a room available."

"Will do! I'll probably get a coffee around 3:30, so I'll ask him then."

"Perfect. Thank you. I'll see you in the morning."

Mama Sharon walks out the door and I get right to work, grateful to have the shop to myself. I check the soil, water where needed, wipe the leaves, dust the shelves, and rearrange the plants to make sure each one gets sufficient light. Since it's still slow, I take the opportunity to clean the windows, organize the card display, and tidy up the restroom. Finally done, I take a step back and admire my work. The shop and plants look spectacular. Go me!

Our intern, Chandra, drops in to pick up a plant, so I seize the moment. "Chandra, do you mind watching the shop for five minutes so I can run across the street?"

"No problem. Take your time."

"Can I get you a coffee, or a snack?"

"Nope," she says. "I'm good. Thank you."

Coffee sounds fantastic right now, and I need to ask Henry about the room, so I head back to The Café for the third time today.

Apparently, it's a slow afternoon everywhere. We haven't had a single customer at the shop since lunch time, and The Café is empty, except for a young lady sitting alone at the corner table, sipping coffee and reading a book. I don't see Henry anywhere, so I ask Veronica, who's sitting at the register thumbing through a magazine.

"Henry around?"

"He's doing paperwork in the back. Feel free to go check, he won't mind." Veronica's voice is warm. I love this café. Everyone is so kind to me.

Walking quietly so I don't disturb him, I head through the kitchen, take a right down the dark hallway to Henry's office, and peek through the window before I knock, just to make sure he's not on the phone or in a meeting.

I see Henry. He doesn't see me, but the look on his face paralyzes me. I want to run, but my body won't move, and I can't seem to look away. His expression is haunted. Vacant. Hollow. As if he just witnessed something horrible. Something is terribly wrong. I need to get out of here!

I slowly step away from the window, then race back out to the front as fast as I can.

Slowing my steps, I take a long, deep breath and try to compose myself before rounding the corner.

chapter 5: The Café

Inhale.
Exhale.
Inhale.
Exhale.
In.
Out.
Now walk in, breathe, breathe, breathe, you're fine, everything is okay.

"Did you find him?" Veronica asks.

I'm shaken to my core, but I try my best to sound lighthearted. "No, I changed my mind. I have to be somewhere, so I'll just send him an email later. It's no big deal, we just want to use the back room next week. Thanks, Veronica!"

"Sure," she says, then returns to her magazine.

I leave and feel terrible for not walking in and checking on Henry to see what was wrong, but I couldn't. It was too much. He looked empty and distraught, and I connected with it—I *felt* it. Henry always seems so happy. I can't imagine what he's going through for him to be in that state.

Thoughts flash through my mind in rapid fire:

What kind of evil is he facing?

What has he done?

Maybe he has a dark secret that's been exposed.

What horrible thing has happened?

Seeing Henry in that state torpedoes me into a frenzy. It takes every ounce of control I have just to function. I thank Chandra for her time and finish my tasks while my insides are churning into knots. My hands tremble as I write an email:

"Dear Henry,

I saw you today. What happened? What have you done? PLEASE TELL ME! Whatever you saw that unraveled you, I've seen it too. I know the same horror and darkness. There's a dread inside of me that I can't shake. I try to ignore it and act like I'm okay, but I'm not okay, Henry! I never sleep. I'm tormented and living a lie. Are you? How do we make it stop? What happened? Please be okay. I'm sorry I walked away. I'm so sorry. Love, Dani."

I press the backspace button and watch the curser erase every word that will never be read or spoken, because there's really no sense in it. Henry and I are worlds apart—all we have between us is The Café.

I stare at the blank page, then rewrite the email:

"Hey Henry, any chance we can use your back room for volunteer interviews next week? Wednesday through Friday in the afternoon would work best for us. Let me know when you can. Thank you! Dani."

The front door opens, and it startles me. It's Mama Sharon's husband, Papa Reg, who is a mountain of a man with big hands, a big voice, and an even bigger heart.

"Hey honey, how you doing?" he asks.

"I'm fine, Papa Reg," I say, trying to steady my voice. "How are you?"

"You sure?" he asks, studying me.

YOU'RE A COWARD, the inner voice screams. *YOU SHOULD HAVE CHECKED ON HENRY.*

"Oh, yes. I'm fine. Just a busy day is all. Did you come to get Daisy girl?"

On cue, Daisy saunters up to Papa Reg, lays her paw on his foot, and stares up at him while her tail thumps on the ground.

He reaches down and rubs her ears. "Okay, old girl, let's get you home."

Papa Reg smiles, we say our goodbyes, and the day comes to an end.

Closing goes quickly this evening. Once I'm finished and the alarm is set, I sit in my car before heading home.

Today rocked me, and I need a minute. I turn the heater on, make a Thrive post on social media, pay my phone and utility bills online, and do some photo editing—anything to keep me from replaying what I saw.

My phone pings with an email alert that sends me reeling. Henry's name is in my inbox.

I panic—did I delete the first email?

I did, didn't I?

DID I SEND HENRY THE RIGHT ONE?

My heart lurches in my chest as I open his message:

"Hi. Of course. You're welcome to use the room anytime from 2:00 until closing. Let Veronica know if we can provide refreshments for you. Be safe, and take good care, my love. Henry."

I read his reply four times for no reason at all, then head home, wondering why we're all falling apart, and what could be haunting this beautiful man.

check on your **happy** friends

check on your **happy** friends

6
When Everything Hurts

I ruminate on the same unanswerable questions:

What is wrong with me?

Why can't I sleep?

Will I always be this way?

Why am I like this?

WHY AM I LIKE THIS?

By the time I get to the shop, I'm a frazzled mess. It takes everything I have just to put one foot in front of the other and show up in the world like I'm supposed to. It was a rough night, and to make matters a whole lot worse, I'm out of coffee.

I'm already depleted, and I've literally done nothing except go through the agony of getting myself ready for work while fighting with the inner voice that's been screaming in my head all morning. Even though I would like nothing better than to drive somewhere far, far away, I have to go to work. It's much easier said than done, but I'm doing it. I have no choice. Mama Sharon is counting on me, and I will *not* let her down.

I arrive at the shop 30 minutes early, which gives me enough time to run across the street and get coffee before I start. If I'm going to function, I *must* have caffeine.

I think of Henry as I'm walking toward The Café. I still can't shake the image of him sitting in his office with that haunted look on his face, and I feel horrible that I saw him like that and just walked away. I can't imagine what happened.

When I pull on the door, it doesn't give. It's locked, which is odd. I take a few steps back and glance at the parking lot. There's not a single car. The rack where Henry always parks his bike is empty too. Very strange. I know today is not a holiday, and if they had to close for some reason, I would think they'd leave a note.

I peer in the window. Everything is dark and still except for the shiny chrome blades of the ceiling fan slicing through the air.

I'm a bit worried, but mostly frustrated that I still don't have coffee. There's no time to go somewhere else, so I drag my caffeine-deprived-head-pounding self back across the street to the shop.

Before I can get the door unlocked, two customers walk up. I'm guessing they're mother and daughter. The woman is attractive and wearing a bright floral skirt, boots, and an oversized, pretty, cream-colored sweater. The teenage girl is wearing all black, and she does *not* seem thrilled to be here.

I greet them. "Good morning, ladies! Please come in. Give me just a second to put my things away and I'll be right with you." I try my best to ignore the growing pressure behind my eyes which I'm certain is because I haven't had a single drop of caffeine.

As I'm putting my things down by the register, I overhear the mom talking.

"Now listen," she says, her voice strained, "I know you're annoyed that I made you come with me, but it's going to be great. You can pick out any plant you want! It will brighten up your room and be fun for you to take care of, okay? Please, honey? Let's just try to have a good day."

I glance up and see the girl looking at the ground. She doesn't respond, and the silence feels heavy. It's probably a good time for me to lighten the mood and introduce myself.

"Thanks for waiting," I say, smiling. "I'm so glad you're here!

chapter 6: When Everything Hurts

My name is Dani."

The mom looks relieved. "Hi Dani, so nice to meet you. My name is Beth, and this is my daughter, Gracie." She offers me her hand. I shake it, then turn to her daughter, who stands motionless, her eyes cast down to the floor.

"Nice to meet you both!" I say, determined to make this a fun experience for them. "How can I help you today?"

I notice Daisy looking at Gracie. She gets up from her bed, pads over, and sits right beside her.

Beth watches Daisy, then turns to me. "We're looking for a plant for Gracie's room. Something she can watch grow and take care of. Right Gracie?" Her eyes plead for some kind of response.

I give it a few seconds, and when the silence feels like too much, I jump back in. "Okay, cool. Let's look around and see what we can find. And Gracie, let me know if Daisy is bothering you. She's a sweet dog—I think she likes you."

"I need to use the restroom," Gracie whispers, her eyes still fixed on the ground.

"Sure. Through those double doors and to your right."

I watch as Gracie slowly makes her way to the back. She's wearing dark, baggy clothes, and she looks unkept, as if she hasn't showered.

I turn to Beth, and I'm surprised to see tears running down her cheeks.

"I'm so worried about her," she whispers. "I didn't know what to do, so I convinced her to spend some time with me today and we ended up here. I've tried everything, but I can't get through to her. I'm afraid she's given up. She seldom comes out of her room anymore, she's barely eating, she won't talk to anyone, and when she does do something, it's with a group of girls who are just awful to her. I feel so helpless."

I lay my hand gently on her shoulder, trying my best to comfort this person I've known for all of five minutes.

"I'm so sorry," I say, and hand Beth a tissue. "I was a total wreck when I was a teenager. We all go through phases, and this might just be a tough one for her, but she'll get through it. I think a plant is a wonderful idea, so I'm glad you came in today. It's going to be okay."

I say the words with more confidence than I feel, but they seem to help, because Beth wipes her eyes and stands a bit taller.

She sighs. "I'm so sorry for unloading on you like this, I'm just a mess today. I haven't slept well in weeks because I've been so worried about her. Thank you for listening, and being so kind."

I nod empathetically. "Please don't apologize. It's fine. And by the way, I'm a total mess and *never* sleep, so you are not alone!"

Beth laughs softly, and I do too—the tension eases for a moment.

Gracie returns with her black hoodie pulled down low over her face.

"Okay, ladies, let's see what we've got here," I say, searching the room for the right plant. I lead them through the aisles. Beth follows eagerly. Gracie shuffles behind us, her gaze pinned to the floor.

I ask her, "Gracie, can you give me an idea of what you have in mind?"

No response.

"Okay, um, do you have pets?" I'm trying my best here.

Gracie shakes her head.

"Okay, what kind of lighting do you have in your room?"

She looks away, silent.

Seconds pass—she doesn't answer.

Beth sighs softly. "She has big windows and gets lots of light and morning sun."

"Great. One more question. Do you want something easy to care for or a plant that might require more attention?"

I look at Gracie, then Beth, back and forth, waiting.

"It doesn't matter," Gracie whispers, so soft I barely hear her.

I show her spider plants, a blooming peace lily, succulents, pothos, and a few more, but nothing seems to catch her attention. I rack my brain, and then it comes to me.

"Hold on, I have a plant I think you'll love, Gracie!" I say with genuine excitement as I run to the back and grab the greenest, most vibrant carnivorous plant I can find. Everyone seems to be fascinated by carnivorous plants, so maybe Gracie will be too.

I choose a spectacular Venus flytrap, grab a pair of tweezers and a container of mealworms from the refrigerator, then bring them out to the front where they're waiting. "Okay, my friends, come join me at the table."

Gracie and Beth follow, and for the first time, I can see Gracie's eyes. They're a stunning ice-blue. Even though she's pale and looks exhausted, I can see how striking and delicate her features are.

I purposely don't make eye contact, hoping she'll follow along. "This is my favorite carnivorous plant, the Venus flytrap. It closes its traps like jaws when prey touches tiny trigger hairs. It's kind of creepy but fascinating! Here, Gracie, why don't you feed her."

She reaches for the tweezers, and I'm shocked. Beth exhales loudly, as if she's been holding her breath.

This is good.

As Gracie nervously places the worm inside the trap, the sleeve of her oversized sweatshirt slips down to her elbow, exposing dozens of cut marks on her forearm.

My heart sinks down to the basement of my chest. *Oh, sweet girl, I've tried that, and it doesn't help. The relief is only temporary. I am so sorry for your pain.*

Beth and I watch in silence as Gracie studies the plant. Her movements are fluid—eyes focused and body more relaxed. It isn't much, but it's something!

I glance at Beth. She's smiling.

After a few minutes, Gracie hands me the tweezers and I watch her eyes fall to the Band-Aids on my fingertips. I quickly move to conceal them, and she looks back down to the floor.

SHE SAW, the voice in my head taunts. *SHE KNOWS HOW MESSED UP YOU ARE.*

I try to hide it, but I pick and pick and pick at my cuticles until they're raw. It's disgusting! Why do I mutilate them? Why is she cutting? Where is our pain supposed to go?

"Do you want this one, Gracie?" Beth asks with a tinge of excitement in her voice. I'm thankful for the distraction.

Gracie nods, and it's the smidgen of hope her mom needed. The tension in Beth's face fades—she instantly looks years younger. Her smile is a burst of sunshine, lighting up her entire face.

The sight of it wows me. Beth is hanging onto her daughter's every word. Clearly she would do anything to help her. I can't imagine that kind of love.

"Wonderful!" I say, feeling grateful for the tiny breakthrough. "You're going to love this plant, Gracie. Let me get her ready for you."

I prepare her plant, slip my card and a care instruction sheet into a bag, grab a jug of distilled water from the back, load them up with everything, and walk them to the door. Gracie doesn't look up, but instead of the floor, her eyes are now fixed on her new plant, and I count that as a win.

Beth hugs me tightly, as if we've known each other for years.

"It will be okay," I whisper in her ear, knowing full well it may not be.

She nods against my shoulder, then lets go.

I'm filled with sadness, envy, and a wave of emotions that confuse me. "Please come back and see us anytime," I say, my words brighter than I feel, "and don't hesitate to call if you have questions. My card is in the bag."

They leave, and my heart aches. *Isn't her love enough, Gracie? I would have done anything for that kind of attention from my mother.*

chapter 6: When Everything Hurts

Lost in thought, I watch them walk away, my thumb brushing over the tiny scars on the inside of my forearm from years ago when I used to cut myself. I remember the relief it brought me in the moment, but the self-loathing that came after was assaulting. When everything hurts, you'll try *anything* to feel better, even slicing into your own skin. I really hope Gracie will be okay. She has a mother who obviously loves her, and that counts for something.

My phone vibrates, snapping me out of my thoughts. It's a text message from Tommy: "Hey. I'm bored. How can I make your day better?"

"If you bring me coffee it will make my whole *life* better!" I respond, eager to finally have some caffeine.

"I'll be there faster than a speeding bullet!" Tommy responds, lifting my mood. He has a way of shifting me out of the darkness, and I'm grateful for it, especially today.

I tidy up the shop, make some phone calls, clean and fill Daisy's water bowl, organize the business emails, and stay busy, trying my best not to think about my horrible mother, the haunted look on Henry's face, my shredded cuticles, and Gracie's scars.

It's been 30 minutes since Tommy sent the message. What could be taking him so long?

Ten minutes later, he comes barreling through the door. "Hey, okay," he says, talking a mile a minute, "that was not faster than a speeding bullet, it was slower than a snail crossing the freeway, but it wasn't my fault. I went across the street to get coffee from your friend Henry, but The Café is closed, so I had to go all the way back across town. Do you know what the family emergency is? Is everything okay over there?"

"Coffee first, please," I say, taking the cup from his hands and savoring the first, delicious hot sip. "Ahhhhhh yes. Finally. Thank you. Wow, this tastes good." I close my eyes, feeling the warmth of the caffeine take hold. "And yeah, I don't know why they're closed, but how do you know there's a family emergency?"

"There's a sign taped to the window," Tommy says while stuffing his face with the biggest, flakiest, most delicious-looking golden-brown croissant I've ever seen. My stomach growls just looking at it, and I can't remember when I last ate.

Daisy notices the croissant too. Tommy grins, rips off a generous piece, and feeds it to her before I can say a word—flaky crumbs scattering everywhere.

"Tommy!" I say, frustrated, "you're not supposed to do that! How many times do we have to tell you? Mama Sharon has made it clear we're not to give Daisy people food—the vet said she's overweight."

"Eating and not sharing is rude," Tommy says, continuing to enjoy the forbidden croissant with Daisy. "Plus, look how happy she is! Right, Daisy girl?"

I hear the front door swing open. It's Trish, our trusted volunteer, who's here to help organize our back room. Her timing is always exquisite.

"Hi Trish!" I greet her. "Hey, do you mind watching the front for a few minutes? I just have to run across the street really quick."

"Sure. Take your time. I got you," she says without bothering to look up. We love Trish.

"Come on, Tommy," I say. "Let's go check out the sign. I have no idea what's happening over there, but I hope everyone is okay." I'm feeling a little anxious all of a sudden. Has something bad happened?

Our timing is perfect, because my friend, Veronica, who works the counter, is walking out of The Café just as we're walking up. I'm instantly relieved. She'll know what's going on.

"Hi Veronica!" I say as Tommy and I get closer.

She turns to face us, and my heart drops. Dread rolls over me and I can tell that something is terribly wrong. Her eyes are red-rimmed, and she looks pale, as if she has seen an actual ghost.

chapter 6: When Everything Hurts

I run to her, my chest tight. "Veronica, what is it? What's happened?"

She falls into my arms, sobbing, and I know my heart is about to be shattered.

"It's Henry. He killed himself. He's gone, Dani!"

check on your **happy** friends

7
If It Were Me

It's been three weeks since Henry took his own life. He worked a full shift that day, said goodbye to his co-workers as if everything was fine, then went home, got a rope, and hanged himself.

Nobody knows that I saw him in his office through the window that same day. I should have done something. *Anything!* I could have walked in and checked on him, or let Veronica know that he was not okay, but instead I did nothing.

What kind of horrible person just walks away?

I keep playing the day over in my mind...

When he gave me my pen back—did he know he was going to end his life? I've literally been holding on to the pen since hearing the news. Rolling it in-between my fingers, trying to sort out the details...

Is that why he told me he wouldn't be there the next morning?

At lunch with Tommy, when I saw a flicker of something in his eyes, why didn't I go back and ask him about it? I should have. I SHOULD HAVE!

That look on his face—is that when he decided?

How long had he been planning this?

From what I understand, Henry's older brother, Grant, found him. There was no note, or anything that would explain what happened or why he did it. He was very much alive, and now he's gone, and no one will ever know why.

Everyone is in shock.

And he did not prepare for it. They say Henry's house was filled with all his belongings. He had clothes in the washing machine and dishes on the counter from his breakfast that morning. Veronica told me he had eaten cereal and fruit—Quaker® Oats, blueberries, and a banana to be exact. I can picture Henry with his curly dark hair hanging down over his forehead, probably still wet from the shower, as he crunched on his cereal and scrolled through his phone.

I can't believe he's gone.

He hanged himself.

How could he?

Grant is trying to get Henry's financial affairs in order, and friends and family are busy sorting through all his belongings so they can get the house emptied and ready to sell as quickly as possible. I'm sure nobody wants to walk in that garage ever again.

Tommy is the closest I have to a real brother, and I cannot imagine walking in and finding him dead. The thought turns me inside out.

YOU COULD HAVE HELPED HIM, BUT YOU DIDN'T. YOU'RE TO BLAME. WHAT KIND OF SPINELESS COWARD JUST WALKS AWAY? YOU, DANI. YOU'RE PATHETIC.

Since it happened, my inner voice hasn't given me a moment's peace. I feel horrible. Just horrible! We were friends, and I cared about him—how could I do nothing?

I've been thinking about Henry nonstop since it happened. Other than our visits at The Café, I didn't know much about him, but we had a special connection. I started most of my days there, with him. I used to park outside The Café and wait for them to open, then early one morning as he was walking in, he noticed me waiting in my car and waved me inside. I told him I had trouble sleeping and didn't want to sit at home alone, so he encouraged me to come for coffee as early as I wanted to—he was always there by 5:00 in the morning. After my first visit, he had my coffee waiting for me—a large hot latte with whole milk, extra shot, and a glass of water, hold the ice.

Sometimes we talked, other times we sat in a comfortable silence, but we always enjoyed our time together before the doors officially opened at 6:00. I never saw Henry outside of The Café, but I told him things about myself that I've never told anyone else, because I felt surprisingly comfortable around him. I'm just now realizing, though, that Henry never told me *anything* personal. He was such a good listener, it never occurred to me to ask him questions about his life. Regret stings. How selfish of me. Henry was always smiling and seemed cheerful, so I just assumed he was happy.

LOOK IN THE MIRROR. YOU'RE NO DIFFERENT.

I flinch at the thought. Others probably do think the same about me...

But Henry? Was there no other way? What will I do in the mornings now that you're gone? I'm sorry. I'm so sorry I let you down!

Today is the day of Henry's "celebration of life," and I decide to wear black—it seems fitting.

As I'm getting ready, I get a text message from Tommy: "Which?"

His question is followed by two pictures: the first is him with his hair down, and in the second his hair is slicked back into a ponytail.

I text back, "Second one. A ponytail looks more formal."

"Excellent. I thought so too. I'll be there in 15 minutes."

Tommy is funny. Every time he does something different to his hair or buys new clothes, he sends me the text, *"Rate the look. And be honest,"* and I always respond decisively. Tommy loves fashion and has always put a lot of thought into his appearance—I think my opinion gives him more confidence. It seems silly, but maybe it's just another way we look out for each other.

I'm picking my cuticles and picking myself apart in the mirror when my phone buzzes with another text—Tommy is here. He's waiting for me downstairs, so I move quickly through my apartment, trying my best to hurry while I'm checking and rechecking things. I grab my sunglasses, stuff some tissues in my purse, lock and double check the door three times—always in threes—then head down the stairs to the parking lot.

Tommy is standing beside the passenger door of his truck, holding it open for me. He looks handsome in his dark gray suit and crisp white shirt. He did not want to go with me today, but I talked him into it. He's my person, and he'll do just about anything I ask, but he's also sensitive. He doesn't handle sad things very well, and I'm not sure what could be sadder than a beautiful soul like Henry taking his own life.

PEOPLE WILL MISS HENRY. THEY'D BARELY NOTICE IF IT WERE YOU, the inner voice whispers.

I struggled with guilt and questioned if I should even attend the services today, but I decided to go because I think Henry would want me there, or maybe I'm just curious to see what happens. Whatever the reason, it's too late to back out now. We're going.

Tommy gives me a quick side hug before I slide into my seat. He closes the door behind me, races over to the driver's side, and hops in.

"You look nice," I tell him. "I really appreciate you coming with me today—it means a lot."

He starts the truck and looks at me thoughtfully. "Of course. I'm so sorry about your friend. It's horrible. I only met him once, but I liked him. I'm just so sorry it had to end this way. I've never been to a suicide funeral before. Ugh."

"Me neither," I say, with dread.

We both exhale loudly, mustering the strength to get through this.

When we pull up to the church, the parking lot is packed, which surprises me for some reason. I guess I felt like Henry was my friend exclusively; just the two of us sitting in The Café morning after morning, but I'm happy to know there are a lot of other folks who cared about him as well.

Tommy opens the door for me and locks his arm in mine as we walk in. I appreciate being able to lean on him, because I'm feeling a chapter 7: If It Were Me

bit shaky. I don't think Henry's death has fully hit me yet.

I can't believe he's gone.

With my hand tucked in my pocket, gripping the pen Henry returned to me, I wait in the back of the room while Tommy looks for two seats together. He weaves between the rows and waves me over. We're a lot closer to the front than I want to be—I prefer to blend in and not be noticed, but every other seat is taken, so the second row will have to do.

We settle into our seats, and I quietly take a few deep breaths, bracing myself as Henry's brother walks up to the pulpit. He looks like Henry, but his head is shaved clean. His eyes are bloodshot, and he seems so distraught I can barely watch him speak.

When he adjusts the microphone, his hands are shaking.

"Hi friends," he says, and then stops. His lips press together hard, and his expression tightens. His pain must be unbearable. It hurts to watch.

He takes a deep breath. "Um, listen, there's a lot I want to say, but I just can't find the words right now. My brother, Henry, was my best friend. He was my hero, and I wanted to be just like him. I thought he was happy, so I'm confused. I don't know why this happened. He had everything going for him. What did we miss? How did I not know? I don't get it!"

He pounds his fist down on the pulpit, then pauses, wipes his eyes, and tries to compose himself. My heart breaks for him. I can tell it's taking every bit of strength he has to continue.

His face shifts from anger to defeat, and I wish he would just stay angry—he looks helpless now, and it's heartbreaking. This man is a complete stranger, but I can almost feel the toll this is taking on him. It's too much. I should have done something!

"I'm sorry," he says. His voice is softer and cracks with emotion as he tries again. "Look, I just want to thank everyone for helping my family and showing up today. It would have meant the world to Henry to see you all here, and it means a lot to me too. God bless."

He leaves the stage and takes a seat next to an elegant woman I assume is his wife. She's wearing dark sunglasses, and it's clear that she's struggling. These people loved Henry. It's obvious how devastated they are.

I'm devastated too.

It's starting to sink in.

Next up is the pastor, and I wonder what in the world he's going to say to us.

He places a Bible on the pulpit and opens it to a bookmarked page. "Hello, dear brothers and sisters. Thank you for being here today as we gather with heavy hearts, mourning the loss of Henry James Santos, a beloved son, brother, uncle, and friend." He pauses, and seems troubled. "Henry's life has been cut short in a way that is deeply painful and difficult to understand. In moments like these, we struggle with questions about suffering, love, and faith, and we wonder what happened. We don't have all the answers, but we must trust and know that God is still in control, and even though we may never understand Henry's suffering or what happened in his last moments, God does. God understands the depths of human suffering in ways we cannot imagine. God is with us, and we will get through this together, as a community."

I glance around the room. Everyone is in tears and Tommy is sobbing. I rub his back gently, trying to comfort him, and realize I haven't shed a single tear. I think I'm still in shock.

"I need to say something," the pastor continues, "and I want to be clear about this. For anyone here who might be wrestling with guilt, please hear me: it's not your fault. The weight you might be carrying, the questions in your mind, and the guilt that tries to settle in—none of it belongs to you. Supporting someone through their pain is incredibly hard. You can love them deeply, and still not be able to stop their suffering—and that does not mean you failed. Sometimes, our love, prayers, and best efforts aren't enough to change the outcome. As we grieve, we can release the burden of guilt and rest in God's grace. And finally, my people, let us remember Henry for the wonderful man he was and the joy he brought to our lives, and let it bring comfort knowing that Henry is finally at peace. He is at rest, and no longer suffering."

The pastor keeps talking, but I don't hear what he's saying. My brain hit the brakes on that last sentence—"He is at rest, and no longer suffering."

The pastor reads a few Bible verses and finishes the eulogy, then the lights dim and the slide show begins. My breath catches in my throat as Henry's smiling face fills the screen. He looks joyful and carefree, as if he didn't have a single worry.

In slide after slide, I watch Henry with his family and friends—images of him with his two nephews at Disneyland, with his brother at the ballpark holding a beer up to the camera, at the ribbon cutting ceremony for The Café, playing baseball, fishing, camping, the finish line at a marathon, and more. In every picture, he looks the same—happy and full of life. There is no hint of suffering.

How did I not see his suffering? Can people see mine?

By the time the slide show is over, Tommy and I are both overwhelmed. We say goodbye to the few people we know from The Café, and I wait in the hallway while Tommy uses the restroom. He's distraught, I can see it. He doesn't do well with death, but I wasn't expecting him to fall apart like this.

I scan the room, looking over the crowd trying to figure out who's who. Everyone looks weary, and I notice they're all comforting each other. I spot a woman who I'm sure is Henry's mom. She has curly hair like his, but it's completely gray. She's ghost-like pale and looks small and lost. We're standing close enough that I can smell her perfume; a musty fragrance that reminds me of my Grandma.

Two young men walk by. They look grief-stricken like everyone else. The tall one leans in and rests his hand on his friend's shoulder. The shorter guy breaks down—his friend tries to console him as he weeps.

It's eerily quiet for a place that's packed with people. The air feels thick and heavy. Shock, grief, and disbelief paint the faces of Henry's loved ones. Eyes are swollen and red-rimmed, some staring blankly, as if they're stuck in a nightmare. Some people bow their heads, their faces clenched in silent pain, and others seem disoriented, as if they've been betrayed.

Finally, Tommy comes out of the restroom looking a little better. He points at the door, and I fall in line behind him for the walk to the parking lot, relieved to get out of here. I suggest we stop for a drink before we go home, and Tommy agrees. Neither of us is ready to be alone just yet.

We arrive at the corner restaurant and walk into the bar. I find a booth while Tommy gets our drinks. It's good to sit and catch my breath—I feel like I just got tossed around by a tornado. Out of habit, I start digging at my nail beds, but quickly stop myself and tuck my hands tightly under my legs.

STOP! YOU'RE IN PUBLIC. SUCH A DISGUSTING HABIT.

I close my eyes, take a deep breath, and reset.

Inhale.

Exhale.

Inhale.

Exhale.

In...

Out...

As I start to calm down, the image of Henry sitting in his office flashes in my mind, but this time he's looking straight at me—his eyes dark and empty.

My heart lurches and a chill shoots down my neck.

"Hey, are you okay?" Tommy asks, his voice jolting me back.

chapter 7: If It Were Me

"Yea, sure, just a little rattled." The words are tight in my throat.

"You were shaking your head," Tommy says, "and you look pale. Are you sure you're all right?" He slides next to me in the booth and places two glasses of red wine in front of us. I'm grateful for the distraction and take a big gulp, not tasting it, trying to calm down.

I sigh. "I'm okay. I just feel awful."

"Me too," Tommy says. "That was an actual nightmare." He raises his glass to mine. "Here, let's toast to Henry."

Tommy looks as worn out as I feel, and I wonder if he'll ever get over this. I wonder if either of us will. I think going was a mistake.

Tommy leans forward, elbows on the table, his eyes filled with tears. "That was a lot to take in. I feel like it changed me."

I'm instantly curious what he means.

I ask, "How so?"

Tommy gazes out the window as if he's searching for words. "I guess, it's just... I don't know, it's just so incredibly heartbreaking! He seemed so alive and now he's gone. It makes me want to make some changes and start living instead of just existing. Sometimes I feel like I'm on a hamster wheel and I'm not going anywhere. I just work, go home, and scroll through my phone, get to bed too late, wake up tired, go to work, and do the same thing over and over, every single day. Did you see his pictures and all the places he's been?"

"I did. It was wild to see that side of his life, because all I knew about him was at The Café. It was obvious Henry had a loving family and lived a fulfilling life, which makes his death even more confusing, right?"

Tommy nods. "Totally. I don't get it. What would make someone do that? How bad does it have to be to end your own life? I mean, even if I was suicidal, I wouldn't choose that way of going out, ya know? It's crazy. He had a good job, owned his own home, and obviously had a lot of people who loved him. He seemed to have it all. But no one knew! They didn't see any signs. But like they say, you never know what people are going through."

I take another sip of wine, my thoughts racing. *You have no idea what I'm going through, Tommy!*

"Yeah," I say, "it's hard to understand. But maybe he really is at peace, finally, like the pastor said."

Tommy shrugs. "I think they just say that to make people feel better. How can he be at peace after *that*? Oh man, I feel wrecked." He looks like he might break down again.

"Me too. I'm just trying to make sense of it," I say, fresh out of words.

"I know. But it *doesn't* make sense. Life sucks."

Tommy looks heartbroken, and I hate it. I say, "Yeah, it sure does," because it's the truth.

"Right?" he says, with passion in his voice. "I just can't shake the image of his brother trying to speak—it's burned into my brain. Henry just destroyed a lot of people's lives, you know? His brother will *not* come back from this."

I feel suddenly protective of Henry. "He didn't want to hurt anyone—I'm sure of it. And maybe it was just too much, and he couldn't take it anymore. Maybe he thought the world would be better off without him."

Tommy stares at me for a long time.

"No," he finally says. "I disagree. I think it was a selfish thing to do. His brother will be haunted by this forever, and what will he tell his kids? That Uncle couldn't take it anymore, and he just decided to check out? They're little kids! Can you imagine if *you* did that, and they had to tell Sammie? It's tragic! I mean, it's bad enough to take yourself out, but not leaving a note seems cruel. They'll never know why. Don't get me wrong, I can't imagine how bad it had to be for Henry to do this, but the whole thing is just awful."

If I did that… *Sammie. Sammie. Sammie. My sweet little bear. I love you every day, all the time, everywhere.*

"That poor family," I say, lost in my thoughts. "Eventually they'll move on from this. They have no choice."

"Hmm," Tommy says. "I know, it's just not that easy for me, Dani. Anyway, let's stop talking about it. My head is pounding, and I don't want to think about it anymore."

We toast to Henry one more time, drain our glasses, and head home, exhausted.

Before I get out of the truck, I ask Tommy a question. "So, how *would* you do it?"

He stares at me with a confused expression. "How would I do *what?*"

"If you were ending your life, how would you do it?"

Tommy considers my words. "Well, I'm trying to overlook the fact that your question is super creepy, and I thought we agreed to not talk about this anymore, but for sure I'd take pills and overdose. I'd be too scared to try anything else. What about you?"

I'd shoot myself.

"I'm not sure, I haven't given it any thought," I lie.

"Good." Tommy looks at me, his eyes pleading. "Please don't think about it. Let's just focus on ways we can live our best lives, okay?"

I nod. "Okay. Great idea. And thank you for coming with me today. I probably shouldn't have asked and put you through that, but I don't know how I would have made it if you hadn't come."

"You're welcome," he says. "Try and get some sleep, I'll talk to you tomorrow. Oh, and Dani? I'll always be here for you. We have each other, and we can tell each other everything. Right?"

I nod and smile. Tommy holds his fist up and I give it a quick bump, then push my tired self out of the truck and trudge up the stairs to my apartment, feeling instant relief when I walk through the door. From my kitchen window, I give Tommy a quick wave so he knows I'm safe inside, because otherwise he won't leave.

Once he's gone, I drop my things, run to the refrigerator, and take everything out to make a veggie sandwich. I pile the cheese on, squirt heaps of mustard on both slices of bread, and add lettuce, tomato, cucumber, avocado, and pickles for added crunch. I grab a bag of Flamin' Hot Cheetos® that Tommy left, and a peanut butter cookie, and take my feast to the couch where I polish off every bite. I can't remember anything ever tasting so delicious.

I don't know what's come over me, but something is stirring inside, and I'm confused by my appetite and sudden energy.

The pastor's words dance in my mind: *"Henry is finally at peace. He is at rest and is no longer suffering."*

I sigh, and wonder what that might feel like—rest, peace, and no more suffering. Maybe I did Henry a favor by running away and not saying anything. Maybe Henry did the only thing he could do for himself. But if it were me, I would have left everything in order, and I definitely would have written letters to my loved ones.

8
Church

It's a chilly, blah, overcast Sunday morning. The clouds are blended into one massive blanket that spreads wide across the sky without even a hint of sunshine. Just flat, dull gray as far as you can see. These kinds of days are not my favorite, and if I could, I would curl up with a book and not speak to a soul, but I know that's not good for me, so I invite Tommy to breakfast instead.

I should have reached out to him sooner, but Tommy can be clingy, and I haven't been in the right mindset to handle "clingy Tommy." Since Henry's service, something has shifted. I don't know if it's me or if it's him, but we haven't talked much or spent any time alone together in over a month, and that is not like us.

I decide to break the ice—if there even is ice—and send him a message: "Hey, champion, good morning!"

He responds in seconds: "Hey, superstar, good morning to you!"

I smile at his text. It's reassurance that he's not upset with me. I should probably just call, but texting takes less effort.

I send another message. "What's good?"

"Everything. What's good with you?"

"Woke up hungry. Do you want to meet at Dino's for breakfast? I can already taste the pancakes. Please say yes!"

"I'm starving but sorry, I can't this time."

"Bummer. Why can't you go?"

"I'm busy."

I'm getting curious now. "I said PANCAKES, Tommy! Busy doing what?"

"I'm on my way to church."

"LOL. For real, what are you doing?"

"I AM for real. I'm going to church."

"Wow! What church and since when?"

"It's called Freedom Church, and I've been going since the weekend after Henry's service. Want to come with?"

I stare at his text in disbelief. Why is he going to church all of a sudden? I *knew* he would struggle after the service. I should *never* have asked him to go! I feel bad. This is my fault. I always screw things up.

"Helloooooo?" Tommy, being impatient as usual, texts me again because I didn't respond fast enough.

I type back, "I'm sorry, I can't make it to church. Why didn't you tell me you've been going?"

"We haven't talked much since the service. Want to meet for an early dinner? I have a lot to tell you."

"5:30 at the barbecue place in the plaza?" I respond, even though the thought of going to a restaurant during the dinner rush sets a storm off in my head—it's the last thing I want to do.

"Perfect. I'm gonna order either ribs and coleslaw or chicken tenders and fries. Maybe both. Woohoo! Grab our table if you get there first. Love you. Bye."

I send a final text. "Love you. See you soon!"

I miss him. Tommy is 34 years old and still acts like a playful little boy, and I love that about him. He literally gets excited over anything—food, a good song, when he sees a ladybug or a dragon fly...

My phone beeps with another text from him: "JESUS LOVES YOU!!!"

Welp, here we go again! Sounds like Tommy is on yet another kick. I should have known. I swear it's *always* something with him. A new girl he's fallen madly in love with, a dog he rescued that he can't live

chapter 8: Church

without, a new workout supplement he claims has changed his life, or a new business opportunity that's going to make him millions. Tommy is just that way. He's always searching for something, and I guess this time he found Jesus. I don't want to discourage him, but I know this is just another phase and soon he'll forget about church and move on to something else.

It's hours until I meet Tommy, and my stomach is growling, so I scan my refrigerator for something tasty, but there's not much to pick from. I grab an apple and save my appetite for dinner. I haven't been to the gym in two days and I'm feeling antsy, so I decide to take a run. I slip on my running shoes and head out the door to the high school football stadium that's just two blocks away. With my ear buds in and the volume turned up, I start jogging at an easy, warm-up pace, and head to the track.

There's not a soul in sight. Awesome.

I take the bleacher steps two at a time, pushing myself as hard as I can. I run up and down the bleachers six times and take five laps around the track, pushing and pushing until I run out of steam. I can feel the sweat dripping down my back as I sit on the stairs, guzzling water, trying to catch my breath. I'm suddenly grateful for gray skies and cool weather; sunshine is overrated.

It's already 3:30, so I hurry back home to get showered and ready to meet Tommy. Hopefully we can have fun and enjoy our dinner, and he doesn't talk nonstop about his newfound faith. Tommy can be a lot sometimes, especially when he's on a new kick, but I do miss him. I smile thinking about how pumped he was over the dinner menu. He's been through a lot, but there's an innocence about him that's endearing. I wonder, what would it be like to live as freely as he does?

I shove all my thoughts and feelings deep down, keeping everything locked tightly inside of me. But Tommy is the opposite—he says *exactly* what he feels, no filter, no hesitation. He never holds back. I'm envious, and wish I could be more like him.

By the time I fight through my shower, get myself ready, and go through my check-every-appliance-three-times ritual, I'm ten minutes late for dinner. I despise being late, but it's Tommy—he won't mind, so I try to let it go.

I spot him right away as I walk into the restaurant. He's sitting at our table, fiddling with his phone, probably texting to ask me where I am. He looks up, and his smile spreads across his entire face as he scrambles out of the booth to greet me.

"Hi!" he says, hugging me so tightly my bones crack.

"Hi!" I say back, delighted to see him—hoping he doesn't notice how bad I look.

HE SEES IT. EVERYONE DOES. DON'T KID YOURSELF. The inner voice begins its assault.

Tommy looks good. His eyes are shining, and unlike me, he looks fresh and rested. He's wearing a shirt I haven't seen before.

"Nice shirt!" I say, knowing he'll appreciate that I noticed. "That's a great color on you—matches your eyes."

Tommy grins from ear to ear. "Right? I've had this shirt forever and have never worn it. I knew you would like it!"

Our server brings us glasses of water and collects my menu before I've had a chance to even look at it. She's cute, with curly blonde hair and eyes as blue as the summer sky. She shows all her perfectly straight, pearly-white teeth as she smiles at Tommy. "What can I get you to drink today?"

"I'll have an iced tea with lemon," he says. He studies the waitress's name tag for a second, then looks back up at her. "Thanks, Christine. Lots of ice please."

I can tell Christine is more than happy to give Tommy all the ice he wants.

She directs her attention toward me. "And for you?"

"Tea sounds refreshing, I'll have the same. Thank you."

Christine keeps her eyes fixed on Tommy. "I'll be back with drinks, and your food should be right out."

I'm confused. "You ordered for me?"

Tommy looks pleased with himself. "I sure did! The dinner rush is coming soon, and since you were late, I went ahead and ordered for us both. I got my favorite chicken tenders with crinkle-cut fries and an order of mac and cheese because I'm starving, and I ordered you a veggie burger with sweet potato fries—extra crispy, and I'm definitely taking a bite!"

I do a happy dance in my seat. "Thanks!" My stomach rumbles. I am *so* ready for my burger.

DON'T LET PEOPLE SEE YOU EAT. YOU'RE A DISGUSTING PIG.

I try my best to ignore the whispered insults, but it's not easy.

Focus on Tommy. Take a breath. You're okay. Everything is fine.

"Okay," I say, "tell me about this latest cult you've joined."

I meet his glare with a forced smile, trying to be peppy. "I'm totally kidding! For real, tell me about church. I want to hear every detail."

Christine shows up with our iced teas before Tommy can respond, and I swear she put on fresh lipstick.

Tommy notices. He smiles big for her.

I think about the iced teas and have to ask, "Why are we not drinking beer? We always have a beer with our food when we come here."

"I quit drinking," Tommy says, not even looking up.

I stare at him with my eyebrows raised. "Wait, what? Since when? First, you spring on me that you're going to church, and now you tell me you quit drinking? Who are you and what have you done with my best friend?"

Christine returns, this time carrying plates piled high with our food. "Veggie burger," she says, putting mine on the table, "and your chicken tenders." She places Tommy's with care. "I added extra mac and cheese for you!" she says, looking at him expectantly.

Tommy gives her a wink.

This is getting ridiculous...

Christine leaves and Tommy digs in. "Oh my gosh, this is so good. How's yours?"

I pick up my burger. The first bite melts in my mouth. The patty is seasoned perfectly, the pickles are nice and crunchy, and the special sauce is so juicy it's dripping onto my plate. "Mmm," I hum, still chewing.

Tommy grins. "Awesome!"

He takes one of my fries, and I try one too. They're done to a crispy perfection, and the ranch dip is fantastic. We toast with our iced teas and spend the next little while sharing our food and enjoying every bite.

I love Tommy. He makes me forget my troubles.

He groans. "Why did you let me eat so much?"

"What? You're full?" I ask, inspecting his empty plate and mine that he finished off. I notice he's eyeing the dessert menu, and we burst out laughing.

"I'm for sure ordering the vanilla ice cream cookie volcano thing with two forks so we can share," he declares boldly.

Oh, how I've missed him!

I chuckle. "No. Please don't order dessert. I'm stuffed, and I can't handle watching you and your new friend drool over each other."

Tommy leans in over the table, grinning. "I think she's into me. I'm going to ask for her number."

I watch in disbelief as he waves Christine over, but instead of asking for her number, he orders dessert.

"You had me going for a minute," I say, smiling.

Tommy winks at me, and we laugh.

Dessert comes, and we help ourselves to the mountain of delicious ice cream and cookie goodness.

"Listen," Tommy says, "I don't know how to explain this, but after Henry's service, I couldn't work it out in my mind. It was haunting me, so I took the pastor's advice and called him. His contact information

chapter 8: Church

was on the program. I kept mine. Anyway, we met, one on one, and he shared some things that got me thinking, and I wanted to explore it. The next time we met he invited me to church, I enjoyed it, and now we're meeting weekly. I'm learning about Christ and who He is. I don't know where it's headed; all I know is I'm going to keep attending. I'm trying to make good decisions for once. You know I've struggled with addiction in the past, and drinking wasn't serving me, so I decided to take a break from it. Henry's service scared me. I've had dark moments where I didn't want to live anymore, but I never planned to actually kill myself. Thinking that someone like Henry chose to take his own life confused me, and it scared me because in some ways I understood it. Life is hard! I had to do something. Anything to add meaning and purpose to my existence. I'm tired of searching, Dani. I need something more. If you haven't noticed, I'm kind of a mess."

"Oh, wow," I say. It's quite a shift from our dessert volcano and the cute waitress. There's pain in Tommy's eyes, and I can feel the weight of his words. It's surprising to hear him talk about dark thoughts—I didn't know he had them. There were times he didn't want to live? No. Not Tommy. There's no way. This is shocking. Tommy is an incredible person. He should never feel this way. He can't. He has to know how special he is!

"Listen to me," I say. "You are *not* a mess. You're amazing. You're literally my favorite person on the planet! I wish I was more like you!"

My cuticles tingle, itching for me to pick at them.

I force myself to leave them alone.

Tommy looks surprised. "Excuse you! Why would someone as perfect as you want to be like me? You've got it all, Dani. You are everything! Everybody loves and admires you!"

His words slice through me, and in my mind I plead with him to understand:

You do not want to be like me, Tommy. I'm not what you think I am. I'm damaged. Can't you see it?

A wave of anxiety crushes in.

SEE WHAT YOUR LIES HAVE DONE? YOU HURT EVERYONE YOU CARE ABOUT. YOU'RE A FRAUD. YOU DIDN'T HELP HENRY, YOU KEEP LYING TO TOMMY, AND YOU PRETEND TO BE SOMEONE YOU'RE NOT. YOU LET DOWN EVERY SINGLE PERSON WHO CARES ABOUT YOU. YOU CAN'T KEEP HURTING PEOPLE LIKE THIS.

The truth hits me, and I feel sick. I really *am* a horrible person. There's no excuse for the things I've done.

I can feel the color draining from my face as my heart slams against my chest.

Tommy must sense something, because he seems worried. "Hey, are you okay? You look pale all of a sudden."

I jump at the opportunity. "Oh my gosh, I ate too much, or something. Ummm..." I dig frantically in my purse for my wallet. "I don't feel well. I'm sorry, do you mind if I take off?"

Tommy puts his hand over mine. "Don't you dare try to give me money, Dani. It's on me. Please go. I'm so sorry you don't feel good. Want me to drive you home?"

"No, I'll be okay. Thank you. Sorry. Let's get together again later in the week, okay?"

Tommy stands and helps me from my seat, always a gentleman. He looks me in the eyes as if he sees something.

IT SHOWS. YOU'RE SLIPPING. YOU CAN'T HIDE MUCH LONGER.

I try my best to steady my voice and not fall apart. "I'm fine. Really. Thanks for dinner. Love you. I'll call you tomorrow, okay?"

He smiles. "Sounds good. I guess I'll just stay here and hang out with Christine."

He laughs, and I manage to, but I'm freaking out inside and I need to get out of here.

"Love you, Dani," Tommy yells as I'm walking out the door.

I force a smile over my shoulder.

"And Jesus loves you too!"

chapter 8: Church

My heart is pounding as I race to my car and drive home as fast as I can, feeling dazed by everything. I rip off my clothes and crawl into bed, hoping for sleep to come—trying to block out the voice inside that won't leave me—

LIAR! it bursts in.

Inhale.

YOU RUIN EVERYTHING!

Breathe.

IT'S YOUR FAULT HE'S DEAD.

Inhale.

YOU'RE GOING TO HURT TOMMY.

"I'm okay. I'm okay. I'm o—"

NO YOU'RE NOT, OK. YOU NEVER WILL BE.

I grip my pillow, bury my face in it, and scream my insides out.

check on your **happy** friends

9
I'm Nothing

I think most people wake up to a few minutes of blissful calm—that sweet, hazy space between dreams and reality before worry creeps in—but it's not that way for me. If I manage to sleep at all, I wake in a complete panic. There's no warning. No transition. One second I'm sleeping, the next I'm bolting out of bed checking to see if the world has ended. On the rare occasion I wake up and experience a few precious seconds where everything feels okay, once my brain catches up, it hits me hard.

The darkness.

The weight.

The fear.

The gnawing dread that rushes in, curling around my chest and tightening its grip.

I do have fleeting moments of happiness when my smile and laughter are genuine, but the dread is still with me, pulsing underneath the surface of my skin.

It's *always* there.

I imagine my life as a long, winding road trip—passing through beautiful places, sharing meals and laughter with good people, and catching glimpses of joy along the way. But most of the time, I'm just gripping the wheel, driving on empty, trying my best to make it to the end without breaking down.

Even as I go through the motions of daily life, there's a dull, constant ache in my chest—a knowing that things won't end well for me. It's the weight of something I've always known deep down. Most days, I picture it—reaching the end of the road, slamming my foot on the gas pedal, and driving straight into a brick wall. It's all over in a bloody, tangled flash—I'm wiped off the face of the earth forever.

I keep telling myself, *I'm okay. I'm okay. I'm okay,* hoping that if I say the words enough, I'll start to believe them. But I don't. I never have. I don't even know what okay feels like anymore. I just smile. Nod. Breathe. Make myself small. Blend in. Fake it. Pretend I'm happy even when I'm falling apart. It's the only way I can survive in a world where I don't belong.

My phone rings and it startles me. I answer, but the darkness doesn't lift. It *never* does.

It's Tommy.

"Hey," I say, trying to sound alive and well.

"Hey! What are you doing?" Tommy asks, his voice full of energy.

"Oh, you know, just slaying the day away—nothing new!" I'm desperately trying to sound like a calm, confident, well-adjusted human being.

Tommy laughs, so it worked. "I like it. You sound extra peppy today. What are you up to?"

I supercharge my voice with false positivity. "Livin' my best life. You?"

YOU CAN PUT YOUR MASK ON, BUT YOU'RE A FAKE.

"Here's the deal," Tommy says. "Me, Sara, Xavier, Andre, and maybe Frank and Lola from the gym are all heading to Santa Cruz tomorrow. I checked the weather and it's going to be in the high 60s and sunny, so it will be perfect! We're gonna hit the Boardwalk, walk the beach, eat all the food—clam chowder, fish and chips, and pizza from Pizza My Heart. Just a fun, chill day with lots of food. I'm not sure about everyone else, but I plan on eating at all my favorite spots. You're coming too, obviously. I'll pick you up around 7:30 tomorrow morning. That work?"

The thought of going makes my insides quiver with anxiety.

THEY'LL NOTICE. DON'T GO. YOU CAN'T. THEY'LL SEE WHO YOU REALLY ARE. YOU LOOK TIRED, WORN OUT, AND DISGUSTING. SAY NO. SAY NO!

My mind spins. I don't know what to say or how to get out of this. Come on, Dani. Think. Think!

I squeeze my eyes shut, draw in a slow, silent breath, and steady myself before I respond. "Oh my gosh, that sounds like so much fun! I wish I would have known sooner, but I can't tomorrow. I already committed to volunteering, and I have lunch with a friend who's coming into town. Such a drag!"

The lies sizzle in my throat.

YOU'RE A LIAR.

"Honestly?" Tommy asks, sounding genuinely disappointed. "Ugh. That sucks. I *really* want you to come."

I cringe at my deceit.

DON'T KID YOURSELF. HE'S PRETENDING. HE DOES NOT WANT YOU TO GO—HE'S JUST SAYING THAT. YOU'RE A BURDEN. YOU'LL RUIN THEIR DAY. RESPOND NOW, BEFORE HE ASKS MORE QUESTIONS.

"Same," I say. "I'm so bummed. Let's plan another trip soon, okay?"

I hope we never do.

"Okay. But it won't be near as much fun if you don't come with. Let me know if things change and I'll come swoop you up tomorrow morning. All I need is a few minutes' notice, and I'll be there. Promise me you'll try. It will be good for you to get out in the sunshine with friends. Gotta go. Love you! Bye."

Tommy hangs up, but I keep staring at my phone. It goes dark, and I seethe, boiling with anger until I scream at it.

"It would be good for me, Tommy? To get out with friends and be in the sunshine? Are you kidding??? Do you know what it takes for me just to get out of bed every morning? That taking a shower and getting ready is a huge, exhausting chore? And every day before I leave my apartment I stare at myself in the mirror and hate, absolutely *hate* what I see!"

I gasp for air, rage rising and pounding throughout my body. I try to stop—to shut my mouth and pull back—but I can't. The screams rip out of me.

"*I hate myself, Tommy*! I lied to you! I'm a fake! I lied because I couldn't bear to tell you the truth. I can't go to Santa Cruz because I *hate* the way I look, I *hate* the way I feel, I *hate* the way I act, and I know *everyone* will see right through me. They'll think I'm pathetic. I can't go because it will take too much effort to pull myself together, keep my mask on all day, smile, laugh, and pretend I'm okay when I'm *not*! I am so not okay! Just the *idea* of going makes me want to throw myself off a cliff. Can't you see what life is doing to me, Tommy? I'm miserable all the time. I can't sleep! I never sleep! There's no relief. It's too much. I want to die!!!"

I throw my phone, overwhelmed. Shaking.

DO IT. YOU'D BE BETTER OFF. THEY'D BE BETTER OFF.

I breathe. In, and out. In, and out.

YOU KNOW IT'S THE ANSWER.

Slowly, the anger dissipates, and sadness weighs in as I drop to my knees and continue my rant in quiet whispers...

"Please don't give up on me, Tommy. Don't leave me. I need you. I don't want to be like this, but I can't fix it. You can't fix it either. Nobody can. This is who I am. I'm so ashamed. I don't know what to do. Nobody sees me. Not even you, Tommy. I'm in pain. I'm weak. I'm scared. I need help."

NO ONE CAN HELP YOU.

My mind races with thoughts of a carefree day with friends at the ocean. I imagine the others living, thriving, and having fun while I'm just falling deeper into my darkness. I cannot comprehend what that freedom feels like. I'll never live that way. I'm different. Damaged.

Messed up. I'm nothing.

YOU'RE WORTHLESS.

I break. My thoughts turn into sobs of defeat.

I can't take it anymore.

I can't do this.

I can't.

This pain is too much.

I can't hold it.

RELEASE IT. YOU KNOW HOW...

Trembling and barely able to see through my tears, I crawl to the kitchen, grab a knife off the counter, and press the blade into my skin—its cold edge is familiar.

Blood drips, but relief doesn't come.

The knife drops to the floor with a clatter as I clutch my arm.

But it's not better.

It's not helping.

I feel even worse.

What have I done?

check on your **happy** friends

10
Circling Buzzards

I wake to the sound of someone screaming in my apartment. Panicked, I race around looking for whoever it is, and then it hits me with the force of a brick to my forehead—no one is here. It's me. I'm the one screaming.

IT'S HAPPENING. YOU'RE LOSING CONTROL.

The nasty inner voice is back with guns blazing.

YOU WILL NEVER HAVE PEACE. YOU WILL NEVER SLEEP.

"I'm fine," I say out loud, trying to ignore it. "Everything is fine!"

THEN WHAT'S THAT? it hisses as I enter the kitchen.

I don't want to look. I don't want to face it.

YOU SAID YOU'D NEVER DO THAT AGAIN.

I grab the knife off the floor and throw it in the sink, rinsing red down the drain until the water runs clear.

YOU FAILED. YOU COULDN'T RESIST.

"I'm fine!"

YOUR ARM'S NOT FINE.

"I'm fine! Everything is fine!"

I storm into the bathroom, repeating the words, but showering is brutal and makes me feel even worse.

The cut stings.

It hurts.

It *burns* with shame.

Drying off. Getting dressed. *Everything* is torment.

I'm trying to pull myself together, but I can't.

Anxiety is building and pulsing through my body as I hurry from task to task. I *need* to get ready for work. I *need* to pull myself together.

WHY KEEP TRYING? YOU'RE NEVER GOING TO BE OKAY. YOU'RE LOSING IT, AND EVERYONE WILL SEE.

I glance in the mirror, and I'm shocked by my reflection. I look AWFUL. How can I possibly show up to work this way?

PEOPLE ARE GOING TO STARE. THEY'LL TALK ABOUT YOU. THEY'LL NOTICE SOMETHING IS WRONG.

I've had enough. I clench my fists and scream, "Stoppppp!"

Inhale.

Exhale.

Deeper now.

Inhale.

Exhale.

Slower.

In…

Out…

It's not working. It is not working!

I'm panting. Light-headed. The room is spinning.

It's okay, it's okay, it's okay, it's okay, it's okay, it's okay, it's okay, it's okay, it's okay, it's okay, it's okay. Everything is okay. I *need* to calm down!

On the couch, bent over with my head between my knees, my breathing slows enough for me to get up, quickly gather my things, and head out the door. I race to my car, frantically scanning the parking lot with no idea what I'm looking for.

My hair straightener.

Did I turn it off?

Yes, I'm sure I did.

I know I did.

chapter 10: Circling Buzzards

YOU IDIOT. NOW YOU'RE GOING TO BE LATE FOR WORK AND YOU'RE JUST GOING TO DRAW MORE ATTENTION TO YOURSELF. YOU KNOW YOU UNPLUGGED IT, BUT WHAT IF YOU DIDN'T? WHAT IF YOUR APARTMENT BURNS DOWN BECAUSE YOU LEFT IT PLUGGED IN?

Reeling, I run back inside and into the bathroom where my straightener sits in its proper place, unplugged, just as I knew it would be. Even though I didn't cook breakfast, I check all the burners on the stove to make sure they're turned off. I check the lights, triple-check the iron, and check my hair straightener once again, because at this point I don't trust anything.

Finally, I descend the stairs, slower this time, because I feel off balance, as if I'm on an escalator.

What is wrong with me?

I need to pull it together!

Traffic is heavy, and the other cars feel dangerously close. I'm convinced one of them is going to crash into me, so I tighten my grip on the steering wheel and brace for the impact.

YOU'RE GOING TO CAUSE AN ACCIDENT. YOU'RE GOING TO CRASH.

My thoughts pace back and forth like a caged animal.

Should I call in sick? Should I slam on the brakes right now? I probably shouldn't be driving. I think I need help.

Breathe. Breathe. Breathe.

Are people concerned because of how awful I look? Can they see it? Do they know? How will I make it through this day?

I have to go to work. I can't mess this up. I can't let Mama Sharon down. Did I lock the door? Am I late for work?

Breathe. Breathe. Breathe.

I consider calling in sick, then quickly dismiss the thought. I *need* to be at work. It's all I have.

This will pass. It will be okay. Relax. Calm down. Everything is okay.

It's 9:10, which means I'm late. Most days that wouldn't matter, but today it feels like the end of the world.

"Mama Sharon, I'm so sorry I'm late!" I yell, rushing into the shop. My voice is much louder than I intended—it doesn't even sound like me.

I hope they don't pick up on my energy. I hope it doesn't show. I hope they don't ask why I'm wearing long sleeves. I *always* wear short sleeves.

Keep breathing. Steady now. I'm here. I made it. Everything is fine.

Mama Sharon studies me. "Well, good morning to you, too! It's good to see that you're human, Dani. I don't think you've ever been late. Ha! Take your time getting settled, and when you're ready, could you please check the plants in the back?"

Is she angry? Is she disappointed in me? I'm going to get fired. I deserve it.

"Got it!" I say, trying to sound like I do every other day, but it doesn't work. My voice, my posture, my expression—everything is off.

THEY'LL SEE RIGHT THROUGH YOU.

As I'm walking to the back of the store, waves of nausea pass over me. The room spins. I'm afraid I might pass out.

YOU'RE HAVING A PANIC ATTACK. YOU'RE HAVING A PANIC ATTACK.

The peace I typically feel when I walk into the shop doesn't come. Instead, my anxiety just keeps building. The plants look different today. Unfamiliar. As if they're decaying. I notice a customer staring, and I *know* he sees that I'm a wreck. I should have stayed home.

YOU CAN'T HANDLE THIS.

I need a minute, so I rush to the back room and accidentally knock over a stack of empty boxes. It scares the hell out of me, and I scream like my soul is being ripped out.

Daisy is at my side in an instant, pawing my leg and whimpering, and before I can get a hold of myself, Mama Sharon and a customer burst in to check on me.

"Dani, what's wrong?" Mama Sharon asks. "Are you okay?" She's looking around wide-eyed and confused. The customer looks terrified.

I pick up a box. "Oh, my goodness, I am so sorry! I didn't mean to scream. I, uh, umm, I accidentally bumped into the boxes and when they fell, it startled me. I'm really sorry."

My eyes fall to the ground. I'm mortified.

YOU'RE STUPID. STUPID! STUPID!

The customer sighs with relief and leaves, but Mama Sharon remains at the door.

"Sugar, are you okay?" she asks. "You look tired. If you're not feeling well, please go home and rest. Everything is fine here."

YOU LOOK TIRED. YOU LOOK TIRED. YOU LOOK TIRED.

I fight back my tears. "No, Mama Sharon. Please. I need to stay here."

I hate how desperate I sound.

She walks over slowly, as if approaching a spooked animal. She lays her hand softly on my shoulder.

I hold my breath. She knows something is very wrong. I know she does.

"Dani, listen to me. Do whatever you need to. If you want to stay, it's fine. If you'd rather go home and rest, that's fine too. Okay? I'm here for you. Do you want to talk about it?"

Without looking up, I shake my head no, and as she's walking away, I whisper without meaning to, "I can't do this anymore."

Mama Sharon turns back. "What?"

I respond quickly, terrified she heard me. "I said I'm, um, I'm just a bit tired is all. I'm fine. Really, I am."

I want to smile and ease her mind, but instead, I just stand there, arms hanging down my sides like they don't belong to me. My gaze fixed on the floor wishing it would crack open and take me under.

I want to disappear.

"Okay," she says, but I can tell she's not buying it. She leaves me alone in the back room, and I'm grateful for it. My shoulders slump and my entire body exhales as I lean against the wall and sink to the floor.

Daisy approaches, nudging her nose against my chest until her forehead is nestled just beneath my chin, as if she's trying to anchor me.

I wrap my arms around her and bury my face in her fur. "What now, Daisy? What am I supposed to do? I'm falling apart. I'm not sure if I have the strength to keep pretending." I whisper to this sweet dog who faithfully keeps all my secrets.

"I can do this," I tell myself. "Just stand up, Dani. Walk out to the front of the store and clean the shelves. Then drink some water. Be charming to the customers. Breathe, Dani. Breathe. You are okay. Everything is going to be fine. Fake it. You can do it. You have no choice."

Somehow, the sky does not fall, and eventually I manage to regain control. It's wild how often I find myself in a frenzy that feels like it will take me out, then suddenly I'll switch back to living my life as if everything is fine and I didn't just completely lose it. It's insanity. Do other people go through this or is it just me?

It's probably just me.

Eight hours feels more like twenty, but I manage to stick it out. Sweet Daisy stays by my side for the entire day. I swear she senses my moods. On my worst days, she always stays close.

Finally, it's closing time, and I cannot get out of here fast enough. The plants, my sweet customers, not even Mama Sharon could save me from myself today. I survived, but barely. The ground beneath my feet still feels shaky.

The drive home is the worst. The inner voice is louder, circling my brain like buzzards waiting to devour me.

My hands are trembling, but I manage to open my apartment door. As soon as I'm in, I lock it and put my back to it, trying to catch my breath.

chapter 10: Circling Buzzards

My head is pounding, so I leave the lights off and run a bath because it's the only thing I can think to do. I gather all my candles, light them, and carefully place them one by one on the bathroom shelf. While the tub is filling with water, I strip off my clothes and add lavender and eucalyptus oils, then swirl them around with my hand. The smell calms my nerves, and the temperature is nice and hot—it feels good on my skin as I ease into it. Resting my head on the back of the tub, I close my eyes and let the warmth soothe my body.

I feel depleted.

I'm tired of breathing.

I'm tired of pretending.

I'm tired of fighting.

SLIP UNDER THE SURFACE AND DON'T COME UP, the inner voice whispers.

I don't think I can do it that way.

MAYBE YOU SHOULD HANG YOURSELF LIKE HENRY DID.

The candlelight casts flickering shadows on the wall, and I'm mesmerized by how evil they look. I stare at them, losing track of time until I have no idea how long I've been in the tub, but my skin is starting to wrinkle, so I pull the plug and watch as the water circles and gurgles down the drain. I stay a few minutes more, my body limp and cold. It takes all of my energy to pull myself out and dry off.

Carrying one of the candles for light, I walk to my desk and trace my finger through the calendar until it lands on today's date, July 14th. I pause, thinking about how much time I'll need to get everything in order, then slowly run my finger over the next 30 days, then another 30 days, another 30, and I stop there, marking the date. I grab a bright red pen from my desk drawer and circle it over and over, pressing harder with each stroke—Friday, October 17th.

Maybe I will, I say back to the inner voice.

I've dipped my toe into the dark water, but it didn't bite back like I thought it would. It feels strangely calm and warm.

People say Henry "lost his battle with mental health," but what if that's not true? What if he actually won? Maybe the joke's on the rest of us—the ones still fighting, still dragging ourselves through each day with no relief.

I close my eyes, trying to quiet my mind enough to sleep, and a sudden wave of calm settles over me. I breathe it in and whisper to myself, "Rest now. It's okay. There's an end in sight."

11
Floating Pills

I know it's a mistake as soon as I swallow the last one.

My throat constricts as panic tightens its hold.

What have I done?

Think, Dani, think!!!

I crouch over the toilet and shove my fingers down my throat. Deeper and deeper, I ram them in until vomit shoots out and splatters everywhere. Sharp cramps seize my stomach. I taste bile as it fills the toilet. Then, sobbing, I do it again, scraping the roof of my mouth as I dry heave—my body weak and empty of everything.

That *has* to be all of it—please let it be over. *Please, please, please* let this be over.

Gasping for breath, I rest my head on the toilet seat and cry as I stare at the floating soup of last night's dinner, acidic bile, and a full bottle of Xanax capsules washed down with wine.

What was I thinking?

Using all of my strength, I pull myself up to the sink and run cold water over my face. I rinse my mouth, trying to ease the burning in my throat, then lean against the wall, waiting for my heart to pick back up and start beating again.

Breathe, just breathe.

I'm still alive.

It's okay. It's okay. It's okay. It's okay.

I squeeze my eyes shut and shake my head, slowly at first, then faster, trying to dislodge the horrible images clawing their way through my mind.

The pills.

Henry's face.

Gracie's scars.

My mother's eyes.

My bleeding cuticles.

The knife.

Smashing my car into a brick wall.

Blood.

Screams.

Darkness darkness darkness…

Weak and empty, I collapse back onto the floor and curl into a ball. My body won't stop shaking, and I can't tell if I'm cold or in shock. Maybe both. Maybe more.

I don't know what possessed me to take all those pills. It was an insane thing to do. I'm desperate for relief and sleep, but I don't want to die—not yet anyway. Not today. I'm not ready, and it would destroy Tommy. It's just that sometimes the despair is so dark and the chaos in my head is so loud that I don't think I can take it anymore. This morning it was too much for me—I acted on impulse and took the pills, and I hate myself for it. I can't lose control like that ever again.

My body stills and my breathing slows enough for me to stand. I look down at the toilet, then pick up the prescription bottle.

Should I try to salvage the pills?

YOU COULD TRY AGAIN.

I quickly flush the toilet, disgusted at the thought of fishing them out of my vomit. I stand over it, watching as the contents of my stomach and the proof of my insanity swirl around and around, disappearing into the pipeline of waste—never to be seen again.

I've had the pills sitting in my medicine cabinet for six months.

chapter 11: Floating Pills

When I was in counseling for a brief period, my therapist prescribed them to take as needed for anxiety—not to take them all at once and end my life. Maybe it wasn't enough to kill me—I don't even know, but what if I waited too long and couldn't throw up? Someone would have found me unconscious with an empty pill bottle, and how would I explain *that*? And what if I did die and there was no note, and nothing was prepared? Just like Henry, I would have hurt the people I love. How would Tommy make it without me?

The thought makes me shudder.

I manage a shower, brush my teeth, and feel a little better, but relief is quickly replaced with a deep sadness that threatens to pull me under.

I don't know what to do, so I call Tommy.

"Hey, Dani." He answers on the first ring, sounding wide awake and cheerful. My throat is on fire, and I can't catch my breath—what do I say to him?

"Hello? Are you there?"

"Hi," I manage to squeak out.

"You okay? Is something wrong?" The tempo of his voice is rising.

"I'm fine," I say on the verge of tears. I hate how desperate I sound.

"I'm putting on my shoes right now and heading your way. Unlock your door and hang tight." Tommy hangs up, not waiting for my response. I know he's on his way, and I'm grateful for it. I can't be alone right now. I don't trust myself.

check on your **happy** friends

12
Bad Decisions

Tommy lives ten minutes from my place, which gives me little time to pull myself together. I sip on lemon ginger tea, hoping it will soothe the fire in my throat. Swallowing hurts—it feels like shards of glass are lodged into my tonsils. It serves me right for acting so impulsively. I still can't believe I swallowed all those pills. No matter how bad it gets, I need to stay in control!

Getting dressed is a struggle, but I manage. I put on a pair of faded soft jeans and a white t-shirt, braid my hair in one long braid, brush my teeth for the fifth time, and flush the toilet once more to make sure the pills don't rise back up to the surface just to spite me.

My life is a mess.

I'm exhausted.

I'm so tired.

Shame and disgust pour over me—I hate how weak I am.

YOU'RE A DISGRACE. A BURDEN TO THE WORLD. WEAK. NEEDY. DESPERATE. UGLY. YOU DON'T BELONG HERE.

I'm too tired to combat the venomous inner voice this morning. I cower under the assault. I deserve this—all of it.

My body feels heavy as I walk to unlock the door for Tommy, then drag myself over to the couch.

I wait, gnawing on my already inflamed cuticles.

Tires screech in the parking lot outside—Tommy has arrived. He probably drove like a maniac.

His footsteps are loud coming up the stairs, and I hate that I made him worry. He rushes in the door and plops down next to me on the couch.

"How's my best friend?" he asks, hugging me gently to his side—his heart pounding so hard I can feel it.

"I'm fine," I whisper, my chest hollow, aching with all the words I can't say out loud.

He pulls me to my feet. "Let's get out of here and take a drive. Come on. Grab your stuff and let's go."

I do as I'm told and grab my purse and sunglasses, mindlessly following his lead.

This is what I needed. Tommy knows me well enough to take charge and not ask questions when I get like this—he's been doing it since we were kids. Back then, it wasn't uncommon for him to find me sitting alone on the curb in front of his house, or at the park, scared and unable to speak. That was his cue to take me on an adventure. Tommy would immediately invite me into a make-believe world where we became superheroes, werewolves, detectives, or anything we wanted to be. No questions asked, we would just play, and he would distract me with fun until I calmed down and found my voice again. It was the escape I needed back then, and it's what I need right now.

The bright sunshine and fresh air slap my face as soon as I step outside; a sign that I am in fact still alive.

I just need to get through this day.

One breath at a time.

That's all.

Tommy starts his truck, I hop in the passenger seat, and my body melts into it. I'm grateful he came right over. Sometimes I'm embarrassed by the way our trauma connects us, but today it feels like a lifeline.

After 30 minutes of driving, my sadness subsides a bit and I'm

chapter 12: Bad Decisions

suddenly curious where we're going.

"Thanks for rescuing me today," I say, my voice raspy and weak. "It was a rough night. I swear the walls were closing in on me."

Tommy nods. "I know the feeling. I've had that lately too. I'm glad you called. Lord knows I've called you a million times. You sound like you're losing your voice. Are you getting sick?"

"No," I say, fighting back the tears welling in my eyes, "I think it's just my allergies. Why are we such a mess?"

"Because our parents ruined us, and life is hard. That's why. But there's good news, Dani. Despite it all, there is hope in Jesus!"

Tommy is smiling as if he has everything figured out.

It irritates me.

"Not that again," I mumble without thinking.

"Not what again? Oh, you mean Jesus?" Tommy smiles when he has every right to be angry.

"I'm sorry. I don't know why I said that." I say, feeling horribly selfish. Tommy dropped everything to help me today and this is how I repay him?

YOU'RE SELFISH. SELFISH. SELFISH.

There I go shaking my head again—a new habit I've picked up when the chaos in my head gets too loud.

Thankfully, Tommy's eyes are on the road, and he doesn't notice my head-shaking craziness. He reaches for my hand, squeezes it, and quickly lets it go. He loves me in a way I don't deserve. I can't bring myself to be honest with him about how bad things are. I feel awful. He opens his heart and tells me everything, and I keep my secrets locked inside.

"Okay, best friend," Tommy says, "we're going on an adventure, but first we're getting some food because I'm starving, and just so you know, it's not going to be healthy. I haven't eaten much lately, and I need BIG food."

Tommy helps me—being with him quiets the chaos.

I ask, "You're not going to Ma's Kitchen drive-through, are you? Wherever you're going, I just want coffee and maybe a water."

I know full well that's *exactly* where he's going, but I ask anyway.

My mind shifts from me to Tommy. I may be a lost cause, but there's hope for him. I need him to be okay. Why hasn't he been eating? He's *always* hungry.

"Why haven't you eaten much? That's not like you." I say.

Tommy nods. "Just some bad decisions and stupid stuff that made me lose my appetite, but I'm okay now. I'm *hungry* hungry this morning, so I'll be fine."

I'm not sure what Tommy means by "bad decisions," but I opt to not ask any more of him. Some things are better left alone.

As usual, there are at least ten cars in the drive-through line at Ma's Kitchen. Normally a wait like this would stress me out, but right now I'm just along for the ride, trying to survive the day.

Finally, it's our turn.

"Thank you for coming to Ma's Kitchen. I'm ready to take your order," the speaker box says.

Tommy grins and leans out his window. "Good morning, Ma's Kitchen, how are you today?" His voice is over-the-top cheerful.

"I'm good, my man!" Ma's Kitchen speaker guy plays along with equal cheer. "What can we get started for you on this beautiful Saturday morning?"

"Glad to hear it, bro," Tommy says. "Okay. I'll take three breakfast sandwiches, hold the sausage on one of them, six hash browns, two coffees with creamer, two waters, and..."—he taps his finger on his chin as he scans the menu, considering his options—"a pancake stack with extra syrup."

The speaker box guy repeats the order back to Tommy without missing a detail.

"Awesome. Yep, that is correct. And one more thing, bro. Can I pay for the order of the car behind us? Can I do that?"

chapter 12: Bad Decisions

I glance at Tommy, curious who all this food is for and why he's paying for someone else.

"Absolutely! That's generous of you. I'll get their order, and we'll confirm if the total is okay when you pay."

"Perfect!" Tommy says, looking overjoyed as he pulls ahead.

"You know I'm not eating, right?" I say, my throat still full of razors from puking up the pills this morning.

Tommy smiles at me, showing every one of his gleaming white teeth. "Oh, you are *for sure* eating. You need a breakfast sandwich with hashbrowns in it. You really do. Trust me on this."

We laugh, and for a second I forget that I'm miserable.

The line inches along, and Tommy hums happily until we reach the window.

Speaker guy greets us. He's much younger than I pictured. He has colorful tattoos covering his arms and neck, and his long, wildly curly hair is pulled back into a huge, puffy ponytail. "Okay," he says, "I got it. It's a large order, so if you need to change your mind just let me know. Their total is $42.00 even. You want to pay both or just yours?"

"Perfect!" Tommy says, handing over his card. "I'll pay it, and one more favor, please. Can I write a message on their receipt before you give it to them?"

Speaker guy raises an eyebrow. "Okay, um, what exactly do you have in mind? I have to look out for my customers, you know what I'm saying?"

"Oh, yeah, for sure. I just want to write that Jesus loves them—hoping it will bless them today."

I hold my breath, wondering how the guy will respond—expecting the worst.

To my surprise, a huge smile spreads across his face. "YEAH! Praise Jesus, that's legit my dude. You got it. Just a sec!"

I'm shocked. I did *not* see that coming.

Speaker guy hands over the receipts and Tommy's credit card.

"Do you need a pen?"

"Thanks!" Tommy scribbles his message and gives it back.

Speaker guy takes a look and smiles. "God bless, my man. Please pull up to the next window for your food!"

Tommy gives him a wave and looks over at me. "So cool! I've never done this before. I haven't even thought of it!"

I'm irritated, and I don't know why. "Please explain this to me, Tommy. Why do you keep saying that to people? I mean, for once, can't you just *not* talk to strangers? Must you tell EVERYONE?" This "adventure" is suddenly too much for me, and I wish I was back home.

Tommy is unphased by my rant. "It's literally my job to spread the good news of the Gospel, so you might as well get used to it," he says calmly.

Instead of being offended, he seems even more delighted with himself.

As soon as we get our order, a car horn honks behind us. "Thank you so much!" the driver shouts. "Praise Jesus!"

Strangers exchange smiles and the air feels lighter, warmer. It catches me off guard and my heart picks up an extra beat. I don't know what Tommy's doing, but nobody else appears to be irritated. These folks seem profoundly grateful. I marvel at how Tommy loves others so generously, as if he has nothing to lose.

Tommy rolls the tops of the bags down tightly to keep our food warm, and we finally get back on the road.

He passes them to me. "Hold these, we'll eat when we get there."

I nod, no longer annoyed with his charades, but simply relieved to be here with him as he seems to be living his best life.

After a while, I notice the streets look familiar. Then it hits me. I sit up in my seat. "This is our old neighborhood! Why are we here?"

"It sure is." Tommy says. "I've been working through family issues with my pastor, and he encouraged me to visit the places from my childhood, and since you lived here too, I thought we could do it

chapter 12: Bad Decisions

together. Maybe it will be good for us. What do you think?”

"I don't know," I answer, hesitantly. I'm staring out the window, taking it all in, and something is stirring inside of me. I'm not sure if it's good or bad, but at least I'm alive and feeling things.

I ask, "Can we go to the park first?" hoping that's his plan.

Tommy nods. "Yep!"

As we pull into the parking lot, adrenaline surges through my body and I feel awake for the first time today. Tommy and I jump out of his truck, race to the playground, and hop on the swings just like old times. We swing beside each other, pumping our legs back and forth, climbing higher and higher until we hear a loud creak and the entire set bends beneath us, as if it's about to break in two.

"Jump!" Tommy yells, and together, we spring forward into the air and land with a thud in the bark.

We're both out of breath and laughing hysterically.

Tommy is wiping the tears off his cheeks from laughing so hard. "Okay," he says, "that actually hurt. We're too heavy for this—that thing is about to break!"

"We almost died!" I say, my anxiety simmering quietly in my belly. This is good. I feel better.

Memories of our park adventures flash in my mind—the sound of our laughter, the squeak of the swing, the smell of the dirty old bark that softened our fall so many times.

This little park holds a sacred spot in my heart. It was our refuge, a safe place for me and Tommy to land when life was cruel.

We stand, dust ourselves off, and Tommy takes off in a full sprint. I know exactly where he's going and quickly run after him. We race to the bottom of the tree and look up. Sadly, there's no treehouse left, just broken boards and a bunch of rusty nails sticking out of the trunk.

"I remember this tree," Tommys says. "It's massive!"

"Me too," I say, as I gaze up at the giant oak. When we were kids, it was more than just a tree, it was our protector. Up in the treehouse, nothing could touch us. I remember climbing the roots like steps, each one lifting us closer to our secret world. The branches wrapped around our little treehouse fort like arms, cradling us gently, as if the tree knew how much it meant to us. Up there, we felt safe—free to dream and just be ourselves.

I sigh. "Everything around here seems so small compared to how I remember it, except for this tree. I can't believe our treehouse is gone."

Our energy shifts as we walk quietly to the only bench in the park. Tommy heads to the truck to get our food, and I sit tight, soaking in the memories.

He's back in seconds. "Okay," he says, his eyes sparkling, "I was starving earlier, and now I'm ravenous, but first, hold our coffees while I prepare your sandwich. You're going to love me for this."

He carefully opens my breakfast sandwich and lays two hash brown patties on top of the egg and cheese, gently squishes it together, and hands it to me with a mini plastic cup of ketchup for dipping. The sandwich is still hot and dripping with cheese—the smell makes my mouth water.

"This actually looks really good," I say, smiling in anticipation of my first bite.

Tommy chuckles. "Oh, trust me, that sandwich will change your life!"

We sit together in the sunshine, me and my best friend, eating delicious greasy food in the park of our childhood, and it feels sweet. It's been so long, I'd forgotten how much fun we used to have playing here. My throat screams every time I swallow, but I'm hungry, and do my best to ignore it.

We sit in silence for a good while, sipping coffee and letting our food digest.

Tommy shifts in his seat, obviously uncomfortable. "I'm stuffed," he says. "Why'd you let me eat so much? That was enough for three people."

chapter 12: Bad Decisions

"You say that like it's *my* job to monitor your food intake," I tease. "Your eating habits are entertaining, Thomas."

He laughs. "Yep, that's me, I've always been a crowd pleaser! Okay, are you ready for our next stop? This one may not be as much fun, but we're doing it."

I choke down my last sip of coffee and walk beside him back toward the truck. He's going to our childhood homes, I know he is, and I'm not sure if I'm ready.

Tommy drives to his family's place first, but it's gone!

He double checks the address. "5016 Sycamore Avenue... Yep. This is it."

We park across the street, get out, lean against the truck, and stare at the clean, modern duplex sitting where Tommy's house used to be. Two cheerful, bright yellow units sit side by side with matching navy-blue front doors trimmed in white. I never would have chosen those colors, but somehow it works. The yard is well manicured, and the identical, cozy little porches have planter boxes loaded full of blooming flowers. It looks warm and inviting—nothing like Tommy's house.

After a few minutes of staring in silence, I nudge him. "I don't know how to feel about this," I say, wondering what he's thinking.

Tommy pauses, then exhales loudly. "You know, this is actually good. Maybe the best-case scenario. The house I grew up in was cold and empty of love—I'm so glad it's gone. I just wish I could have been here to watch the demolition. I would have loved to bash in those walls."

Just as we're getting ready to leave, a young woman pulls into the driveway of one of the duplexes. I watch her closely, forgetting it may seem a bit strange that we're parked here staring at her house.

She turns in our direction, her hand shielding the glare of the sun. "Can I help you?"

"Hi, we're just admiring your place," Tommy shouts across the street. "I grew up in the house that used to be here. Have you lived here long?"

"I'm sorry, I'm in a hurry," the woman says sharply, gathering her groceries from her trunk.

We take that as our cue to leave.

Tommy opens his door, but he doesn't get in. "Thank you," he shouts again. "Sorry we bothered you. Have a good day! Jesus loves you!"

I don't know what his deal is or why he keeps repeating himself to strangers, but he needs to stop. It's too much!

The woman turns around, her hair whipping angrily across her face, and I know this is not going to be good. She shifts her groceries to one hand and gives Tommy the middle finger. "No thanks, loser!"

Tommy giggles as we drive away.

"Doesn't that bother you?" I ask, curious why he seems okay with everything these days. Not too long ago, that encounter would have crushed him.

"Not one bit," he says matter-of-factly. "It's fine, not everyone is open to hearing the good news of Christ, but that won't stop me from telling them. I'm relieved that's over. I'm never coming back here. I don't need to. But," he says, driving slowly in the direction of my house, "are you ready to go to your old place?"

The route is familiar; I've walked it many times. "Ready as I'll ever be," I say, anticipation rising in my chest with the force of a raging riptide.

I add in a whisper, "I hope mine is destroyed too."

"Me too," Tommy whispers back. "I hated your house as much as I hated mine. Maybe even more."

It turns out my old house is not destroyed or made new or preserved or anything. It's a dark, dingy, condemned shack of a place not fit for anyone to live in—just like I remember.

Tommy pulls over to the curb and cuts the engine. "Woah," he says,

chapter 12: Bad Decisions

staring out the window. "It looks like no one has done a thing to this place in decades. It's awful."

I stare in disbelief. "It's worse than awful. It's pitiful and dirty, just like my childhood."

"We can leave. You don't ha—"

"No. Let's go check it out," I say as I reach for the door.

"You sure?"

"Nope! Not sure at all."

I might regret this, but I walk up the driveway leading to the house where I lived until my Grandma Vee saved me. It terrifies me to think what might have happened to me if she hadn't.

The sky is blue today, and the sun is shining brightly, but that's the only color I can see. The siding, once painted white, is now chipped and faded into dull shades of decay. The grass, the garden, and the trees are all dried up and dead.

A cyclone fence wraps around the house and a sign is nailed to the front door that reads: "*Condemned – No Trespassing*," but we walk up anyway.

Yellow tape drapes across the front door like it's a crime scene, which strikes me as funny, because in my mind it IS a crime scene.

Peering through the broken window, I can see signs that people have been here. Old blankets are rolled up in the corner and broken glass, aluminum foil, burnt spoons, syringes, and other drug paraphernalia are scattered all over the floor.

Tommy takes my hand and gently leads me to the front porch. "You're not going inside, it's dangerous."

Grateful to be led, I take a seat next to him.

"You okay?" he asks.

"Probably not," I say, honestly. "It's just so depressing here. How did I live this way?"

I sweep my gaze across every corner of the property, looking for something *not* horrible to focus on, but there's nothing—it's all gray and lifeless. This isn't a home. It never was.

"Yep," Tommy says, "it's not the most cheerful place, that's for sure. Hey, I need to go to the truck for a minute. You okay?"

"I'm fine. What do you need from the truck?"

Tommy doesn't respond, which is odd.

As I sit here, my eyes drift to a dry, barren spot on the property where the garden used to be, and memories rush in…

The sun is shining so brightly I have to squint to see my dad's face. He's smiling. Together, we pick tomatoes from the garden. I pop one in my mouth; the taste is warm and sweet, making my mouth water. The air is filled with the rich, refreshing scents of fresh basil and mint. Dad tells me he has to leave and that I'll be okay. He kneels down until his eyes are level with mine. Tears run down his face. I wipe them away and ask him what's wrong, but he doesn't answer me. I'm confused because I thought we were having a good day. His voice shakes when he speaks. "Just stay quiet, my little Dani girl. Try to stay quiet and make yourself small. You'll be fine." I'm confused and scared, but I believe him. If he says I'll be fine, then I will be. He gets in his truck. My mother is screaming and throwing things at him. I run as fast as I can as he drives away because I want to go with him—I don't want him to leave me! I run faster and faster, but I can't keep up. He drives away and I'm left standing alone in the middle of the road with no shoes on.

Tommy nudges me. I was so lost in thought I didn't hear him come back.

"Are you okay?" he asks, and I notice something is off in his voice.

My mind feels fractured—as if being here and seeing all this has broken me into pieces. I was so young—too young to have my dreams shattered. When my dad left, he took my hope with him, leaving me with nothing.

Why didn't he take me with him?

chapter 12: Bad Decisions

HE LEFT BECAUSE YOU'RE A BURDEN TO EVERYONE. NO ONE CARES ABOUT YOU.

I break into tears. "I think I've seen enough. Let's go."

"Okay." Tommy sounds panicked. "Go get in the truck. I'll get our things off the porch and be right there."

I run as if someone is chasing me—years of held back tears pouring down my face.

I feel calmer once I'm in the truck, but I can't stop crying. My nose is running, so I pop open the glove compartment, looking for a tissue.

An empty brown prescription bottle falls out. I catch it and read the label. It's Adderall, #40 count, prescribed on August 3rd to Christine Hanes.

Hmmm. I check the date on my phone. Today is August 6th.

I glance up just in time to see Tommy heading toward the truck. I throw the bottle back into the glove compartment, slam it shut, wipe my face with my shirtsleeve, and hold my breath. My mind is flooded with questions.

Why does Tommy have an empty prescription bottle of Adderall?
Where are all the pills?
Who the hell is Christine?
Why did my dad abandon me?
Why did I take all those pills this morning?

Tommy hops in, buckles his seatbelt, and takes off. His hands shake as he grips the steering wheel.

"That was a lot," he says. "You okay?"

My stomach clenches. My jaw tightens. What the hell is Tommy doing?

"Yeah. You keep asking if I'm okay. Are YOU okay?" My tone is accusatory.

"Me? Yeah, I'm fine," Tommy says without looking at me, and for the first time today I notice deep lines on his forehead and dark circles under his eyes.

Feeling defeated, I lean my head against the window as we drive. Worse than the run-down, pitiful shack I used to live in is me and Tommy. What an absolute mess we are.

"What is it?" he asks. "You've got something on your mind."

I'm sure he won't be honest with me, but I decide to call him out.

"Okay. I was looking for tissues in your glove compartment and I saw the pill bottle. Who is Christine Hanes, and why do you have her prescription of Adderall?"

Tommy keeps his eyes fixed on the road. "Christine is that server from the barbecue place in the plaza. I met her a while back when you and I went to dinner. The blonde with big blue eyes who was flirting with me, remember?"

I nod. I do remember.

"We dated a few times, but I quickly learned she's not good for me. She's a bit aggressive, and sometimes that draws me in. Plus, one of her boyfriends is a pharmacist and gives her an endless supply of Adderall. Anyway, she called me out of the blue and in a weak moment I agreed to meet up with her. We went out, I drank way too much, and she loaded me up with Addie. I lost my appetite because I've been popping them like candy for the last few days. I finally stopped, and slept all day yesterday, which is why I was so hungry this morning. Earlier, when we were sitting on the porch, seeing our houses was too much for me. I was starting to panic, so I went to the truck and popped the last of the pills, which are kicking in right now. Huge mistake. I'm sorry."

I'm shocked at his honesty. I don't think I wanted to know this.

"Tommy, pull over, you need to throw up! Let me drive, we need to get to the hospital right now! Are you trying to kill yourself?" I'm yelling, but my throat is so inflamed it comes out like a strained whisper.

"Hey, hey, no, it's okay. I promise," Tommy says softly. "Calm down. I am not trying to kill myself—I do not want to die, Dani. I promise you. And I'm not going to throw up, it's too late for that, and besides, I

chapter 12: Bad Decisions

hate throwing up. I've done this a lot, and I know the drill—my heart is racing, I'm going to be amped for a while, I'll get paranoid, shame will come, I'll hate myself and fall into depression—but then, I'll be okay. I promise. It was stupid, okay? I know it was. I won't do it again. I don't know why I did it this time."

I speak before thinking, tears streaming down my face, "What about Jesus, Tommy? If you love Him so much and He loves you like you say He does, then why did this happen? I thought all that changed, and you were better?"

Tommy smiles weakly, his eyes brimming. "Listen, Dani, it's true. I *have* changed and I *am* better. The beauty of Christ is that He loves me as I am. With all my flaws and weaknesses, He *still* loves me. This was a mistake, but it does not define me. Years ago, this setback would have sent me into a spiral of more bad decisions, but that's not who I am anymore. God's grace is abundant. Sanctification is a process. Christ understands the battle of my flesh, and lately, instead of turning to Him, I've been relying on myself, and that *never* works. I'm going to get back into my healthy routine, read God's word, ask for forgiveness for the millionth time, and pull my strength from Him. I know you struggle, but you always stay in control. It's different for me. I'm an idiot. I'm sorry I upset you. I hope you can forgive me."

I want to tell Tommy about the pills I took, and how I made myself throw up. I want to tell him that I'm out of control—that I'm drowning in self-loathing and shame. That I'm scared of dying, but I'm even more afraid of living. I want to share the broken parts of me that no one can see. I want to be open and honest like he is, but I can't. I don't say any of those things. Instead, I take Tommy's hand and tell him the only truth I feel certain of.

"I love you, Tommy. Forever. No matter what. And you're not an idiot. You are amazing and you're going to be fine." I'm desperate for him to believe me.

He raises my hand to his cheek and rests his face against my palm. "I'm so sad about our treehouse," he says, his voice small and thick with emotion.

"I know. Me too." I feel depleted.

We drive the rest of the way home in silence, our hands locked tightly together. Tommy keeps his eyes on the road, and I keep mine on him, watching for signs of the pills he swallowed. I scan his face, glistening with sweat, and watch his hands grip the steering wheel a little too tightly. I notice the fabric of his shirt pulsing and shifting as his heart pounds in his chest, and I wonder if it might explode.

13

The Incident

Another day has come and I'm still here.

I'm trying.

I'm doing my best.

Work is in full swing. The bustling energy shifts my weary brain from my misery to what's happening right here and now at the shop.

Mama Sharon is explaining to customers that we're having repairs made, but to come on in anyway. Tommy is using a drill in the corner, and the loud whirring makes it hard to hear anything else. I watch him, looking for signs of Adderall, but he seems okay today. It was an emotional weekend for both of us—I hope he's feeling better, and I *really* hope he's done with pills. *I* sure am. My throat is still raw. Every time I swallow it's a sad reminder of how weak and desperate I am.

I close my eyes and shake my head, trying to erase the weekend from my mind and focus on the shop. *Thank goodness for this shop.*

Last night, after closing, a heavy shelf fell off the wall and made a big mess on the floor. The mounting bolts tore out, leaving holes surrounded by chipped and cracked sheetrock and paint. Thankfully, we hadn't restocked yet, so no plants were damaged. I called Tommy early this morning to see if he could help us, and he answered on the first ring.

Tommy—being Tommy—rushed over and got right to work. First, he cleaned the floor using his Shop-Vac, and then he prepped and repaired the wall, so we were finally able to open our doors at noon. The shelf was damaged, so he hauled it off, and he's currently unboxing a brand new one to install. In his real job, Tommy writes code for a big tech company. He works from home and has a flexible schedule, which is great for us.

Tommy has become an unofficial handyperson for Thrive. Mama Sharon pays for materials, but Tommy refuses to take any money for his time, so she gives him food. I can only imagine what she has in store for him after he finishes this job, probably her famous jerk chicken with rice and peas, which is his favorite. It's a wonder he stays so trim with all the food he consumes—he eats more than anyone I've ever known!

It's a warm August day and breezy outside, so I prop the front door open and let the fresh air flow in. Today hasn't gone the way we planned, but there's something about the activity and the buzz in the air that gives me renewed energy. I needed a break from the circus in my head, so this feels good.

Sales are slowing for the afternoon, which gives us time to get the shelf back up without it being too much of a distraction for our customers. I take advantage of the break and start cleaning out the junk drawer below the register. Mama Sharon notices me organizing and gives an approving nod, but then there's a shift on her face as she looks past me. I turn to follow her gaze and my eyes land on him. It's Gabe, the customer with an impressive beard and a girlfriend.

Daisy bolts for him before I can say a word, and then Tommy jumps to his feet. "Gabe, my man! What's happening?"

Gabe looks surprised. "Tommy, I didn't expect to see you here! What's up?"

The guys greet each other with a hand slap and a quick side hug, then Gabe bends to Daisy, ruffling her fur as her tail wags like crazy.

"What are you doing here?" Tommy asks.

chapter 13: The Incident

Gabe glances at me. "Just stopped by to buy a plant. What are you working on?"

Tommy shows him the shelf project.

Gabe surveys the tools and shelf pieces scattered on the floor. "I'm just killing time this afternoon, so I'm happy to stay and give you a hand with this."

Tommy is clearly thrilled. "Thanks, bro! I'll take all the help I can get. Oh, have you met Mama Sharon and Dani? Mama Sharon owns the shop, and Dani runs it; they both know everything there is to know about plants. Dani and I grew up together and have been best friends forever."

"Yes!" Mama Sharon jumps in on the conversation as if she's been eagerly awaiting her turn. "We *have* met. He was in a while ago buying a plant for a friend. Isn't that right, Gabe?"

Gabe flashes a brilliant smile for her. "Yes, ma'am, that is correct."

"No, no. My friends call me Mama Sharon," she says. She gives him an inquisitive look. "Well, did she like it?"

Gabe chuckles, rubbing his beard as if he's embarrassed. "About that...yeah, she did. In fact, she liked the plant more than she liked me, because a few weeks after I gave it to her, she dumped me for her yoga instructor. But it's fine, Mama Sharon, I feel like I may have dodged a bullet."

Mama Sharon pats him on the back and winks at me. "Is that right? Well, that's her loss, and for the best it seems."

I realize I haven't said a word—I'm still trying to figure all this out.

"So how do you two know each other?" I ask, my eyes shifting back and forth between Gabe and Tommy.

Tommy looks amused. "Gabe is my brother-in-Christ. He goes to my church."

"Okay," I say, feeling a bit shocked, "this day is full of surprises!" I wink back at Mama Sharon. "I'll leave you guys to it. I've got work to do!"

Mama Sharon grabs my hand, leans in close, and whispers, "Told you, sugar."

I nudge her playfully and can't help but wonder what brought Gabe back in. Could he really be here just to buy a plant?

Tommy and Gabe get to work on the shelf, which has turned out to be much more difficult to assemble than we thought it would be, but I don't mind. I'm riding on the breeze of the day; feeling something I can't quite put my finger on—I feel connected, and comfortable in this moment. Like I belong here.

An hour later, the guys are still battling the shelf, and I'm starting to fade from lack of sleep, so I decide it's time for some caffeine.

"I'm making a coffee run, who wants what?" I ask the group.

Tommy's eyes light up. "Caramel Frappuccino extra whip, please."

Gabe looks at him with eyebrows raised. "Bro, do you know how much sugar is in those drinks?"

I answer for Tommy. "I've told him, but he doesn't care one single bit. Gabe, what can I get you?"

"I'll just take a plain black coffee. Thanks Dani. Do you need help?"

I knew it—I knew he would take his coffee black.

I smile. "Nope, I got it. Thank you. Mama Sharon, what can I get you?"

"It's 3:00 sugar, you know I don't drink coffee this late. It would keep me up all night. I don't know how you youngsters handle all that caffeine!"

Note to self, maybe lighten up on the coffee—it can't be helping my insomnia.

"Okay," I say, "hold down the fort and I'll be right back."

"Get snacks!" Tommy yells as I'm heading out.

I yell back, "You got it!"

As I'm crossing the street to where my car is parked, I catch myself smiling. It's turning out to be a far better day than I expected. I notice the inner voice has been quiet—it's probably exhausted from

chapter 13: The Incident

screaming at me all weekend. I don't care what the reason is, I'm just grateful for the break.

As I'm driving, my mind drifts to Henry. I miss the days when I could just walk across the street to The Café and he'd be there, greeting me with a big grin on his face and my coffee ready.

Are you at peace, Henry? I hope so. I miss you every day.

There are no coffee shops nearby, so the little market down the street will have to do. Their coffee is decent, and they'll have snacks for Tommy. Thankfully, it's not super busy, so in less than ten minutes I'm driving back with drinks balanced on my lap and a bag full of food—a couple of apples, cheese sticks, pretzels, and a big bag of Flamin' Hot Cheetos®.

Hopefully the guys are almost finished with the shelves so we can get everything back in order before we close this evening.

As soon as I arrive at the shop, I hear Daisy barking, which is unusual. I sense something unsettling in the air that wasn't here before. Carefully, I set our drinks down so I can try to figure out what's going on.

Tommy rushes over to me. The look on his face makes my stomach drop. "Dani, listen, you might want to get out of here. Just turn around and go back to your car, right now."

"What?" I ask. "Why?" I try to see past him. He's in the way, and an older woman is standing in the back of the shop next to Gabe and Mama Sharon.

"Dani, please don—"

I'm already around him.

"Don't," Tommy says, then sighs.

I stop dead in my tracks and stare, studying the woman's face, trying to piece together what it is about her that seems oddly familiar.

A cold wave sweeps through me. I blink a few times, not trusting my own eyes, but it's her.

It's been at least ten years since I've seen her. Ten years with no contact. Not a single word, and now she's here.

It's my mother.

If it weren't for her dark, soulless eyes, I may not have recognized her. Her once imposing physique is now thin and frail. Her hair used to be long, thick, and curly, but now it's thin and completely gray. Her skin is a sickly shade of yellow, and the deep lines on her face make her appear much older than she is. It's clear that her bitterness and all the years of drinking have taken their toll.

Anxiety slams against my chest—I didn't think I would ever see her again.

My body reacts before my mind can comprehend what's happening. My pulse skyrockets, my face feels flushed, and every muscle tenses. My instincts scream for me to run and disappear, but I'm frozen—I can't move.

My mind is racing with images of my childhood—the shouting, the abuse, the neglect, and all the times I literally begged for her attention.

Fear rises from somewhere deep inside me, rippling through my body in waves as the gravity of this moment hits me.

My breathing is heavy.

The room is spinning.

She stumbles toward me, and I catch a strong smell of alcohol.

She's drunk.

How could she just show up here, after all these years? How did she even find me?

I can feel myself shutting down, pulling away.

The room spins in slow motion...

I see Mama Sharon standing in the corner, her hand covering her mouth as if she's in shock.

Daisy whimpers, pressing her body protectively against mine.

Gabe is walking toward me, a distraught look on his face.

Spit is spraying from my mother's wrinkled lips—she's yelling,

chapter 13: The Incident

but I can't make out her words. Her voice—I remember it. Deep. Cold. Laced with cruelty. I want to pretend it doesn't affect me, but it still coils under my skin, unraveling me just like it did when I was a little girl. She damaged me beyond repair.

Tommy reaches for me—I feel his arms wrap around my waist, trying to hold me up, but I'm falling. I cling to him, trying to hold on, but I'm slipping away. My ears ring. My vision blurs. The edges melt, and then everything fades to black.

check on your **happy** friends

14
Kindness and Lies

I wake to sunlight filtering through the curtains. Squinting, I try to focus, but my head feels heavy, like it's wrapped in a fog. I drag my hands over my face, trying to collect my thoughts, but everything is a blur.

I search for my phone. Where is it?

What is going on?

I'm not at home.

The realization slams into me.

I bolt upright, blinking, trying to figure out where I am. The room is unfamiliar—strange walls, a strange smell. I start to get out of bed, but there's a pinch on my arm—then my vision clears, and it hits me.

I'm in the hospital.

There's an IV in my arm.

I'm so confused.

Mama Sharon is beside me. Her long arms wrap tightly around my shoulders.

"Mama Sharon, what's going on?" My voice is hoarse and shaky.

She pulls me in close to her chest, her hands smoothing over my hair. "Shhhh, child. Everything is fine. You just breathe and let me sit with you for a minute. You've been through a lot, sugar. Just take some deep breaths for me, please."

I squeeze my eyes shut, trying to fight back the tears that are welling up inside of me. I feel groggy. I don't understand why I'm here!

Slowly, the fog lifts...

Yesterday.

The shop.

My mother.

The abuse.

It all comes flooding back.

I whisper, "Oh my gosh, Mama Sharon, what have I done?"

"Nothing, honey." Her voice is soft and comforting. "You haven't done anything wrong. Not a thing. You are okay. Everything is going to be fine."

The door creaks open.

"Good morning, Danielle. I'm Doctor Marshall. I admitted you. I'm sure you have a ton of questions for me, but first answer one of mine. How are you feeling?"

I close my eyes, trying to calculate how to respond to her question so I can get out of here quickly. "I'm good! A little confused, but I'm okay."

I force a smile, but it's weak. My lip trembles and my tears are brimming. I swallow hard, trying to hold it together.

Doctor Marshall is eyeing me closely. "Okay, well that's good to hear. Miss Sharon, would you mind stepping out for a few minutes so I can examine Danielle? You can join the others in the waiting room."

I turn to Mama Sharon. "Others in the waiting room? Please tell me it's not Tommy and Gabe."

She smiles softly, with love in her eyes. "It most certainly *is* Tommy and Gabe. Listen to me, sugar, you don't bother yourself with anything but rest. Your healing is coming, my girl. I promise you that." She pats my hand gently, smiles at the doctor, and steps out.

Doctor Marshall stands right next to me. "Now tell me how you're *really* feeling."

I look at her but don't speak. I can't.

chapter 14: Kindness and Lies

"Okay, just relax. Let me check your vitals, and then we'll talk."

I nod and sit perfectly still.

She checks my temperature, my pulse, shines a light in my eyes and instructs me to look from side to side, and then checks my blood pressure with an electronic cuff.

She removes my IV as she's talking. "You were severely dehydrated when you came in, so less coffee and a lot more water, okay? Add some lemon to it for taste if you care to. And honestly, Danielle, I kept you overnight because of fatigue. I know you endured a traumatic event yesterday, but I think you were exhausted as well. I can see the signs. It's important that you take it easy for a while. After some fluids and a solid nine hours of sleep, you look better. Other than slightly elevated blood pressure and a rapid heartbeat, your condition has stabilized. This has been stressful for you, so I'm not surprised you're still anxious. And listen, I know your life has not been easy. Your friend, Tommy, provided a brief history. Do you remember what happened yesterday and how you got here?"

I think for a moment. "I remember everything that happened at the shop and when my um, she, I mean, my mother was there. But I must have blacked out, because I don't remember the rest or how I got here."

"Your mother. Yes," Doctor Marshall says, her voice lower. "I'm gathering this is a strained relationship?"

I immediately look down and begin picking my cuticles.

"Yes," I whisper.

"Okay, well apparently you collapsed and someone called the paramedics. You regained consciousness right away, but seemed to be in shock, so they brought you in and I decided to keep you overnight for observation. I gave you a mild sedative and you fell into a deep sleep. Have you been having a lot of anxiety? Any trouble sleeping?"

I look her straight in the eyes and lie. "I've been a little stressed, but nothing horrible, and I sleep okay."

She nods. "On average, how many hours of sleep would you say you get?"

I keep my gaze fixed on hers and lie again. "Probably five to six hours a night."

She gives me a worried look. "Over an extended period of time that's going to catch up with you, my friend."

I laugh on the inside—*if she only knew!*

"Do you feel safe in your current living situation?" she asks, her voice turning serious.

Okay. Here we go. *Be confident. Be clear.*

"Yes," I say, trying my best not to blink. "I feel safe. I live alone."

"Good. Overall, do you have a strong support system? I know you have friends here today. Do you have more friends, family, or a faith community?"

I've got this. I've got this.

I try to sound confident. "Yes. All of it. I have amazing support."

"Good…" She shifts her posture slightly. "I'm required to ask this next question. Danielle, have you had thoughts of harming yourself or others?"

Answer quickly. Don't hesitate!

"Oh, my goodness, no, never!" I say, my voice louder than it should be. "I have lots of support and I'm happy. My life is good!"

Please believe me. Please believe me.

Doctor Marshall looks down at her notes. Quietly as I can, I exhale the breath I've been holding.

She faces me again, and I tense. There's something different about her expression.

"Danielle…"

I wait, but she just looks at me. She's not saying anything. I ask, "What?"

"Are you sure?"

Don't let her get to you!

chapter 14: Kindness and Lies

"What do you mean?"

Her eyes drift down, and I follow her gaze to my lap.

To where my arm rests.

With my shirtsleeve rolled up over my elbow.

With gauze taped where she removed the IV.

And to the skin of my forearm, exposed as I pick at my fingers...

She sees.

"That's a pretty bad cut," she says.

I stare at it. "It was an accident."

"And all those scars?" she asks softly.

I shiver, and my voice catches. I don't talk about these things.

"Well?"

Lie!

I whisper, "Accident."

"Accident," she repeats.

I nod slightly, still staring at my arm.

Get it together, Dani. Say something. Lie!

I look up. "With a cactus."

We lock eyes. She knows it's not true. I can see it. She's deeply concerned, like maybe she understands, but what can she do? She can't make me talk or admit to anything.

Doctor Marshall sighs. "Okay. Here's what we're going to do. You need resources. I'm sensing you're dealing with a lot. Trauma and stress can really take a toll on us. I'm going to prescribe you a mild sedative that should help with your anxiety, and I'll give you a list of natural remedies for sleep that you can pick up from any health food store. If they don't work, please let me know and I'll prescribe you a sleep aide to use on occasion, just so we can get you back into a good cycle."

She pauses. "I'm also going to have a behavioral health specialist come and speak with you. I'm sure you're ready to get home, but please listen to her. She'll present some resources, and I encourage you to consider counseling, Danielle. You need support, and sometimes healing comes when you talk through your trauma. Does that sound okay?"

"Sounds great," I lie, again. It doesn't sound great—it sounds awful.

"Thanks," I say as she gets up to leave.

She looks at me thoughtfully. "You have people who really care, Danielle. I hope you'll let them help you. Get some rest, and let me know if you need anything. Here's my card."

I nod and do my best to smile.

As soon as the door shuts, I yank my sleeves down, dash into the bathroom, and make the mistake of looking in the mirror. Bloodshot eyes, swollen face, yesterday's make-up smudged and half worn off, my hair sticking up every which way—a total mess.

Cupping cold water in my hands, I splash it over my face until I feel more alert, my skin tingling from the cold. I turn the water to hot, soak a towel, then press my nose into the middle, letting the steam clear my senses.

Like a hidden treasure, I find a hygiene kit with toothpaste, a disposable toothbrush, and a hairband. I use all of it.

Relieved, I glance back in the mirror, then break down into tears once again.

Pull it together or they'll never let you out of here.

Pull yourself together!

I hear the door open and brace myself for the behavioral health person and the questions they'll probably ask me.

I feel exposed. Like everyone knows.

What did Doctor Marshall say to them?

I open the bathroom door to find Tommy, not the hospital staff. He rushes in and hugs me so tightly I can barely breathe. He looks as bad as I feel.

"Are you okay?" he asks. "How are you feeling?"

"I'm okay. I'm okay. I promise. I just really want to go home.

chapter 14: Kindness and Lies

They're going to have one more person come talk to me, then hopefully I'll be released. Where's my car? Can you drive me home?" I'm trying to make sense of everything. My mind is mush. I can't believe I just slept nine hours.

The tension leaves Tommy's face—now he just looks tired. He takes my hand and guides me to the hospital bed, where we sit side by side, eyes fixed on the worn-out linoleum floor.

He hugs me again. "It's going to be okay. I promise you it will. And just so you know, no one blames you for anything. Your mom was awful. I can't believe she just showed up out of the blue! I was freaking out the entire time. I'm so sorry. This whole thing brings back crappy memories. I hate it."

I nod. "Me too. It was horrible, but I'll be okay, I promise."

I need Tommy to believe me. I need *everyone* to believe I'm okay. That is the last time anyone will see me like this—I will *not* lose control again.

Tommy's eyes are bloodshot, and I wonder if he slept at all.

He sighs. "It sucks, but we knew she'd eventually show up. Maybe it's good that it happened, so we don't have to worry about her anymore. After that, I'm sure she'll leave you alone for good."

"Maybe," I say. I don't have the energy to put on a front for Tommy. "I'm just so tired of it all."

The behavioral health specialist enters the room and Tommy leaves. I'm glad she's here—I'm anxious to get this over with. She has a clipboard, a checklist, and a big stack of paperwork I'm hoping isn't all for me. She talks briefly about the effects of trauma and stress, then provides a list of community resources, a 24-hour crisis hotline, and a list of recommended therapists. She is kind and thorough—I can tell she genuinely cares.

She rests her hand on mine. "I don't know your story, but we all have struggles. I hope you take good care of yourself. Here's my card, call me if I can help you with anything, okay?"

She's so nice I feel like I might cry—I guess it's all I do now.

"Thank you so much," I say, sincerely. "This is really helpful, and I appreciate your kindness."

I study her business card and slip it into my pocket so I don't lose it. Her name is Clare—it suits her. Clare loads me up with a folder stuffed full of information and I thank her repeatedly.

As soon as she steps through the door, the discharge nurse comes in and reviews my aftercare plan:

- ❑ Pick up prescribed medication from the pharmacy.
- ❑ Select an over-the-counter sleep aid from the Physician's Approved List and take as directed.
- ❑ Increase daily water intake.
- ❑ Ensure adequate and consistent rest.
- ❑ Review counseling and support group resources provided. Consider initiating as appropriate.
- ❑ Contact physician with any questions, concerns, or changes in condition.

I thank the discharge nurse over and over again because like the others, he is incredibly kind. I feel like a complete idiot putting everyone out like this when there are other people who really need help. I'm so embarrassed.

Finally, I head to the waiting room and am relieved to see Tommy sitting alone.

He stands. "Hey, you ready to go? I thought you might need a minute, so I asked Mama Sharon and Gabe to leave. They both said to let you know they're thinking about you and praying for you. Here, let me take your stuff." Tommy carries everything, and I'm glad, because even after all that sleep, I'm still exhausted.

We drive home in silence, both of us struggling to make sense of why life is so hard. Yesterday was devastating for Tommy. I can see it in his eyes, and it makes me feel horrible that I'm the one responsible. He deserves better.

YOU'RE NOTHING BUT A BURDEN. YOU HURT EVERYONE AROUND YOU. LOOK AT THE MESS YOU'VE MADE.

The voice is back—louder than ever.

"What pharmacy are we going to?" Tommy asks.

I shake my head, trying to silence the inner voice before I respond.

"All I want to do right now is go home and take a shower. I'll drive myself to pick it up later. It will be good for me."

Tommy nods in understanding. We pull up to where my car is parked and he cuts the engine, lays his head on the steering wheel, and stares down at the floorboard. He looks like he did when we were young—broken and scared.

"We're going to make it, Dani. Okay? We have each other. That's all we need." I hear the heaviness in his voice.

I do my best to smile, but the tears are threatening to spill again, so I don't speak.

Tommy sits up and clears his throat. "Hey, Mama Sharon said for you to take a few days off and get rest. She'll see you Monday, but if you're still not ready, she said no worries. I'm heading home. If you need anything, I'm just a phone call away. I can be there in ten minutes."

I appreciate Tommy so much. I hug him tightly. "Thank you for everything, and I'm so, so sorry. Please go home and get some sleep. You look awful."

He raises his eyebrows. "*I* look awful? Have you looked in the mirror lately?"

We burst into laughter instead of tears—because sometimes you just have to. If we didn't laugh, we might completely fall apart.

"Okay," Tommy says, "I'm going to go home, eat the snacks you bought me yesterday, inhale the cookies from Mama Sharon, and then I'm going to pass out for at least ten hours."

The heaviness is gone from his voice, but when he looks at me, his eyes are still red. "Seriously," he says, sounding confident for the first time today, "if you need me, I'm here. Get rest. Love you forever. We're going to be okay. I promise."

I wish I could believe him.

Tommy gathers my things, hands them to me, and I watch as he drives away.

My body aches. My mind is reeling. But there's relief because I'm finally alone. I pull the business card from my pocket and trace my finger over Clare's name. I consider keeping it, but instead, I walk over to the dumpster and toss it in along with the folder full of paperwork from the hospital—I won't be needing any of it. I glance at the prescription for anxiety meds but decide to toss it as well—I'm not going through that again.

The drive home is quick. I barely register it.

As I trudge up the stairs to my place, self-loathing gnaws on my bones. I hate myself for wasting everyone's time. I hate this feeling of being exposed. But mostly, I hate my repulsive mother for ruining my life.

15
Angels Singing

Morning comes.

The sun rises.

The sky is still blue.

I don't know how the world keeps turning or how I'm still here, but somehow, I am.

Today is a big day, and if I'm not careful, I could spiral into a full-blown episode of—I don't know what—but it wouldn't be good. I need to pull myself together. I don't want to disappoint Tommy by not showing up, but this will not be easy. For starters, I barely slept, but to make matters even worse, I somehow managed to drink an entire pot of coffee because when night terrors come—and they always do—I'll try *anything* to stay awake. I'm definitely awake, but the caffeine shakes are at full throttle.

The other reason I'm a mess is because this will be the first time I see Tommy, Gabe, and Mama Sharon since the incident with my mother.

Since it happened, I haven't been able to muster the courage to face them or even step foot in the shop. I know they'll look at me differently, and I hate the fact that they saw me fall apart. Mama Sharon graciously told me to take all the time I need, and so far it's been a couple weeks, but the truth is, I may never go back.

My phone buzzes with a text. It's Tommy. Again.

He's already sent five messages this morning pleading with me to come, telling me how excited he is, and reminding me of what time it starts. This is a big day for him—one that he's been looking forward to, and I don't want to let him down. I can't. I have *got* to get it together and show up, no matter what.

What I thought was just another of Tommy's latest fads turned into a serious, real life change for him, and today at 3:00 this afternoon, at Freedom Church on Mission Boulevard, Thomas David Goodwin will publicly declare his faith by baptism. He wants to tell the world that he loves Jesus, and the more people watching, the better. He loves an audience, he always has.

Tommy's faith has changed him in big ways. He's sober, he's taken a pause from dating, and he seems to be focused on becoming a better man. He tends to drag me along on all his escapades, but not this one. It seems deeply personal, and he hasn't talked much about it.

I'm not sure what I believe. My parents never took me to church or talked to me about God or the universe or anything, and honestly, I've never given it much thought. But if there really is a God, and if He is as good as everyone seems to think He is, then why hasn't He shown up for me? I don't even care anymore. It's too late for me, but I'm thrilled for my friend. Tommy deserves the best, and if finding Jesus makes him happy, then it makes me happy too.

Gabe and Mama Sharon offered to pick me up so we could all ride together, but I prefer to drive myself so I can leave whenever I'm ready. I've only been to church a few times, and I've never attended a baptism, so I have no idea what to expect, and I'm nervous about it.

I study my reflection in the full-length mirror one last time. I chose a sleeveless, fitted dress that falls just above my knees. It's a pale rose color that matches my lipstick perfectly. My heels are soft beige with thin straps that wrap around my ankles and crisscross in the front. I let my hair air dry so it's extra fluffy and curly. I decided to let it fall freely instead of pinning it back like I always do. I've become quite

chapter 15: Angels Singing

good at hiding my true self; make-up and clothes can do wonders. A little concealer, and no one should notice my arm. I rotate it to catch the light in the mirror. *I can barely tell.*

It's time to go, so I close my eyes, take a deep and cleansing breath, and head to my car.

Worries tumble through my mind on the drive. I hope no one mentions the incident with my mother. I just want to forget it ever happened and put it behind me. I tell myself to calm down and walk into the church with confidence. It's the only way I'll get through this.

Traffic is light so I arrive early, and I'm grateful for the extra time. I add gloss to my lips, run my fingers through my hair, take one last desperate look in my visor mirror, and head inside. My nerves are shot, and my heart is pounding, but I don't have a choice now—I need to go through with this.

THEY ALL KNOW THE TRUTH. THEY'LL BE WHISPERING BEHIND YOUR BACK. THEY THINK YOU'RE CRAZY.

I tell myself to ignore the inner voice and focus on acting confident. *Breathe. Don't listen. Let it go.*

I'm surprised when I walk into the church—the setting is much different than what I expected. Because it's Tommy, I thought there would be bright lights and a rambunctious crowd, but it's quite the opposite. The soft, warm lighting creates a peaceful atmosphere, and I immediately feel the need to slow my steps and walk softly.

I stop and look around, taking in the uniqueness of this beautiful church. The roof is high and vaulted, with six huge wooden beams that stretch from the floor all the way up to the ceiling. The walls are an exquisite mix of brick and stone, and the pews are shiny, polished wood. You can tell it's been well taken care of.

At the front, next to the stage, are vases filled with long, silvery-green eucalyptus branches that spread a sweet fragrance throughout the room. Flickering white candles line the stage, and dozens of pots full of cream-colored gardenias sit on the floor next to the altar.

The stained-glass windows are gorgeous, but by far the most striking feature is the massive wooden cross that hangs high on the wall at the center of everything.

Someone taps my shoulder—it's Tommy in a black suit, handsome as ever. He looks excited, and much better than the last time I saw him.

"You made it!" he says, and hugs me tightly.

I smile. He's literally glowing. "Did I have a choice? You only sent me a dozen reminders this morning."

He grins. "Because I wanted you here for this!" He spins around. "How does my hair look?"

"Ten out of ten."

"Cool." Tommy looks pleased.

"Big day, huh?" I ask, trying to be encouraging.

"Yep! It's HUGE for me. I hope I don't bawl my eyes out up there, because that would be embarrassing, but who cares, right? I'm so excited!"

"I'm excited *for* you! And I must say, you look amazing." I fix his collar and straighten his tie.

His eyes are burrowing into mine. I know this look. It means he's about to spring something on me, so I ask, "Why are you looking at me like that?"

Tommy rolls his eyes. "There's someone I want you to meet, and it's not "like that," but she's special. Will you wait here for just a second? Also, you look stunning! Are you okay? I mean, are you doing okay, really?"

I nod. "Yes. I'm taking care of myself, so don't worry about me. And yes, I'll wait, but hurry, you have water to splash around in!"

Tommy rolls his eyes again, then walks away. As soon as he leaves, I see Gabe heading in my direction. I brace myself, hoping he doesn't bring up the incident.

"Hey." Gabe has a soft smile on his face as he approaches me.

chapter 15: Angels Singing

"Hey," I say back, my stomach tangled in knots.

"I saw you walk in, so I got you a coffee. Latte with whole milk double shot, right?"

I'm amazed. "Yes! You remembered? I do *not* need more caffeine, but I'm totally drinking it. Thank you so much, Gabe. That was thoughtful of you."

Gabe raises his coffee cup to mine and toasts, "Cheers to Tommy finding Jesus. It makes me so happy."

I'm curious, so I ask, "Does it? How so?"

He looks directly at me. "Because finding Christ saves your life."

I raise my eyebrows at him. "You sound certain of that."

"It's the only thing I *am* certain of, Dani," he says without hesitation.

I'm not sure how to respond, so I'm relieved when Tommy walks up with his friend—she's lovely with a quiet confidence I like right away. "Hey," he says, "so glad you're both here! Dani, this is Vanessa—Vanessa, this is my best friend, Dani, who I've told you about. And you already know Gabe."

I'm shocked. I haven't heard her name before. Vanessa has a wonderful smile, and she's looking at Tommy as if he hung the moon.

"Great to meet you, Vanessa!" I say.

She takes my hand, "Dani, I've heard so much about you. Lovely to finally meet you too!"

"Hey," Tommy says before I can respond, "we gotta go. I'm up soon!" He takes Vanessa's hand, and they disappear into the crowd.

Gabe offers his arm, which I take. "C'mon, let's go find our seats next to Mama Sharon and Papa Reg."

I'm elated that Papa Reg is here too. This is turning into quite a celebration!

Arm in arm, we make our way to Mama Sharon. She looks like a vision dressed in vibrant oranges and reds from her head wrap all the way down to her fabulous silver flats. Big gold hoop earrings dangle against her smooth, dark skin, and she is absolutely stunning.

She smiles warmly and pats the seat next to hers for me to sit.

Papa Reg stands up to greet me, towering over everyone. "How you doing, honey?" His voice is booming as usual.

I smile. "I'm good, Papa Reg, and you're looking handsome as ever!"

He chuckles and waves me off.

I take my seat next to Mama Sharon. She leans over. "You look lovely, sugar, I'm so happy to see you!"

I whisper back, "I was just going to say the exact same thing to you! I love you, Mama Sharon. I'm so sorry about everything." My voice cracks with emotion—I'm mortified about what happened.

Mama Sharon takes my hand in hers and pats it gently, then looks at Gabe, who is sitting on my other side. "Okay, you two, let's pay attention now, this is a big deal for Tommy, and we don't want to miss a thing."

We settle into our seats, our eyes glued to the stage in front of us.

Vanessa, Tommy's friend, walks out first with an acoustic guitar strapped over her shoulder. She adjusts her microphone and flashes a smile at someone in the front row—Tommy. The look she gave him was quick, but I definitely saw it. Something about the way they look at each other seems special, even if they *are* just friends.

One by one, band members take the stage. It's an interestingly diverse group. The drummer has long dreadlocks with a bandana tied neatly around his forehead. The lead and bass guitarists look like they could be brothers; both are clean-cut with collared shirts and slacks. And the keyboard player is striking with long, straight blonde hair, thick, black-rimmed glasses, and wide bell-bottomed jeans. The moment they step on stage, you can feel it—they seem excited to be here, like something wonderful is about to unfold. The dread in my stomach has been replaced with anticipation. I can hardly wait for whatever is next!

Once the band is settled into their respective places, the church grows quiet—so quiet, all I can hear is the gentle breathing of the

chapter 15: Angels Singing

people sitting around me.

The lights dim until it's almost completely dark, and then a soft spotlight shines down on Vanessa. The rest of the band is hidden. Vanessa's eyes are closed, her chin tilted up, her body moving slightly, as if she hears music the rest of us can't. She remains like that for a while with her guitar hanging by her side, and then she steps up to the mic.

"Amazing grace..." She sings, acapella, breaking the silence. Her voice is captivating and not at all what I expected. It's deep and smooth as she pours out the lyrics of a song that even *I* recognize.

Vanessa's voice is just a whisper, so sweet and sultry that I find myself fighting back tears. It grows steadily with power and soul as she sings, and then she swings her guitar from her shoulder and starts strumming.

The band joins in. The spotlight fades and the lights get brighter. The band sounds incredible with each instrument weaving together and building in momentum, echoing throughout every corner of the sanctuary.

A screen with the song lyrics drops down, Vanessa signals, and the entire congregation rises to their feet and sings along. The church comes alive as the song progresses, and Vanessa's voice booms with so much power it gives me goosebumps. I glance around the room, overwhelmed by what I see—arms raised up, hands outstretched, people swaying to the music and singing freely with so much life pulsing in the air that the church is vibrating. I'm completely in awe.

Tommy is standing in front, his eyes closed, one hand on his heart and one raised above his head with fingers spread wide. Mama Sharon's body flows in natural rhythm with the music as she sings at the top of her lungs, and even papa Reg is tapping his foot and belting out the words. I notice Gabe is standing perfectly still, singing softly with his eyes fixed on the cross. I can't read the look on his face, but he seems completely absorbed like the rest of us.

Little did I know, the worship team was just getting started! They play five more songs, each filling the room with so much energy and joy that I feel breathless. Lyrics for each song dance on the big screen, so everyone joins in, including me. At one point, I look up, fully expecting to see angels hovering above and singing with us. I'm so overcome with emotion that tears spill from my eyes.

Gabe notices, and hands me a tissue.

I feel embarrassed and whisper to him, "I don't know what's wrong with me, I'm so embarrassed. I can't believe I'm crying!"

Gabe smiles wide. "Dani, please don't be embarrassed. I get emotional too. Just let the music wash over you. Feel it and enjoy it!"

Something about his words gives me confidence, so instead of overthinking it, I decide to take his advice and experience these moments fully.

By the time the music ends, I'm speechless. It was a rush that cannot be explained, and there's still more to come! I wipe my eyes, breathe deeply, and brace myself for whatever is next.

Pastor John takes the stage, thanks the worship team, welcomes the congregation, and instructs us to greet the people next to us.

Gabe and I immediately turn to each other and embrace. "I'm so glad you're here," he whispers in my ear.

I want to hold on to him forever, but he pulls away and greets the guy next to him. Mama Sharon and Papa Reg are doing the same, so I follow along and introduce myself to the young couple sitting in front of me. The church is buzzing as people greet each other, and then it ends as quickly as it started.

The pastor signals for us to take our seats. The rooms grows quiet once again, and he leads us in prayer.

He starts into a message. Each time he shares from scripture, Gabe opens his Bible to the correct page and holds it up so I can read along. It's a small, but incredibly thoughtful gesture that makes me feel included.

chapter 15: Angels Singing

Pastor John looks over the congregation. "A public baptism dedicated to the Lord Jesus Christ is a deeply symbolic and meaningful event in the life of a believer," he explains. "It's a ceremony in which someone publicly declares their commitment to Jesus, acknowledging His role as Savior and Lord in their life. It's a declaration of faith, an outward symbol of inner change. The person getting baptized commits to much more than the ceremony you will witness today. This is a lifelong commitment to live in a way that reflects Jesus's teachings and values, aiming to grow in faith, love, and service to others. It's a way of saying to the world, 'I am a follower of Jesus.'

"The ceremony of baptism represents the death, burial, and resurrection of Jesus. When the person is submerged in, or sprinkled with water, it symbolizes dying to their old way of life—leaving behind sin and past mistakes and being spiritually 'born again' into a new life, now centered on Christ.

"It truly is an honor that today, I have the privilege of performing the baptism of a young man I have grown quite fond of over the last several months. His name is Thomas David Goodwin." Pastor John smiles. "We call him Tommy."

"Some time ago, I spoke at a service to honor a young man who tragically took his own life. Of all the services I've attended, the ones involving suicide are by far the hardest. Suicide is a deeply painful and difficult thing to understand. I did my best to point the attendees to Christ that day, and I tried to speak words of comfort, but let me tell you, it is a mountain of a task. Suicide is NEVER the right option, and while we might not understand the darkness and pain that the person who takes their own life must be facing, we know that the *only* answer is Christ. In Him there is *always* hope, no matter how bad the struggle. Friends, God is greater than our pain. He is life. He is breath. He is sufficient!"

The pastor's words shake me. I was not prepared for this.

"Anyone who knows Tommy would tell you he feels things deeply.

Tommy is an open book, and we love that about him. On the day of the service, something happened—Tommy left consumed by fear. He was deeply confused and struggling, so much so that he was finding it hard to function, so he reached out to me. I met with him and shared the good news of the Gospel. Tommy believed, as many do, that if you're a good person, it saves you a spot in heaven. I explained to him that salvation is only promised when you accept Jesus Christ as your Lord and Savior. We spoke often, and over time, something began to shift. I saw it with my own eyes, and Tommy has never looked back! So yes, church, today is extra special for me. But before we get to the baptism, Tommy would like to say a few words."

Wait. What?

I turn to Mama Sharon. "Did you know he was going to speak?"

Mama Sharon shakes her head but keeps her eyes on the stage. "No, I didn't, but I'm not surprised. God is going to use Tommy in mighty ways, just you wait and see."

I glance at Gabe. He shrugs his shoulders; he didn't know either.

Drawing a deep breath, I fix my eyes on Tommy, who is so much braver than I am.

Tommy takes the microphone from the stand and holds it, pacing the stage confidently. "What's up, Church! Ya'll are looking GOOD today! Can you hear me okay?"

The congregation laughs. Tommy is beyond endearing.

"We can hear you loud and clear, brother!" Gabe yells.

Tommy smiles, then his expression turns serious. "Thank you all for being here, it means a lot to me. I'm going to share a little about my life, but before I do, I want to be clear about something. I am not sharing for sympathy or as an excuse for any of the horrible choices I've made. I share my story only to give hope to anyone here who is struggling, and to show how Christ has changed me."

Tommy's voice cracks with emotion. "I grew up in a violent home. I never felt safe there. Love was something you had to earn. I was

chapter 15: Angels Singing

desperate to be loved and would do just about anything for attention. I happily lapped up any scraps that were thrown at me. I was like a beaten-down dog who still wags its tail when you pet it. The only happy memories I have of my childhood took place in a treehouse built at the top of a massive oak in my neighborhood park. It was a secret place for me and my best friend, Dani. We met there every chance we had. Sometimes we snuck out late at night and brought our flashlights so we could find our way in the dark. We brought books and toys and talked for hours. We told each other stories, sang songs, and talked endlessly about only happy things. That treehouse was my refuge. It was the only place I felt safe. Dani had a tough home life too, but we found comfort in that treehouse and in each other. It's a friendship I treasure to this day."

Tommy looks directly at me and smiles, and I'm afraid I might fall apart. I loved that treehouse!

"I've been addicted to everything you can think of," he continues. "By 12 I was addicted to porn and that stayed with me for years. You name the drugs, I probably took them. In high school I was popping over 100 milligrams of Adderall a day, and if you don't know about Adderall—that's a lot more than anyone should *ever* take. In college I drank every chance I got, I took advantage of women to fulfill my sexual desires, I popped pills, snorted cocaine, and would do just about anything to numb myself. There was even a time I contemplated overdosing on purpose because being six feet underground sounded a lot better than facing another day. I was empty and constantly searching for an escape. And then, recently, I went to a funeral of a guy who could have been me. He seemed to have everything going for him, but he took his own life, because for him, facing another day was out of the question. I hated that service because everyone was shocked and wondered how he could do something so horrific, but I wasn't shocked, and that scared me. I *understood.* I actually *could* imagine doing that, and the feeling terrified me. I praise God for leading me to Pastor John and this church. During one of our many meetings, he said something that got my attention. He told me that God has a plan and a purpose for me, and that all I needed to do was follow Christ and He would lead me to a life worth living."

Tommy smiles. "After talking to Pastor John, I remember thinking, oh man, I can definitely follow this Jesus guy. I've been chasing things and following people my entire life. That comes easy for me! But this time was different. This time I was following someone who would change my life in ways I never imagined. This time I was following my Savior, Jesus Christ. His Word tells me I am loved. I am seen. I am known."

Tommy doesn't bother wiping away the tears falling from his eyes.

I'm holding my breath, because now I KNOW I'm going to fall apart!

"You see," Tommy says, "when I was a boy, I was told over and over again that I was worthless. I was told that I was a mistake and would never amount to anything, and I believed it. I wore those words on my heart my entire life, and *believed* them. But now I know that it was all a lie, because God NEVER makes mistakes."

The tears subside and Tommy is beaming. "I'm so excited to get baptized and feel the cleansing that washes away my sins. Knowing I am forgiven and made new makes me grateful to be alive and standing here in front of you today."

Tommy pauses, his eyes searching the crowd. "Listen, when I was a little boy, that treehouse was a safe place for me. It was a place where I felt the love of my best friend. It was a place where I wasn't judged, and I could be my true self. And now, I don't need a treehouse anymore, because I've got Jesus. He *is* my treehouse. He's my shelter, my friend, my safe place. Christ is where I belong. Never condemned, never judged, only loved and accepted, just as I am—a broken man who loves Jesus."

Tommy's face breaks into a huge grin as he turns to Pastor John.

chapter 15: Angels Singing

"Okay, I'm ready, it's go time! Let's do this!"

The pastor practically runs to Tommy, shakes his hand vigorously, and takes the microphone as he's wiping tears from his eyes. "Now those, God's people, are the words of a soul saved. Praise Jesus!"

"Praise Jesus!" The congregation repeats it back, loudly, and with the passion of ten thousand voices.

There's a hush in the church as the pastor leads Tommy to the baptism pool. He speaks softly, they meet eyes, smile, then bow their heads together in prayer. The smiles stay on their faces as they step down into the water. Pastor John guides Tommy deeper, dipping him under for just a few seconds, then raising him up, and they embrace.

The entire congregation leaps to their feet with a thunderous boom that makes me jump. The applause is so loud I swear the walls are shaking.

There is not a dry eye in the house.

I stand in amazement, flooded with feelings I can't explain.

Tommy—my sweet, emotional, passionate, brave best friend—just brought an entire congregation to tears. I don't really understand what just happened, and I don't know anything about Jesus, but there is no denying I witnessed a miracle today. I'm so glad I came. I whisper under my breath, just in case He *really* is real, "Thank you, Jesus, for saving my friend."

check on your **happy** friends

16
Fleeting Hope

After the baptism, we all wait in the church lobby for Tommy, who has changed out of his wet clothes and is now busy shaking hands and giving hugs to a swarm of people who seem to adore him. Tommy gave a powerful testimony today, and the congregation was moved by it. It moved me too.

Finally, the crowd clears and Tommy walks up to us with Vanessa by his side. "Let's get some food," he says. "All of us, together. Please! I'm starving!"

Everyone, including Papa Reg, looks at Mama Sharon, because even though we're adults, Mama Sharon is the one in charge and we all know it.

Papa Reg nudges her gently. "The diner down the street has the best pancakes and hashbrowns in town. I'd be happy to drive us, my darling."

Mama Sharon gives an approving nod, and like one big happy, hungry family, we head to the parking lot and pile into Papa Reg's gigantic, midnight blue SUV. Gabe holds the door open for Mama Sharon, Vanessa and I hop in the very back, and Tommy and Gabe slide into the middle seat.

I was worried about my anxiety and almost didn't come along, but I quickly dismissed the thought because I knew Tommy wouldn't have it, and besides, my mind is still reeling from the service, and I don't want to leave them all just yet.

It's a quick, quiet drive to Dino's Diner. Like me, I'm sure the others are lost in thought about what we all just witnessed. I still can't get over Tommy's testimony and how honest he was. I could never do what he just did—not in a million years could I stand in front of people and share the ugliness of my past. But before I can take that thought any further, we arrive at the diner.

As soon as Tommy gets out of the car, Mama Sharon hugs him tightly. "I am so proud of you! I know it wasn't easy to speak about your struggles, but you blessed every person in that room today. It was an incredible testimony, and I had no idea you were such a powerful speaker. God bless you, Thomas!"

Gabe follows Mama Sharon with praise for Tommy, then Vanessa and Papa Reg chime in, and then all eyes are on me. I can't find the words, so instead, I hug him and whisper in his ear, "The treehouse!"

"The treehouse!" Tommy whispers back.

The sweetness of the moment continues as we walk into the diner. The clanging of dishes and folks chatting fills the room, as do the smells of freshly brewed coffee, cinnamon rolls, and warm, baked bread. My stomach growls and I'm suddenly famished.

A tall, red-headed server named Kip leads us to a table in the back where it's a bit quieter. Kip rushes to pull out a chair for Mama Sharon to sit, and I can't help but smile. Even this young man senses her presence—she has that effect on people. I'm not sure what it is about her that demands respect, but I've felt it since we first met.

The six of us find our seats and mine is in-between Mama Sharon and Tommy. Sitting next to my two favorite people is exactly where I want to be in this moment.

Kip hands us each a menu. Tommy takes his but doesn't even look at it. "Kip," he asks, "what's your favorite thing on the menu?"

Kip is visibly excited. He smiles. "Bro, the chicken-fried steak with eggs and potatoes covered in gravy is bomb!"

chapter 16: Fleeting Hope

Tommy smiles back. "Yep! That's what I'm getting. Thanks, man."

Kip pours our coffee into little white ceramic mugs that remind me of the ones my grandma had stacked up in the cupboard right above her coffeepot. I smile at the memory and enjoy what must be my tenth cup of coffee today. Caffeine jitters are no joke! I make a mental note to cut down and drink more water like the doctor suggested.

Kip pulls out his pen and notepad, ready to take our orders. Everyone picks *big* food. Tommy orders Kip's favorite and a few sides, Gabe and Papa Reg order steak and eggs, Mama Sharon gets a vegetable omelet, Vanessa picks French toast, and I order my favorite blueberry pancakes with a side of fruit.

I know this is just breakfast with friends at a local diner, but it feels more like a feast with people who have something special to celebrate. I'm happy for Tommy, and I'm grateful to be here with him. When I woke up full of dread this morning, I had no idea what an incredible day this would turn out to be.

Our new friend, Kip, delivers our food, and everyone laughs as he struggles to make enough room on the table for Tommy's massive meal—country-fried steak with all the fixings just as Kip described, an extra stack of pancakes piled high, a side of bacon, and a huge cinnamon roll.

I glance around the table, looking at each one of my friends as they enjoy this moment, and I'm suddenly aware of the lightness I feel in my chest. When my eyes land on Gabe, he notices and gives me a quick wink—I wink back and find it hard to look away. The conversation is light and easy as we eat, and I can't remember when I last felt this comfortable.

The inner voice is silent.

My mind is quiet for once.

We all ask for to-go boxes because none of us were able to finish our food, except for Tommy, of course, who ate every single bite of his and is now complaining that he's too full.

When the bill comes, we all reach for our wallets, but Mama Sharon waves her hand in the air, stopping us. "Reg, would you be a dear and pick up the tab?"

Papa Reg nods. "Your wish is my command, my darling."

Gabe, Tommy, Vanessa, and I all object and extend our hands full of cash over to Papa Reg.

He looks at us with his eyes narrowed. "Ya'll going to upset Mama Sharon and try to give me your money? Or are you going to graciously thank her and do as she says?"

Like little kids, we put our money away and thank Mama Sharon, who looks quite pleased with her husband. We breathe a collective sigh of relief and burst into laughter.

With happy hearts and full bellies, we leave our table full of empty dishes and head to the parking lot.

The ride back to the church is quiet until Papa Reg speaks, "Tommy, son," his voice commanding and strong, "what you did at church today took guts. You shared things that are deeply personal, and I'm guessing you've kept some of that to yourself for a long time. When you give your testimony like you did today, it not only brings you healing, but it gives others hope. There was a big crowd, and I'm sure there were folks struggling, and maybe, just maybe, your story will give them enough hope to keep going. You seek guidance from the Lord, Thomas, and He will direct you, and remember, Mama Sharon and I are here for whatever you need. You hear me?"

Papa Reg's words go straight to my heart, and I have to fight back tears.

"Yes, thank you, sir," Tommy says. "I hear you, and I'm very grateful." He turns to each of us. "Thank you all for coming. I needed you with me today."

Without saying a word, Vanessa reaches over the seat and lays her hand on Tommy's shoulder. He rests his own on hers.

chapter 16: Fleeting Hope

My eyes drift over to Gabe, who is looking at Tommy and beaming with pride.

We make it back to the parking lot and everyone piles out one last time. There are more smiles and hugs and laughter, and something in the air that I can't quite put my finger on, but it feels like love. It feels like hope.

I drive home with all the windows down, letting my hair fly freely, and it feels good. I think about Tommy and Papa Reg's words and the tears start falling, but I don't mind, it's a welcome release.

Tommy *was* brave today. Like mine, his life has been a constant battle, but he handles it differently than I do. He lets his feelings pour out into the world, revealing his deepest, darkest pain, and he doesn't care who knows. That's the difference between me and him. I can't speak of my pain, because I'm still in it—it's part of who I am, but I'm not going to let that weigh me down today. Nope! Instead, I decide to turn the music up and let this feeling—this glimmer of something good—wash over me as I enjoy the rest of the ride home.

On a whim, I stop at the flower shop and buy two dozen of my favorite bright yellow roses. The buds are still closed, so I'm excited to watch them open up into full bloom.

As I'm walking from the flower shop to my car, my phone alerts me with a text message.

It's Tommy: "Thank you for coming. I love you! Jesus loves you! And I think Vanessa loves you, too!!!"

I smile as I text him back: "You were magnificent! I'm happy you found Jesus and Vanessa! Love you!!!"

Tommy replies with a dozen smiling emojis, and I feel like my heart might burst with love for him. What a wonderful friend he is. I really am thrilled he found Vanessa. He deserves happiness!

Pleased with myself, I drive the rest of the way home, rush into my apartment, and arrange the roses in my tall, clear glass vase. I set them down in my bedroom, move them to the coffee table, then decide to leave them on the counter by the kitchen window where the morning sun streams in. Pausing to admire the bouquet, I make a quiet promise to myself to buy flowers more often.

Ready to relax, I kick off my heels, step out of my dress, put on my comfy clothes, and tie my now wildly poofy hair up into a bun, and just as I'm about to warm up the rest of my blueberry pancakes, my phone beeps with another text.

It's so like Tommy to keep sending messages. Sometimes it's a bit too much, but after such a special day, I don't mind at all.

I look at my phone, smiling expectantly at what Tommy has to say next.

But the text isn't from Tommy.

And I don't recognize the number.

My stomach lurches as I read the first message: "Danielle. This is your mother."

This cannot be happening.

Another message: "Call me right now."

My throat constricts. The color drains from my face.

"This is your mother! You don't get to ignore me!"

My phones rings. It's the same number. It's her.

I can't answer it. I *won't* answer it.

Another message comes right after: "PICK UP YOUR PHONE!"

My phone rings again.

Then another message, and another, each growing more aggressive.

"Don't make me come find you. Call me right now!"

Before I can catch my breath, another hateful message comes. Her words spit venom from the screen.

My heart is pounding so hard I can feel it all the way to my temples. I'm like a walking jack hammer—this is a nightmare!

I can almost hear my dad's voice. "*Dani girl, just be quiet. Stay in your room and make yourself small until your mother calms down.*"

I throw my phone across the room, hoping to make it stop, but the screen continues to flash as the text messages and voice mails keep coming—one alert after another—stacking on top of each other like bricks on my chest. I crouch in the corner, sobbing, feeling the weight of my pain crashing over me. Day after day I try my best, but it's not enough. I'm not like Tommy. There is no hope for me.

check on your **happy** friends

17
Fire in the Sink

As soon as I wake up, I know I can't go in to work today. I didn't sleep, and I'm exhausted. Most days I can push through, but not today. There is just no way.

I take a long, shaky breath, and try to muster enough courage to call Mama Sharon.

She answers on the second ring. "Morning sugar, how's my girl?"

The warmth of her voice splits me in half.

"Morning, Mama Sharon. I'm not great, and I hate to leave you stranded, but I can't come in. I know this is supposed to be my first day back, but I need more time. I'm sorry. I'm so, so sorry."

Please please please don't be disappointed in me.

"Sugar," she says, not missing a beat, "don't you worry about a thing. There's no need to be sorry. Tommy, Gabe, and our new volunteer are available if I need them. Stay home and do what you need to do. Can I help with anything?"

The weight on my chest lightens. "Thank you so much for that. You know I never want to let you down. I was fine and I had the best day with you all yesterday. Then somehow my mother got my phone number and started harassing me. She called me last night and left cruel voice mails and sent dozens of hateful text messages and I didn't sleep. I've blocked her and I'm changing my phone number, but I'm struggling today. I'm so sorry."

The truth slips out before I can stop it, and just like that I fall apart.

"Oh honey, you precious girl. I am so sorry! Can I come and sit with you? Do you need Papa Reg to do anything? You should notify the police and file a report just in case. Please come and stay with us. I'll wash the sheets and have the guest room ready."

I pull myself together—quickly. I don't want her to worry about me.

I fake a more confident tone. "Oh, you are so kind. Thank you, Mama Sharon, you have no idea how much I appreciate you, but I think I just need some time alone. I'm safe. She doesn't know where I live, and she can't call me anymore. This will blow over, I'm sure of it. I just need to rest and put it behind me. But thank you for offering. Thank you so much."

"Okay," she says, "I understand. Remember we're just a phone call away. We love you, Danielle. Everything is going to be okay. Take the time you need. I have coverage for the whole week, so don't worry about anything. Call if you need us. I love you. Bye bye, sugar."

"I love you too. Thank you so much."

I drop to the floor and sit with my eyes closed, trying to piece myself back together.

Inhale.

Exhale.

Inhale.

Exhale.

Deeper this time.

Inhale.

Exhale.

Hold it.

Inhale.

Exhale.

My heart slows down and my shoulders slump.

The last 24 hours have been a whirlwind.

Yesterday was amazing, I'll never forget it. Listening to Tommy give

chapter 17: Fire in the Sink

his testimony, watching his baptism, being in that gorgeous church with the music blasting, and spending time with people I care about… It was incredible. By the time I got home, something had shifted. A light and beautiful feeling came over me and I felt a smidgen of hope. It wasn't much, but it was something! Then I received the first text message from my wretched mother…

"This is your mother."

Those four little words were a blade in my back—she ruined everything and buried every last bit of hope I had. Of course she did. She's the demon in my head—ripping me open, twisting my thoughts, dragging me deeper into the darkness.

After the messages finally stopped, I managed to doze off just long enough to have a horrible nightmare. It was shockingly vivid, and I remember every detail. My dreams have always been filled with blurry images. Most I can't recall when I wake up, but something has changed, because all morning my mind has been flooded with specific memories and clear pictures of my childhood.

I *have* to do something to get control over this. It seems to me, if I can't get rid of the demons that keep chasing me, then maybe it's time to stop running and face them head-on. I'll write down everything I remember, and maybe I can make some sense of it.

I've done enough research and read enough books to know that my anxiety and sleep struggles are because of the trauma I endured as a child, but nothing has ever been clear. My memories have always come in fragmented flashes. I couldn't make complete sense of them, but that's not the case now. There must be a reason all this is happening— it's time to stop living in fear and take back control.

My mother neglected me, which is why I ended up living with Grandma Vee. But it wasn't just neglect, she was abusive as well. She's my birth mother, but she did *not* take care of me. She never loved me, in fact, she seemed to despise me. What did I do to deserve that?

Hopefully, if I record the details of my dreams and memories, then maybe I can start putting the pieces together.

I'll treat the nights like a research project with the goal of capturing and recording every memory and image that shows up in my head.

I'm strangely excited because I have a plan, and it just might lead to answers.

The next four days are a blur. I toss and turn so much that my bones ache, but eventually the images come. I document everything I can remember and get into a steady rhythm of journaling. The hours pass quickly as I fill the pages, and even though the hidden horrors of my childhood are coming alive, at least I feel in control again.

Journal Entry: *It's dark, and I'm trying to sleep, but I hear yelling and bottles breaking. My mother is screaming at my dad. She's slurring her words, yelling louder and louder, while dad stays quiet. He seems afraid of her. My chest heaves in and out. I can't breathe.*

Journal Entry: *The room is white with bright lights over me. I'm in a bathtub and the water is so cold I'm shivering. There's slimy green mold in the corners of the tiles. My mother is screaming in my face. She tells me the neighborhood kids won't play with me because I smell bad. She says I'm dirty and I should be ashamed of myself. Her face is so close that her spit sprays on my cheeks. Her eyes are narrow and dark. Her face is twisted in anger. Dad walks by and I know he's going to help me. I'm relieved. My teeth are chattering but I smile because dad is here. He looks me in the eyes but then quickly looks away and keeps walking. He's not going to help me. I stop crying and hold my breath as I scrub my skin until it hurts. I didn't know I smelled bad.*

Journal Entry: *My mother slaps dad hard across the face. It knocks him back, but he doesn't say anything. I watch as he calmly removes his glasses and cleans them with the pale blue handkerchief he keeps in his pocket. His face is bright red where her slap landed. He hugs me and cries, and now my mother is screaming at both of us. I cover my ears and scream too.*

chapter 17: Fire in the Sink

I keep writing. I remember our house being a disgusting mess. Empty vodka bottles littered the kitchen counter. Garbage spilling out from the can onto the floor. There were piles of trash and dirty laundry all over, and even then, as a little kid, I felt shame and embarrassment because of the way we lived. I was always hungry. When my dad was there, we had fruit trees and a garden full of fresh vegetables, but after he left, the only food I ate came out of a box.

I remember watching the garden die after my dad left. My mother hated the garden, probably because my dad and I spent so much time in it. The garden was the only thing that brought us joy, but it reminded her of him, so after he left, she wouldn't allow me to go near it. I was scared of getting in trouble, so I just sat on the broken-down porch, watching the ants swarm the rotting fruit lying on the ground beneath the fruit trees. The once thriving plants in the garden began to droop and wither, just like me. Green rows of shiny, fresh vegetables became a tangled mess of weeds and dead plants. It was as if all the colors in the world faded, dried up, and rotted into the ground. Watching our garden die was quite possibly the saddest thing I've ever witnessed in my entire life.

I write and write until my hand hurts from gripping the pen. Sleep and awake time blur together. A rush of memories and dreams rolls through my mind like a slide show. I record over 50 journal entries of everything I can remember, asleep and awake, and as I thumb through the pages of notes, I feel sick.

This isn't helping me at all.

It's making things worse.

I flip through the journal, searching for something to hold onto, but there's nothing there except the madness of my childhood.

Grandma Vee was my angel. She saved me. After dad abandoned me, I went back and forth between my mother's and Grandma Vee's houses a lot. And then my mother disappeared—she never came back to pick me up. For a long time, I worried she would show up, but as the months passed, I started to relax, thinking she might not come after all. Grandma Vee and I made a decent life for ourselves; we were all each other had for many years. I was crushed when she died. I felt an emptiness I had never felt before, as if I had no one left who really loved me. When I found out she left me her life savings, I cried for three days. She was so loving and generous. Grandma Vee was everything to me.

A hard truth to face, if my memories are accurate, is that my mother also abused my dad. That bothers me, but what bothers me even more is the realization that he left me there.

Alone.

With her.

Knowing the monster she was.

How *could* he?

My mother was *terribly* cruel. The physical abuse was awful, but the verbal abuse was much worse. Her hateful words still scream in my head every day. Demeaning, intimidating, scolding words that should never be spoken to an innocent child...

But there's something else...

I read the entry again: *My mother isn't home, and there's a strange man sleeping in her bed—suddenly he's awake and walking toward me— I'm terrified—I try to run but my legs won't move. Screaming screaming screaming but no sound comes out.*

Fragmented images run through my mind. I know I witnessed things I shouldn't have, and that my mother often had strange men over after my dad left, but...

It hits me like a slow, dark wave—a realization too ugly, too devastating to take in, but it's here now in jagged memories bookmarked in my brain. I press it down, trying to make it disappear, but my mind keeps looping back to that same, sickening page.

What else happened?

What did they do to me?

chapter 17: Fire in the Sink

I don't—I *can't* remember, but I know it.

I think I was hurt in other ways.

Anxiety is rising. It's a nauseating dread I feel inside of me that I've never been able to put into words.

Inhale.

Exhale.

I can't face it.

I slam the journal shut.

I thought this was a promising idea—that it would bring me some clarity. I thought it would answer questions about my past, but all it's done is make me feel worse. In my mind, my dad was always my hero. He was handsome, with broad shoulders and a high-pitched laugh that made me laugh too. He was kind, taught me everything he knew about plants, played games with me, tucked me in at night, and read books to me. When he was home, there was less chaos. But if he truly loved me, how could he leave? I was an innocent little girl. I needed to be loved and protected. It was his job to do that, but he didn't do it. He was a coward. He was weak and selfish, and I *hate* him for it.

I'm done with this. No more digging into my past. No more searching for good in a pile of trash. I thought if I skimmed off the surface, I might find something worthwhile underneath, but instead it's just rotted, murky water that fumes with a stench I can't escape. I'll never be free from my mother and the demons that haunt me. This is who I am!

One by one, I tear out the pages of my journal and rip them into tiny pieces. When I'm done, I scoop the shredded paper up by handfuls and carry it to the kitchen sink, pile it into one big mound above the drain, strike a match, light it on fire, and watch it burn.

check on your **happy** friends

18
Sunflowers

There was a time when I could sleep in, but not anymore. If I catch any sleep at all, I'm always up long before the sun. This morning is no different; I've been wide awake and staring at the ceiling for hours while my mind spins and twists with intrusive thoughts.

I don't want to get up, but I need coffee, so I make my way into the kitchen and then remember the one thing I wasn't supposed to forget yesterday. Coffee. I'm out of coffee. I was planning to pick some up after running errands, but it was late, and I forgot. Being out of coffee after a sleepless night is *the* worst.

The other thing I forgot last night was to eat dinner. My stomach is growling, so I check the fridge, which sadly has no breakfast-y things like eggs or yogurt, or even bread for toast. Since there's nothing here, I decide to go out. It's 7:00, which is the exact time the new café downtown opens.

Motivated by my need for caffeine, I skip a shower, get ready quickly, go through my obsessive rituals in rapid fire, grab my laptop, head out the door, and drive straight to the Village Café.

I'm relieved to see only a few cars in the parking lot. It's Sunday morning, which means a lot of folks—including a growing number of my friends—are getting ready for church, so it's a perfect time to check the place out.

I walk in the café and sigh—I'm glad I came. It's warm and cozy and smells like coffee, fresh pastries, and everything wonderful. As I'm looking around, a server with flawless golden skin and a headful of gorgeous black curls greets me.

"Morning! Is this your first time visiting us?" she asks as I'm admiring her beauty.

"It is!" I say, trying to match her energy. "I was out of coffee at home and looking for a quiet spot to perch for a while, so I decided to come and check out your place."

"Great! I'm so glad you're here." she says warmly. "Here's a menu. Find yourself a table anywhere you like, and I'll be right over. What can I get started for you to drink?"

I notice the tag pinned on her blouse—her name is Nia. "Wonderful, thanks Nia. I'll take a latte, double shot with whole milk."

She smiles brightly. "Coming right up!"

I survey the seating options and choose the big cushiony chairs tucked in the corner next to an assortment of potted plants and shelves packed full of colorful books. Out of habit, I examine the leaves of a massive fiddle leaf fig that reaches all the way up to the ceiling—they're a deep, glossy green, which means the plant is well taken care of. Good for them.

Nia returns with my coffee. I can hardly wait for my first sip.

"Thank you!" I say. "My morning just got a whole lot better."

She smiles again. "You are most welcome. Have you had a chance to look at the menu?"

"Yes. I'll have a white chocolate raspberry scone, please."

Nia brings my scone and a glass of water, then leaves to greet a young family.

I take a bite, grateful for the quiet. The scone is flaky and melts in my mouth, a nice not-too-sweet taste that blends perfectly with my coffee.

Settling in, I place my laptop on the table and set my purse on the empty chair across from me. Making sure no one is watching, I slip off

chapter 18: Sunflowers

my shoes and take some calming breaths, trying my best to relax. With my eyes closed, I roll my shoulders and turn my head slowly from side to side until my neck pops, releasing the tension in my back.

That's better.

I take a few more deep breaths, then open my eyes to a little girl standing right in front of me.

"Oh hi!" I say, startled.

She waves at me even though her sweet face is so close I can feel her breath.

I ask, "How are you this morning?" suddenly amused by this little person.

She gives me a thumbs up and flashes a toothy grin. "These are my new jamas, see the sunflowers on them?" Her voice is thick with sleep, but her eyes are wide and sparkling as she points to the flowers on her pajamas. I'm guessing she's around Sammie's age.

I muster as much enthusiasm as I can. "Wow, look at all those sunflowers! Those are the cutest jamas I've ever seen!"

She seems pleased with my response. "I can count all the way up to 20, but not right now because I'm going to eat a blueberry muffin with mommy and daddy. Maybe after we get to go to the park. Do you have sunflower jamas at your house?" She looks at me with her perfect little eyebrows raised high.

"No," I say, "but do you know what? I think I might get some because yours are so cool!"

She nods approvingly, then skips over to join the couple who must be her parents.

She is the cutest little thing. Her wavy brown hair is sticking up every which way, as if she just rolled out of bed. She has huge, deep brown eyes, dimples on each of her round cheeks, and she looks comfy in her bright yellow sunflower pajamas that she's so proud of. Her parents turn to me and wave.

"She's darling!" I say to them.

"Thank you!" they respond, smiling proudly.

I watch as the little girl runs toward her father with both arms raised. He bends down and gently gathers her up, holding her close to his chest as she nestles into him.

I can't bring myself to look away.

The three of them walk to their table, smiling and chatting as they go, the dad carrying his bouncy little girl in his arms while the mom gently smooths her hair behind her ears. The dad pulls out a chair for his wife, then gets his daughter settled into hers. The way they tend to each other seems effortless, as if some unseen force of love weaves them together in a perfect, harmonious way.

I squeeze my eyes shut as I rack my brain trying to think of a fun family outing, but I can't come up with a single one. Instead, my mind is flooded with ugly flashbacks of my childhood—begging my mother not to be angry with me, my parents screaming at each other, clothes that didn't fit, bare cupboards, empty vodka bottles scattered all over our cluttered house, and the hunger pangs that used to churn in my belly.

I cry a little as I pick at my scone. I'm not upset because of my horrible childhood; I'm upset because even now nothing good lasts. I walked into this café enjoying myself, but then dark memories came flooding in, and I feel beaten down. Again.

I *do* have good days. I've experienced thousands of special moments like the one just now with little miss sunflower girl. I have friends who seem to care for me, a job I enjoy, and all those things are wonderful in the moment, but the feeling never lasts. I always end up back in the ugly darkness of my past. It's a predictable, vicious cycle. Each joyful experience is quickly overshadowed by my pain; it pumps in my veins and eats at my flesh, and I'm certain it will never go away.

I hear a crash and glance over at the family. Looks like the little girl knocked her dad's glass over, spilling water everywhere.

I watch and listen closely—trauma raging in my head.

chapter 18: Sunflowers

"Un oh, I had an oopsie," the little girl says as she watches the water drip onto the floor.

My focus shifts to the dad—I'm surprised to see him smiling.

"It's okay sweetie pie," he says softly. "Can you get some napkins and help daddy? Accidents happen, sweetie, let's just be more careful next time, okay?"

The tension fades and my heart rate slows down. I'm relieved for the little girl.

She nods and starts pulling napkins from the dispenser on the table. Before her parents can stop her, she takes way too many, throws them in a heap on the floor, and stomps on them. The napkins dissolve into a soggy mess, which seems to delight her. I can see the mom and dad trying not to laugh as the three of them work together to gather up the pile.

I keep watching as they clean up the mess. I would have gotten backhanded for an accident like that, and berated for wasting so many napkins.

But it's obvious to me the little girl isn't afraid; her mind is full of happy thoughts like sunflower pajamas and blueberry muffins. My little body would have been jolted by the slap, and I would have cowered in shame. I can still remember the way I would scold myself for being bad. My mind would race, trying to think of ways to make it up to my mother so she wouldn't hate me even more. The contrast between my family and this one is shocking. I don't know why my parents didn't love me, but it's clear that these parents love and cherish their precious daughter. I imagine her life will be wonderful, and it makes my heart happy for her.

I've been so distracted watching the family that I didn't notice how full the café has become. I scan the room, suddenly curious about everyone. There are folks enjoying breakfast together, couples chatting, teenagers drinking iced matcha and scrolling through their phones, and I can't help but wonder who else here is pretending to be okay when they're really not. Am I the only one?

It occurs to me that most of my friends are probably at church right now worshiping a God they believe saves souls, but what about *my* soul? What about *me*? While they're praising Jesus, I'm sitting alone in a café preparing to research questions about death because I'm getting to the end of my rope. I don't want to live this way anymore. I can't.

Ready to get to work, I slip my feet back into my shoes, twist my hair up in a clip, and glance around the room—making sure no one is too close. With my laptop fired up and connected to the Wi-Fi, I start to type, but then hesitate. My chest is suddenly tight. It feels as if I'm taking a big risk—as if just typing the words will somehow expose me to the world.

I recognize my own paranoia and do my best to push through it. With trembling hands, I pull up my search engine and type in my first question:

"What happens after you die?"

My screen fills with results—links and sources and paragraph after paragraph of information. I skim through dozens of pages. It's nothing I haven't heard before, so I try a few more questions:

"Is there relief or peace after you die?"

"Is death really the end, or is there something else beyond it?"

"Is heaven real?"

I scroll through the endless opinions, beliefs, and perspectives generated by my questions, but none of it addresses what I want to know.

I type another:

"Does suicide affect what happens to a person after death?"

I click on search, but I don't get a list of results like before. Instead, a message is centered on my screen:

Help is available

Speak with someone today

988 Suicide and Crisis Lifeline

24 hours

chapter 18: Sunflowers

There are links to call, text, chat, or visit a website. It's free. It's confidential.

I check my surroundings again, then move the mouse over the button to chat.

THEY CAN'T HELP YOU, the inner voice taunts.

I shiver. Maybe not, but what can it hurt? I press on the mouse, almost hard enough to click it, but I hesitate.

YOU'RE TOO FAR GONE.

I stare at the link and the little pointer hovering over it.

TOO DAMAGED. TOO DIRTY. TOO MESSED UP.

Inhale.

Exhale.

Memories flash in my vision. He's coming. I can't make a sound.

REMEMBER?

No. I squeeze my eyes shut.

Inhale.

Exhale.

Deeper now.

HE'S THERE. I'M SOMEWHERE ELSE.

REMEMBER??

Inhale.

Exhale.

Fear. Trembling. Shame.

REMEMBER?

"NO!" I yell, bolting up from my chair, breathing hard and fast.

My eyes dart around wildly.

Everyone is looking.

YOU'RE FILTHY.

In. Out. In. Out.

I'm shaking. I need to get out of here!

I slam my laptop shut, grab my things, throw a twenty on the table, and run for the door.

Nia is in the way. "Thanks for coming!" she says. "I hope we'll see you again!"

"Yeah," I whisper, trying my best not to burst into tears.

She stops me. "Hey, is everything okay? If something upset you, please let me know and we'll make it right."

I push past her, out the door, towards my car and start bawling.

"Hey," someone says, touching my shoulder.

I flinch, startled.

"Are you okay?" Nia asks. "What's going on?"

Pull yourself together!

I don't look at her. "I'm okay."

She's standing next to me. "Do you need help? Can I get you anything?"

I pause, trying to collect myself. How nice of her to even notice.

Push it down. Fake it. The end is in sight.

"No," I say, swallowing the huge lump in my throat. "Thank you. I'm fine. Everything was just lovely. I was problem-solving something and feeling a bit overwhelmed, but I have a plan, so I'm just going to focus on that and not worry about the details."

"You sure?"

"Yes," I say honestly.

She smiles softly. "I'm so glad. And I get it! I *always* have a plan for *everything*. It's the only way I can live." She takes a few steps back. "Thanks for coming. I hope to see you back soon."

I smile a genuine smile because she's absolutely right. Having a plan really is the only way to live, and I do have a plan. The rest is just details, and since nobody—including the internet—knows for certain what happens after death, I just have to believe it will be better than this.

As I drive home, the questions rumble through my mind. After I'm gone, will I rest in peace, or will my nightmare continue? I don't know Jesus, but I've always been a good person, and I do my best to be kind to others. If heaven is real, then I'm hoping my good deeds

chapter 18: Sunflowers

are enough to get me in.

I stop at a red light and glance to my left at a run-down house on the corner that sits back away from the street. The paint is chipped, there's trash piled up everywhere, and a few broken-down cars are parked in the driveway, but right next to the sagging wooden fence is a row of sunflowers standing tall and facing the sky.

Even with all the wreckage and filth around them, the sunflowers still shine brightly, and something about that makes me think of Henry. Maybe because today was my first visit to a coffee shop since The Café closed. Or maybe it's because even though Henry must have felt like his life was ugly, all I saw in him was beauty. I miss him and want so badly to know where he is and if he feels anything at all.

"Are you at peace, Henry? Was it worth it?" I ask out loud to my empty car, hoping my beautiful friend can somehow hear me.

The light finally turns green, and as I head home, I think about the little girl and wish I would have asked her name, but I didn't, so I come up with my own: Marigold. Yes, I think her name should be Marigold. Vibrant, beautiful, and always searching for the sun.

check on your **happy** friends

19
Something Unexpected

Shockingly, last night I managed to get four solid hours of sleep, which hasn't happened in forever. I have energy, and I need to get out of my apartment, so I send a text to Mama Sharon: "Good morning, need some help at the shop today? I think I'm ready to come in."

She responds immediately: "Absolutely. I'll see you there!"

I manage my morning struggles better today because I'm actually looking forward to being back at the shop. I finish my coffee, get dressed, and head out with plenty of time left. The crisp morning air fills my lungs and refreshes me. I'm going to do my best to forget about everything and just try to focus on being present.

I need a good day.

Just one good day.

The phone rings as soon as I walk in the door. Mama Sharon is busy with customers, so I rush to answer it.

"Good morning," I say. "Thanks for calling Thrive. How can I help you?"

"Hey, Dani, it's Lyle. I wanted to let you know we just received a shipment of carnivorous plants, but they're going to sell quickly. If you want some, you better come today."

I glance at Mama Sharon, who is still busy. "Thank you, Lyle. Let me see what I can do. Hopefully, I'll see you soon!"

I need a vehicle. Tommy isn't available, and our van is out for repairs, so I'm not sure what to do. Just when I think we're out of options, Gabe drives up in his big black Chevy pickup truck.

I seize the opportunity.

"Nice truck," I say to Gabe as soon as he walks in the door.

He looks surprised. "Thanks, and hello to you too, Dani."

I respond with a serious look on my face. "I don't have time for pleasantries today, Gabe. Do you have plans for the next few hours?"

He raises his eyebrows. "Umm, nothing that can't wait. I stopped by to find a gift for my little buddy who lives next door to me. He turns seven tomorrow and he's into plants, but other than that work is covered, so I'm free. What'd you have in mind?"

"A plant adventure," I say, not smiling.

Gabe's eyes narrow. "Hmmm, I'm sensing this adventure could be dangerous?"

"Could be." Still not smiling.

"And since you're eyeing my truck, I'm guessing I'm the getaway driver on this potentially dangerous mystery plant adventure?"

I nod, trying hard not to laugh, thrilled he's playing along.

Gabe rubs his beard for a few seconds, as if considering his options, then flashes a brilliant smile. "Let's go!"

"Woohoo!" I blurt out with genuine excitement. I want these plants!

I grab my purse and coat and shout, "Mama Sharon, we'll be back in a bit!"

"Okay!" she says. "Drive safely, Gabe. And Dani, we're low on inventory, so use your judgment and buy whatever you think our customers will like." She gives me a wink, and Gabe and I head out the door.

Being the chivalrous man that he is, Gabe rushes to the passenger side of his truck and opens the door for me. We hop in, buckle our seatbelts, and off we go.

"Aren't you going to ask me where we're going?" I ask.

"I'm guessing we're picking up plants, but I was afraid if I asked too many questions, you might have to kill me." I can hear the playfulness in his voice.

I laugh. "Okay. Not to spoil the mystery, but today's adventure is to Half Moon Bay—Sunshine Nursery to be exact—to pick up house plants and a bunch of carnivorous plants. We have to go today because they'll sell out fast. Also, we'll accomplish two things, because a carnivorous plant is the *perfect* gift for your little friend."

I brace myself for his response, afraid I've asked too much of him. Heat rises in my chest and I'm suddenly embarrassed.

HERE YOU GO AGAIN ACTING LIKE A FOOL. WHY WOULD HE WANT TO WASTE A DAY WITH SOMEONE LIKE YOU?

Before he has a chance to speak, I add, "I'm sorry, Gabe, I really am so sorry. I should have told you before we left. I was trying to be mysterious and charming, hoping to entice you into saying yes, but if you don't have time, it's fine. You can drop me back off at the shop."

Gabe bursts out laughing—a joyful, deep laugh I haven't heard before. It catches me off guard and I start laughing too. Pretty soon, we're both laughing so hard we're in tears.

Trying to compose myself, I ask, "What is so funny?"

Gabe is wiping his eyes. "Oh man, I'm sorry. But when you said you were being mysterious and charming to entice me, it struck me as funny. It might just be the cutest thing you've ever said, Dani. Listen, I can't imagine a scenario where I would say no to you—ask me anything, anytime. Honestly, if you asked me to run across the freeway, I'd probably do it."

We laugh some more, then Gabe pulls into a coffee shop and parks. He unlocks his phone and hands it to me. "Here, how about you put in the address, and I'll get us some coffee."

He gets out, and my mind starts doing cartwheels.

Maybe this will be fun! He makes me laugh, and he's willing to take time to help us at the shop, so why not just enjoy the day? What's the harm? I think I can warm up to this idea.

YOU'RE UGLY. HE KNOWS IT. HE SEES IT. HE FEELS SORRY FOR YOU.

I feel a rush of unease as the inner voice lets me have it. It's right. I have no business doing this, but I'm here now, so I might as well try and make the best of it. Besides, this isn't about spending the day with Gabe, it's about getting plants for Thrive.

I close my eyes, take a long, deep breath, and decide to enjoy this trip and try to focus on only positive things.

I find the navigation app and enter the address to the nursery, then Gabe returns and hands me my coffee.

He puts his in the cupholder and buckles his seatbelt. "Double latte extra shot with whole milk for you, and a good old black coffee for me."

He remembered!

"Thank you, it smells delicious."

"You're welcome, and yes it does."

We stop at a gas station so he can fill the tank, and when I offer to pay for it, Gabe just rolls his eyes and tells me to keep my money. This guy impresses me—he's a gentleman, and something about him puts me at ease.

As we merge onto the freeway and head toward Half Moon Bay, Gabe turns the music on.

"Do you mind?" he asks, glancing at me.

"No, not at all. I enjoy music."

"What do you listen to?"

"Everything!" I say, feeling light. "Sometimes classical, sometimes alternative rock, Motown, R & B, hip hop, and once in a while country. Did I forget any genres?"

"You did! My favorite—Christian worship music."

I don't know why I'm surprised, but I am. "Well, well, well, Gabe. I took you for a Rock n' Roll kind of guy."

He smiles. "I do like Rock n' Roll, especially the old stuff, but more than anything I love music that's uplifting and keeps me grounded,

chapter 19: Something Unexpected

and that's what worship music does. Have you listened to much of it?"

"I haven't. Mama Sharon sometimes plays it at the shop, and now Tommy listens to it too. I was impressed with the music at his baptism, but I haven't listened to it on my own. Maybe I should."

"Maybe you should." Gabe echoes my words.

He turns the music up as we drive, his hands softly tapping the steering wheel in rhythm with the beat. I close my eyes and listen. The piano is lovely, and the violin is a melody all on its own. It takes me a few seconds to follow the lyrics...

"So, you think you're too far gone—you're not."

"You think you're not worthy of love—you are."

"Stop believing the lies and find your truth in Christ."

"You are never too far gone, there is always hope."

"Jesus saves, Jesus saves, Jesus saves."

I turn to Gabe to ask about the song, but something makes me hesitant to speak. He has a distant look on his face, as if he's suddenly miles and miles away. His hands were relaxed before, now they're gripping the steering wheel tightly. I watch as he slowly moves one hand and rests it on his chest, as if he *feels* the words and the song is weaving through him.

I wait a few more seconds then ask, "Hey, are you okay?"

Gabe seems to snap back from wherever his mind was. "Yep! I'm okay."

He exhales slowly—a soft smile spreading across his face. "This song is special to me. Whenever I hear it, my mind drifts back to a time when I was struggling. The lyrics are a good reminder of how far I've come and how Christ saved me. That's something I never want to forget."

"You really believe Christ saved you?" I ask, trying to understand.

His expression turns serious. "Yes, Dani. I *know* He did. Have you ever been so broken that you wanted to give up?

If he only knew.

"Not really," I lie, regretting that I asked the question.

He glances at me. "Never?"

I do my best to smile. "Can we change the subject, please?"

Gabe nods. I can feel his eyes on me as I shift my attention from him and the music to the beautiful day outside.

The sky is full of dense white clouds, and the sun is glistening on the water as we cross the San Mateo bridge. I've always been nervous driving over bridges, but oddly it hasn't crossed my mind today.

"It's gorgeous outside, Dani," Gabe says. "Put your window down and feel the breeze."

As soon as I press the button, a rush of wind blows through the cab and whips my hair around my face. The air smells fresh and cool; an invigorating mix of sunshine and saltwater. Gabe's music is drowned out by the noise, lost in the whoosh of passing cars and the distant sounds of seagulls. It's a rush I wasn't expecting, and I leave the window down for a good while, soaking in the moment. When the wind gets to be too much, I put the window up and fall back against my seat, feeling breathless.

Gabe glances at me. "Felt good, right?"

We meet eyes for a split second.

HE'S SEES IT. YOU'RE UGLY. PATHETIC. The inner voice hisses just as I'm about to respond.

Quickly looking away, I flip down the visor mirror and try to collect myself. I'm shocked at my appearance. I look tired and wrung out. Mortified, I try running my fingers through my hair, but it's a tangled mess.

Gabe grins. "Leave it just like it is. I love your wild hair, Dani."

I ignore his fake compliment. I know he's just trying to make me feel better about myself, but it's not working. It's making me feel worse!

Please don't look at me. Please don't look at me. Please don't look at me.

Gabe keeps his eyes on the road, and I'm relieved. It gives me a minute to catch my breath.

chapter 19: Something Unexpected

I don't have any hair ties, so I scan his truck looking for something and notice a ball cap. I grab it and ask, "Do you mind if I wear this?"

"Not one bit," he says. "Please do."

I adjust the back strap of the hat, gather up my hair in a high ponytail, and pull it through so it's off my neck, which feels better. Digging in my purse, I find my dark sunglasses and put them on.

"Better?" Gabe asks with a huge smile radiating across his face.

"Much," I say, relieved to be covered.

My mind scrambles to make conversation, so I do what I always do, put on my mask, smile, and direct the attention away from me.

COME ON GIRL, YOU CAN DO IT. SMILE. FAKE IT.

I study his face and try to think of what to talk about, and then it comes to me—the girl, the plant, just talk about him!

"How's yoga girl?" I ask.

He looks confused. "Who?"

I press him. "You know, that girlfriend you bought the staghorn fern for? The one who ran off with her yoga instructor. Remember her?"

Gabe laughs. "Ohhh, *that* girl. Yes. I vaguely remember."

We laugh, and I decide to push a little more. "We have 15 minutes left until we get there, want to play a game?"

The mask is secure. Better now. It's okay. It's okay. It's okay. Distract him. Don't make eye contact.

"Sure," Gabe says, his voice playful, "but be prepared to lose, because I always win. I spy? Three truths and a lie? License plate game? Rhyme Time? Build-a-Story? What do you want to play?"

I'm shocked by his enthusiasm. "Ha! I was thinking Ask Anything. I'm the asker and you're the answer-er, and you have to be honest."

"Ahhhhhh, okay, I'm down. But when you're done, it will be my turn. And just in case, let's include a 'pass' so if a question makes either of us uncomfortable, we can pass and not answer, okay?"

I'm never answering your questions. You don't want to know anything about me.

"Sure!" I lie.

I ask my first question. "Have you ever been married?"

"Yes," he says, to my surprise.

"Oh, okay, are you *still* married?"

"Nope, the divorce was finalized four years ago. She was amazing and we really were in love, but we were young, and I was stupid. I drank a lot back then and I didn't cherish her like I should have; it was on me. I think she would have stood by me through most anything, but I was reckless and drinking all the time. I lost my job and ended up in jail with a DUI. I wasn't walking with the Lord then, and I hate that I hurt her, but I was a broken man. I heard she remarried, and he treats her well. I'm thankful for that. Soon after she left me, I found Christ, and He saved me."

I sit back in my seat, quietly processing his answer.

How can he share so openly? I could never.

"Next question?" Gabe asks casually, as if he didn't just share intimate details of his past with me.

"Woah. I need a minute to process everything you just shared. Are you always this open?"

"Yes. I don't typically offer details of my private life, but if you ask, I'll tell you. And I won't lie about anything, Dani. I will always be truthful."

You would lie if you were me. My life is a lie.

"How long were you married?" I ask, suddenly curious about a million things.

"Just two years. We dated in high school, so we were together for seven. We had plans for a family and everything. Again, it's sad, but she deserved better. I'm not the same man I was then; not even close. She did the right thing, and looking back, I can see it was a blessing."

"How so?" I ask.

"Jesus changed me. He changed everything. It's hard to explain, but there was a time when I thought about drinking every single day from the moment I woke up. Alcohol took over my life, and everything I had slipped through my fingers. I was a mess. My ex-wife is a Christian. She had been praying for me for months, but nothing changed. In fact, I got worse, and eventually she couldn't take it anymore, so she packed up and moved back into her parents' house and filed for divorce. Then one awful morning, I woke up in a drunk tank at the county jail. I'll never forget that feeling. It was freezing cold, my anxiety was out of control, and I had a horrible hangover. I couldn't remember anything from the night before and I had an overwhelming sense of dread—wondering what I had done. When I was finally released, I had no one to call. Not a single person came to mind who would come pick me up. That realization hit hard. It made me feel so lonely that I ended up sitting on the curb and bawling my eyes out. I was so sick of myself that the fear of staying the same was greater than the fear of change. That's when I cried out to the Lord, and He began to work on my heart."

I can hear the sudden crack of emotion in Gabe's voice. "I'm sorry. I shouldn't have asked. I didn't mean to pry into your past."

He looks at me tenderly. "Oh man, Dani. Please don't apologize. The truth is, I love talking about Jesus, and how He turned my life around. It's my favorite thing to talk about. My emotions come from a heart full of gratitude. Seriously, it was a rough road, but it led me to Him, and for that I'm forever grateful. I ended up moving here, started a construction company that has been quite successful, and recently bought a house where I live with my dog, Rex. I joined a church, got my head right, and haven't had a sip of alcohol since."

He lets out a loud sigh. "Any more questions? Or have you had enough for today?"

"Just one more question for now," I say, and we burst into laughter.

"How did I know you were going to say that? Fire away!"

"Did she kill it?"

Gabe looks confused. "Kill it? Who? Kill what?"

I laugh. "The plant. Did yoga girl kill that gorgeous staghorn fern I picked out for her?"

He laughs that same, boisterous laugh. "She did. Cold blooded murder."

We both laugh again, the mood suddenly lighter, the inner voice quieting down.

Gabe claps, then rubs his hands together excitedly. "Okay, it's my turn to ask questions. Are you ready?"

I smile mischievously. "Oh wow, it appears we've run out of time. There's the nursery and my plants are waiting! Come on, let's get moving!"

Gabe parks and we hop out of the truck, eager to stretch our legs and breathe in the fresh air. I'm relieved to be here.

Lyle spots me as soon as we step inside the nursery.

"Dani, you made it!"

"How are you, my friend?" I walk into his outstretched arms, and even though it's only been a month, he hugs me as if we haven't seen each other in years.

"Lyle, meet my friend, Gabe. Gabe, this is Lyle. I didn't have transportation today, so Gabe graciously volunteered to bring me so we can load up with some of your gorgeous plants!"

Gabe smiles brightly as he shakes hands. "Good to meet you, Lyle. Nice place you have here. I'd love to look around if it's okay."

Lyle jumps at the opportunity to show off his nursery. "Dani, your carnivorous plants are tagged in the back, and our new shipment came in from Florida. I'll give Gabe a tour while you shop. Be sure to check out the new rare section."

"Oh, I can't wait to see what you have in stock!" I grab a cart and head for the plants. "Have fun, you two. I'll meet you back inside in about 20 minutes."

The guys take off for their tour and relief washes over me. Alone, with these plants, is exactly where I want to be.

I roam through rows and rows of gorgeous, lush greenery and

chapter 19: Something Unexpected

brilliant flowers—always impressed by how organized and tidy Lyle keeps his nursery. My heart does a little happy dance as I grab several trays and begin filling my cart. I load it full with a fabulous assortment of houseplants, then leave it at the register and fill another with four flats of carnivorous plants, a five-gallon Dracaena Compacta, and a stunning fourteen-inch Ficus Decora Tineke.

Plants are an instant mood boost for me—it's as if they hush the chaos in my head. I breathe deeply one more time, filling my lungs with the rich, woodsy aroma of damp soil and fresh greenery, and then make my way back to the guys.

Lyle and Gabe are standing by the register, chatting. They seem to be enjoying themselves.

We visit for a few more minutes while the clerk is inspecting and boxing our plants. When she's done, Lyle helps us load everything into the bed of Gabe's truck.

We say our goodbyes, Gabe double checks that the plants are secured in the back, and then we head out. In my rearview mirror I can see Lyle waving to us. I wave back and yell out the window, "Thank you, Lyle. See you soon!"

"That nursery was something else!" Gabe says. "And Lyle seems like a good man. He's a believer, did you know that?"

"Believer in what?" I ask.

Gabe smiles. "In Jesus. He follows Christ. Did you know that?"

I didn't, and I'm wondering why Jesus seems to come up in every conversation I have with Gabe.

I ask him. "You talk about your faith a lot, why is that?"

Gabe takes a moment. "I didn't realize that, but it's good, actually, because Christ is my identity, Dani. When you've been as low as I have been, and the Lord pulls you out of the darkness and gives you a second chance, you don't forget it. Anyone I talk to is going to hear about my faith because it's who I am."

He has no idea of my darkness.

I quickly change the subject. "Lyle is a great guy and he's been good to us. He liked you. Not nearly as much as he likes me, but I could tell he liked you."

Gabe chuckles. "I can see why you're his favorite, but yeah, I think we connected."

"I would say you impressed him. You impress me, too, actually," I say, surprising myself.

"Excellent. I'm trying." Gabe's voice is soft, and the look on his face makes my heart race.

UGLY. The inner voice stirs once again. *DIRTY. PATHETIC. SHAMEFUL. HE SEES IT ALL.*

I moan at the cruelty. I can't help it.

Gabe doesn't notice. "Do we have time to grab some food for the drive back? I'm hungry. Are you?"

"Famished!" I lie, feeling nauseous.

Sound peppy, Dani! You can do it.

I pull out my phone. "Let me call the shop and check in really quick." My voice comes out too high-pitched.

I hate myself.

YOU SHOULD. YOU'RE DISGUSTING.

Mama Sharon answers on the second ring. I ask how it's going. Business is slow. There's no rush for us to get back.

I point at the windshield. "There's a place up the way that has amazing clam chowder and the best sandwiches around. We can grab something to go if that works for you?"

Gabe nods. "Sounds perfect."

To save time, I call in our order. Salami with cheddar cheese and the works on sourdough for Gabe. Veggie spinach wrap extra avocado hold the onions for me. We decide to share a bag of salt and vinegar chips, and I order each of us a bottle of water.

When we arrive, I pay the bill before Gabe can say a word. He hesitates, then thanks me.

chapter 19: Something Unexpected

I wave it off. "I'm the one who needs to thank *you*, Gabe. This was a big deal today, and I appreciate it so much. So does Mama Sharon. You've become a huge support to the shop, and we are so grateful."

"It's my pleasure, Dani," he says, and I can tell he means it.

We settle in for the drive back with napkins and sandwiches on our laps, and the chips open between us.

"Mmm," Gabe says. "Man, this is the best sandwich I've had in a while. I'm going to have to try the clam chowder next time we're here."

I catch the "we" in his sentence, and my heart picks up an extra beat. *NOT HAPPENING. THAT'S NEVER GOING TO HAPPEN.*

"You'll love the clam chowder," I say. "It's Tommy's favorite." I'm trying to sound like a happy, normal person—this is exhausting.

The sun is low in the sky and shining like crystals on the water as we drive back over the San Mateo bridge. I notice that Gabe hasn't turned the music on, and I'm grateful for the quiet.

"We're getting close to the shop," he says, "so is it my turn to ask you questions?"

I sit in silence.

"Hello? Did I lose you?" Gabe chuckles. "Can I ask you questions now?"

I answer before I can think about it. "Please don't."

I can tell he's surprised, so I explain. "I'm sorry. It's just that, I can't right now. Um, since you were so open about your past, I'm afraid you'll ask me questions about mine, and I don't want to talk about it. As you know, my childhood was a nightmare, and to be honest, I'm kind of a mess. I don't need to be rescued or saved, I just want to enjoy the rest of this day, right here, right now with you, and not think about anything else."

THERE YOU GO AGAIN, OVERSHARING. STOP TALKING!

Gabe reaches over and places his hand on top of mine.

I hold my breath, staring at my disgusting shredded cuticles.

HIDE YOUR HANDS!

I slip them under my legs and sit perfectly still, hoping Gabe will speak first.

He returns his hand to the wheel. "Fair enough. But if I may, I'd like to tell you something. You don't even need to respond if you don't want to, okay?"

Dread rises in my throat. I choke it back and decide to shut this conversation down quickly. I am *not* a charity case!

"Okay, but before you do, I want you to know that I appreciate how kind you are to me. And I don't want to get into any more details, but, um, let's just say I have things I'm working on. I'm just not someone to invest your time in. You know what I mean?"

I'm slipping, Gabe! Don't you see it? I'm not who you think I am.

Gabe clears his throat. "Okay, well, that's a bit confusing to me. And no, Dani, I don't know what you mean. Listen, this isn't me being kind to you like it's some sort of obligation. I enjoy being around you. When I walked into the shop that day searching for a plant for yoga girl…"

He chuckles under his breath, and it helps me calm down.

"I was a bit bold," he continues, "because I thought I would never see you again. I told you that I thought you were beautiful. Do you remember?"

"Not really," I lie. I remember every single word.

"Well, I meant what I said, and I've thought about you every day since. And this is where it gets hard to explain, because you don't really know me. You don't know my intentions. You don't know my heart. You don't know the respect I have for you. But I care, and I want to get to know you better."

His expression is serious. "Does that makes sense?"

I sink down into my seat.

Please don't look at me.

"But there's something more here," he says. "It's something unexpected, and I'm certain God is leading. I think you're struggling

chapter 19: Something Unexpected

more than you let on, and God has put you on my heart *many* times. I want to send you scripture, invite you to Bible study, and encourage you, but I don't because it might be weird. I want to pursue you, Dani, but as a man of God. As a trusted friend to start with, and God willing, someday maybe a whole lot more than that, but I'm not trying to rush anything. I want to be near you because it just feels right, and I want you to know Christ like I do. And by the way, *everyone* is broken, Dani, and *everyone* needs a savior. You just don't realize it yet."

I can feel Gabe glancing between me and the road, and I feel like I should respond, but I can't think of a single word to say. And if I try to speak, I'm afraid I'll start bawling my eyes out.

After what feels like forever, Gabe looks at me. "I know I said you don't have to respond, but I wish you would say something. Anything at this point." He sounds a bit defeated.

YOU THINK HE LIKES YOU? the inner voice mocks.

"I'm going to use my 'pass' right now," I say, "but I had fun on our adventure, and I really, really like your beard."

Gabe starts laughing again, pulls up in front of the shop, cuts the engine, and turns to face me. "Are you doing the mysterious, charming thing again?"

"I am!" I declare, relieved he doesn't push it.

We hop out of the truck, unload some plants, and carry them into the back room of the shop.

As we finish, I turn to Gabe. "Me too."

He looks at me, eyebrows raised. "You too, what?"

I look him directly in the eyes. "You're something unexpected for me too, but it's not that simple."

YOU'RE AN IDIOT. WHY WOULD YOU SAY THAT?

Gabe's smile lights up the entire room. "Oh, yes, it IS that simple. At this point, I'm just asking for your friendship, okay? Trust what you're feeling, Dani. Let God lead us."

I don't know God!

Gabe takes a piece of paper from the counter and writes on it. "I'm certain you already have it, but in case you don't, here's my number and email. Put them in your phone and call or message me whenever you want. I'm here for you, Dani. For whatever you need."

I take the paper from him and slip it in my pocket.

Mama Sharon walks in. "Well, it looks like we have a lot of unboxing to do! Dani, let's take some pictures for social media; these plants are gorgeous! Thank you for your help, Gabe. Did you two have fun?"

Gabe and I lock eyes. "We did, Mama Sharon," he says. "It was a beautiful day."

After he leaves, I decide to go ahead and put his contact information in my phone, then remember the plant for his next-door buddy.

I text him: "Hey, it's Dani. You forgot the carnivorous plant for the little birthday boy! Come back tomorrow, and I'll have it ready for you."

He responds right away: "Just when I thought the day couldn't get any better. See you tomorrow, Dani. Sleep well."

As I'm wrapping up the plant, I feel anxiety rising in my chest. Who am I kidding? I'm disgusted by the way I laugh and pretend to be okay around Gabe. I want to scrub it all off—every word, every smile, every moment I acted like I might be interested in him. Even if Gabe really does like the version of me I've allowed him to see, it's not real—none of it is real. I dig my nails into my wrists as hard as I can, wishing I could rip my skin off. I'm upset, but my eyes are dry because it's not sadness I'm feeling, it's shame—thick, hot, and choking.

20
Shadows of My Soul

It's early at the shop on a Saturday morning. Mama Sharon and I are busy working on last-minute preparations before we open the doors at 9:00 for our big sale. We've been blasting pictures of our plants all over social media for weeks leading up to this day, and we're hoping for a big turnout.

I watch Mama Sharon's hands as she tends to the plants. Her long, slender fingers exude grace and elegance as she works. She gently wipes down the leaves, checks the soil moisture, and prunes with great care and precision. She doesn't rush. Mama Sharon is the most patient, gentle person I have ever known.

As we work side by side with Daisy girl lying between us, I decide to ask a question that's been swimming around in my head all morning. "Mama Sharon, have you ever wondered what your life would be like if you could change your past? Do you know what I mean? If there was a way you could rewrite your own story?"

Mama Sharon doesn't look up, but I can tell she's considering my question.

"Yes," she says, "I *have* thought about that, but I don't dwell on what could have been. God has carried me through much suffering, and I've always come out on the other side stronger, so now I leave my life in His hands. It's better that way—to trust God and live in the moment instead of regretting the past or worrying about what the future holds."

She makes it sound easy. I AM my past; I can't separate myself from it.

"I'm sorry for whatever you've been through," I say. "You are one of the kindest people I know. I hate to think of you suffering."

I'm always curious about other people's struggles. I want to know because it makes me feel less alone in mine.

Mama Sharon stops what she's doing and turns to me. "Well, sugar, when we were young and newly married, Papa Reg and I wanted a child. In fact, we were hoping for several children. We loved our life together and believed the only thing missing was a big family of our own. For years we tried. We tried desperately to have a baby, and the stress was beginning to take a toll on me. Finally, a miracle happened. I got pregnant. We were beyond thrilled! We celebrated and prepared, and then four months into my pregnancy, I miscarried. There were complications, and we learned that I would never be able to have children."

Mama Sharon's eyes are glistening with tears. "It was one of the most difficult times in my life."

I put my arm around her, gently squeezing her shoulder. "Oh, my gracious," I whisper, searching for the right words. "I am so sorry. I had no idea."

She pats my hand, takes a handkerchief from her pocket, and wipes her eyes. "After we lost our baby, I cried for weeks. I couldn't eat, didn't sleep, and could barely find the strength to get out of bed. I lay on the floor of our decorated nursery that would never be used, and I wept as the walls of grief closed in on me. For hours I stared at my empty arms and the empty crib, with an ache in my bones and an emptiness inside that shattered me. I turned away from Reg, I cursed the Lord, and I hated my body for betraying me. You see, I was so excited when I got pregnant that I didn't wait to prepare. I bought clothes, blankets, books, toys, and had names picked out. I loved our baby and couldn't wait to meet our little miracle. And then my precious, growing child—

my happiness, my dreams, my entire world—was ripped from my womb, and I couldn't bear it. It was too much for me. Those days were hell on earth, and I was inconsolable."

Mama Sharon grips the edge of the table as if trying to steady herself. There's a rawness in her voice that I haven't heard before.

"I screamed," she says, closing her eyes. "I cried and thrashed around in bed until I was nothing but a lifeless heap of misery. I felt abandoned by God, and my faith was wavering."

She looks at me, her eyes dark and narrow. "Dani, do you understand what I'm saying?"

I shake my head; I don't understand.

"Losing my child was the worst thing that had ever happened to me, but losing my child *and* my faith brought me close to the end. My pain began to overshadow my hope. Every unanswered prayer felt like a betrayal from God. My whole world became darker, and darker, as I questioned the very source of my peace and strength. I stopped praying, and didn't go to church for months, but then do you know what happened?"

I look at her expectantly, my heart pulsing.

"I felt the Lord's presence." Mama Sharon lays her hand on her heart and closes her eyes, as if the memory still beats in her chest. "The peace, love, and life-giving grace of Jesus washed over me, and finally, after a horrible year of grieving, I found a sliver of faith to cling to. It was then that I realized Christ had not abandoned me; He had been with me all along. I was the one who turned away from Him. After that I kept going, even when I didn't feel like it. Healing was slow and steady. I asked for help, and I found support. I leaned on Reg, and gave my suffering to the Lord, and soon after that, I was filled with a deep longing to love and serve others."

She wipes away a tear. "I dove into God's word, and Psalm 23 became my anthem. I read it over and over until the words were etched in my heart, and I believed them. I began to pray again, and eventually made my way back to church. Weeks later, the pastor announced they were taking up a collection for a young homeless woman and her newborn baby. She had recently escaped a violent relationship and was staying at a local women's shelter. When our pastor stood at the front of the church and asked the congregation to search our hearts for how we could bless this woman and her baby, Papa Reg and I immediately knew we were being called to help, and that's exactly what we did. We helped in every way we could. Tiffany, the young mama, got back on her feet again and built a beautiful life for her and her son, Michael. Papa Reg and I walked through the entire journey with them. As you know, Michael grew up into a successful, godly man, who is like a son to us. He began calling us Mama Sharon and Papa Reg when he was just a toddler, and it stuck! Michael met and eventually married his wife, Mandy, and they had Samson, who has been the sweetest blessing in our lives. You know how much we love our Sammie, and my word, does he ever love you!"

She pauses and smiles softly at me.

"God kept presenting us with opportunities to help children and their families, and let me tell you, even though I lost my baby, God has allowed me to pour my love into dozens of precious children who've needed me. I've come to realize that I *am* a mother and grandmother to many. Indeed I am."

"Oh my gosh!" I say, amazed that we've never had this conversation. "Michael and Sammie? I didn't know the back story of how they came into your lives. Wow!"

Mama Sharon has joy written all over her face. "Things don't always go the way we want them to, Dani, but God's ways are higher and better, so instead of fretting about the future, Reg and I live each day for the Lord and trust in Him."

She takes a seat, but she's clearly not finished.

"Dani, I know you don't understand this yet, but even *I* struggle with my faith sometimes. As Christians, we don't get a free pass. We all suffer. Everyone struggles. But the difference is, when your world is crumbling and everything *seems* to be falling apart, there is still hope in Christ. There is still faith. Even if it's as small as a mustard seed, it's enough. I know you've suffered, sugar, and I know you need healing. I can see it. My hope and prayer is that you'll seek the Lord and find just a smidgen of faith in your soul. God has a plan for you. I hope you believe that."

She sees my suffering? It shows?

I swallow, trying to hold it together. "You're the closest thing to a mother I have. Thank you for loving me like you do, and allowing me time with Sammie, and I am so, so sorry for your loss."

Despite my efforts, my tears flow. I'm painfully aware that I should be comforting Mama Sharon, but instead, she is comforting me.

"Listen," she says, "I want you to know that I'm at peace. God led us on a beautiful journey; He gave us a purpose and loved us through that difficult season of life, and our faith is stronger because of it. He will do the same for you."

Before I can think, my words come spilling out. "I don't have faith and God isn't leading me."

Mama Sharon places her hands firmly on my shoulders and looks directly into my eyes. "Maybe God is leading you right now."

She pauses, and I can see she's choosing her words carefully.

"Dani, I wasn't planning on sharing my story with you today, but my spirit led me to. God places people in our lives not by chance, but according to His perfect plan. That day when the pastor asked for help for Tiffany and little Michael, we had no idea what God was doing or where He was leading us, but we trusted Him, and it turned into an incredible blessing. You just hold on, darling girl. Keep your heart and your eyes open. Seek Christ and watch what happens."

Her grip on my shoulders tightens as her eyes search mine. "Do you understand?"

I don't understand. I'll *never* understand.

Before I can respond, she pulls me in for a hug. "God has you right where you need to be. Everything is going to be okay."

We dry our tears and steady ourselves, both glancing at the clock—it's nearly time to open.

Mama Sharon laughs. "Look at us! We're a mess! Let's take a break, wash our faces, and get ready for the wonderful day ahead of us. We have ten minutes, then I'll meet you out front. You okay?"

I nod, wipe my eyes, and take a deep breath before heading to the restroom to freshen up.

Ten minutes pass in a flash, and the next thing I know, our eager, plant-loving customers are lining up at the door.

Mama Sharon turns up the music, flips on all the lights, and gives me a thumbs up. "I think we're ready, Dani. Open the doors and let's see what the day brings!" She smiles, and I notice all the traces of pain have vanished from her face.

I switch our sign to OPEN, unlock the door, and greet the ten customers who are waiting in line. The first is one of our regulars.

"Good morning, Anthony!" I say, trying to leave the heaviness behind like Mama Sharon did.

"Dani, my friend, please tell me the philodendron silver sword is still here."

"It sure is! She's waiting for you on the shelf in the back, next to the register."

Anthony breaks into a happy dance as he makes a beeline for his plant.

Next is Jasmine, and I already know what's she's looking for. "The carnivorous plants are right over there," I say, pointing. "Shane is going to LOVE them!"

Jasmine claps her hands in delight and heads straight to the carnivorous section.

Customers flow through the shop in a steady stream, and plants are literally flying off the shelves. I enjoy days like this when the hours pass quickly and the shop hums with activity. It energizes me, and there's no time to think about anything except for what's right in front of me—wonderful customers and fabulous plants!

We get a break from the rush at noon and collapse into our chairs. As if he could hear our stomachs growling from miles away, Tommy walks in carrying two coffees and a hot veggie pizza with extra cheese. It's exactly what we need.

He smiles. "I knew you ladies would be busy today, so I brought you some food and caffeine to keep you going. I gotta run. Have fun!"

He leaves as quickly as he came.

"Thank you!" Mama Sharon and I yell as he's walking away.

We relax and put our feet up for the first time since this morning, and it feels good. After a few minutes of enjoying our pizza, we start planning the rest of the day.

Mama Sharon looks at her schedule. "I have Thao, the new volunteer you recruited, coming in at 2:00 to lead the kids in a coloring project, so let's get their table set up with crayons, coloring books, and maybe some stickers."

I nod as I bite into my second piece of delicious cheesy pizza. "Yep, I'll do that first. Then I'll bring some inventory from the back and restock the shelves. Look how empty they are!"

Mama Sharon scans the room, smiling proudly. "This is great. Better than I hoped for. Okay, I'm ready, hand me my coffee and let's get moving."

I cram the last bite of pizza into my mouth, we lift our coffee cups and tap them together in a quick cheers, and then I get back to work preparing for the afternoon rush.

Thao shows up right on time, and within minutes she has four little ones coloring and playing with stickers. Their giggles fill the room like a joyful song.

As I'm watching for customers, a patrol car pulls up directly in front of the shop. The police officer walks in dressed in full uniform, complete with a radio strapped to his side and a gun holstered on his hip. The air presses in, my chest tightens, and my thoughts race.

Is he here for me? Does he know something? Did the hospital call him?

Whatever he's here for, Mama Sharon is already moving to greet him. I'll let her handle it.

"Good morning, officer!" she says brightly. "How can I help you?"

I glance up and freeze—he's looking right at me.

"Good morning! Mama Sharon, correct?" he says, his voice low and husky, matching his stocky build.

"Yes! How did you know?"

"I don't forget a name! I'm Officer Matteo Conti, but my friends call me Teo." He turns toward me. "Hi Danielle, mind if we talk for a minute?"

"Is everything okay?" Mama Sharon asks.

He motions me over. I walk up and stand right next to Mama Sharon, my heart pounding with every step.

Is my mother behind this? What's happened?

Officer Teo smiles. "I just wanted to check in." His voice is low, like he doesn't want the customers to hear. "Danielle, I was the first officer on the scene when you fainted. I'm glad to see you're looking better. How are you doing?"

"You're here to check on me?" I ask.

"Yes. We care about our community, and this plant shop brings a lot of joy to this town. We want you to know we're here whenever you need us."

My pulse slows, and my face flushes with embarrassment.

I just want to forget that day ever happened.

"Well," Mama Sharon says, "isn't that something? Thank you, Officer Teo. God bless you. Knowing we have your support means a lot. Danielle is family, and we're all relieved to have that day behind us. Thank you for checking in."

Officer Teo's smile grows wide with pride. "To protect and serve,

chapter 20: Shadows of My Soul

Mama Sharon. That's what we're here for. I'm glad to know everyone is doing well. Here's my card—call if you need anything."

"Thank you," I say, feeling grateful and embarrassed, "for everything. I appreciate your kindness, and I really am terribly sorry for any inconvenience I caused."

He smiles. "No need for that. It's our job, Danielle. We're happy to help whenever we can. And actually, while I'm here, my son is starting preschool next week and needs a gift for his teacher. My wife suggested a plant, but I don't know a flower from a weed, so I could use your help."

"Certainly!" Mama Sharon says. The tension breaks as she guides him away to browse the shop. I watch him kneel next to the kids table, chatting with them, giving high fives, and answering questions about his uniform. He pays for his plant, and as he's heading out, I hear Mama Sharon invite him and his family to our annual barbecue. Mama Sharon is that way. If you're kind to us, she's going to feed you.

As the day passes, the pace doesn't slow until just before closing, and then, finally, our last customer walks out the door.

Together, we survey the shop that now looks as if a tornado tore through it.

"I'm exhausted!" Mama Sharon says, as if reading my mind.

I smile. "Me too, but it's a good kind of exhausted."

"Indeed, it is. Thank you for today, you were spectacular. Our customers adore you."

I wave off the compliment, but it means the world to me.

We begin our closing process, working together in a comfortable silence. I sweep the floor, straighten and wipe down the shelves, break down boxes, turn on the humidifier, and take out the trash while Mama Sharon runs a sales report.

Just as I bag the last of the garbage, I hear my phone beep with a text message. My heart leaps when I see it's from Gabe:

"Hey, I was reading the Bible today and felt led to share this scripture with you, it's one of my favorites:

Psalm 23 - A psalm of David (NLT)

"The Lord is my shepherd;
I have all that I need.
He lets me rest in green meadows;
he leads me beside peaceful streams.
He renews my strength.
He guides me along right paths,
bringing honor to his name.
Even when I walk
through the darkest valley,
I will not be afraid,
for you are close beside me.
Your rod and your staff
protect and comfort me.
You prepare a feast for me
in the presence of my enemies.
You honor me by anointing my head with oil.
My cup overflows with blessings.
Surely your goodness and unfailing love will pursue me
all the days of my life,
and I will live in the house of the Lord
forever."

As I'm reading Gabe's text, something familiar tracks in my head. "Mama Sharon, that scripture you talked about this morning... The one you said you read over and over until it was written on your heart? Remind me which one it was?"

"Psalm 23," she says. "The scripture that brought me back to life."

I'm holding my breath as I double-check Gabe's text, and sure enough, it's Psalm 23.

I'm curious, so I ask, "Have you talked to Gabe today by chance?"

chapter 20: Shadows of My Soul

"No, I haven't. I need to call him and thank him again for helping us get all those plants from the nursery. Why? Is everything okay?"

"Yeah, everything is fine, I was just wondering," I say, trying to gather my thoughts. I sense the ground has shifted underneath me, and I don't know what to make of it.

I text Gabe back, "Thank you!" because it's all I can think to say.

We finally finish cleaning, turn out the lights, lock the door, and walk to the parking lot, arm-in-arm, Daisy padding happily behind us.

"What a day!" Mama Sharon says, sounding tired, but happy. "Thank you for our talk this morning, sugar. I hope you know I'm always here for you. And thank you for all your hard work. It looks like we had one of our most profitable days today, and that has a lot to do with you."

I smile. "I'm so glad. I'm grateful for this job, and for you."

"I'm grateful too," she says as she hugs me tightly. "Now go and get some rest. I'll see you in the morning. Come on, Daisy girl, let's get home."

She lets Daisy in her car, then turns to me. "Ready?"

I shake my head slightly. "No, please go on home. I'm going to enjoy the fresh air for a few minutes before I head out."

Mama Sharon smiles, waves goodbye, and drives off.

Too tired to think, I lean back against my car and take a minute to unwind. I yawn, stretch, and let my gaze rest on the sky full of soft, pillowy, pink and orange clouds. As the minutes pass, the sun dips, and the colors deepen into fiery red flames dancing across the horizon, and for just a moment, time seems to stand still.

My mind drifts, recounting the day...

The distant look in Mama Sharon's eyes as she described her suffering.

Sammie and the joy he brings me.

The sweet sound of children giggling.

Anthony doing a happy dance, the taste of cheesy pizza, smiling faces, and the familiar aches of my pain, my fears, and the dark secrets of my past all tangle into a knot in my chest that pulls and tightens with each breath I take. Even on good days, like today, my heart feels as empty as Mama Sharon's arms after she lost her baby, but I don't have a husband to lean on, or even a little bit of faith to cling to, so what's left for me? What am I supposed to do?

The cool night air drifts in and snaps me back from my thoughts, and I feel even more exhausted.

I glance at the horizon, now just a faint glow under a darkening sky, then bring up Gabe's message:

"Even when I walk
through the darkest valley,
I will not be afraid,
for you are close beside me."

I doubt the words apply to someone like me, but there's a little place hidden deep inside the shadows of my soul that wonders if maybe, just maybe, they do.

21
A Shift

I've had two good days in a row, which, at this point, just feels like a cruel trick—a reminder of what I can't hold on to. It's always the same. A good day comes, and then the darkness doubles down, even more punishing than before. It presses harder, and I just let it. I sink into it. I know how this is going to end, so why keep fighting?

I've noticed a shift inside of me since that morning at the Village Café. When I ran out, I felt ashamed, defeated, and empty inside, but soon after, I just felt incredibly foolish. Looking back, it's wild that I actually believed I could find answers on the internet that would change things. I pecked at my keyboard for hours, nervously looking over my shoulder as if someone might be secretly trying to catch a glimpse of what I was typing, but the truth is, not a single person in the café cared, or even noticed me.

Since that day, I've been quietly surveying the wreckage in my life. The deeper I've dived into the damage, the less I've slept, and the more vicious the inner voice has become. But things are beginning to make sense.

They say the truth hurts, and it's true—it hurts terribly. For me, it feels like being stabbed in the same spot over and over again until I'm left with a gaping wound that will never heal. But the pain is necessary, because with it comes acceptance, and with acceptance comes a strange sense of relief.

The truth is, I *am* weak. I *am* damaged. I *am* a coward. There's no denying it.

It's pathetic that I would search the internet looking for answers, trying to ease my mind. Was I hoping for some kind of assurance that I won't burn in hell? I'm already there!

Nothing matters, and nobody really cares—*that's* the truth.

Another truth revealed is my desperateness.

I hate it.

I hate it so much.

As a child, when my mother abused me, instead of running away or trying to get help, I would cling to her even tighter, literally begging her to love me. I was *desperate* for her love. I've lived my entire life in a state of desperation. I'm desperate for approval, hungry for attention, and constantly looking for crumbs of reassurance that people don't hate me, but lately I've come to realize something—when I'm gone, none of this will matter. Everyone will think I'm a coward, and they couldn't be more right.

I know that Gabe, Papa Reg, some friends at the shop, and especially Tommy and Mama Sharon will be hurt when I'm gone. But just for a little while. Soon they'll forget about me and get on with their lives.

And Sammie. Sweet Sammie. He's young and probably won't remember the time we spent together, but I hope he never forgets how much I love him—*every day, all the time, everywhere.*

Everyone I know has been through struggles. I'm fully aware that there are many people who have fought through much worse than I have, and they've come out on the other side stronger because of it. But not me. I'm weak. I don't have a triumphant comeback story like Tommy and so many others do. I don't have a savior who's going to swoop down from the heavens and rescue me. I'm just a sad ending—that's it.

My whole life I've tried to prove that I'm someone I'm not, and I

chapter 21: A Shift

can't do it anymore. I'm tired of trying to quiet the voices in my head that are screaming the truth, so I'm just going to let things be. I don't have any more questions. My soul is parched and empty.

I'm just here until I'm gone.

I glance at the clock and am surprised how late it is—I need to get going. We're closing the shop early today for plumbing repairs, so I have to make sure we open on time. We notified our customers that we're closing at noon, but with all the new plants we have in stock, I expect it will be a busy day.

It exhausts me just thinking about being around people with my stupid life-is-wonderful mask on. My brain is foggy—it's like I'm fighting against an invisible force that's dragging me down. It's getting harder and harder to function, but I *have* to show up. Mama Sharon is counting on me.

Before leaving, I take a quick glance in the mirror, and I'm shocked at my appearance. I look like an old, worn-out shoe that should be tossed in the trash, but it really doesn't matter anymore. Let them look. Let them notice. I don't care.

I manage to get to work on time and have everything in order for when we open our doors at 9:00, but my energy is zapped, and I could sure use some coffee. Just as I'm wondering if I have time to run and get some, my phone beeps with a message from Gabe: "Morning! Tommy and I are heading to the shop to get everything prepped for the plumber and we're stopping for coffee on the way. Can I bring you one?"

"Yes please!" I respond, then pause, staring at what I just typed—at the exclamation point I added on the end. I do it all the time out of habit, whether I feel it or not, but this one...

I'm struck with a realization. My heart isn't thumping in excitement at Gabe's message. I'm not smiling in anticipation of seeing him today. I'm glad he's bringing me coffee, but that's it. There's nothing else.

There's nothing. I feel *nothing*.

Moments later, the shop is full of customers buzzing around looking at our new displays. I do my best to greet them as I usually do, but my smile is wearing thin.

SMILE, DANI. ADJUST YOUR MASK.

Tommy and Gabe finally walk in with coffee in hand, and Tommy rushes to greet me. He's smiling brightly and looks so full of life that I can hardly bear it. Seeing him this way, so happy to see me, tightens the sadness around my heart, and I have to fight back tears.

"Missed you girl!" Tommy says. "I'm so glad you get to see me today!" He laughs at his own joke, oblivious to my agony.

I nudge him playfully, trying to act like myself, but I'm not sure who that is anymore.

I put on a cheerful tone. "I'm happy you get to see me too, Tommy!" I say, hoping no one notices that I'm falling apart.

I'm trying.

I'm *really* trying.

Gabe hands me my coffee. I take it without looking up.

"It's your usual," he says softly. "You look pretty today, Dani."

I shudder. "Please don't do that." It comes out sharp and irritated.

"I'm sorry?" he asks, looking genuinely confused.

"You don't need to tell me I look pretty. It's not necessary," I say, then turn abruptly to help a customer.

I know he's laughing on the inside. I'm tired of people making fun of me. I've had enough.

As the hours pass, the shop becomes utter chaos. The plumbers come early while Gabe and Tommy are still moving things around. Mama Sharon and I apologize to the customers and ask them to finish their shopping so we can close. It's not safe; there are too many things on the floor that folks might trip over, and I can see the concern on Mama Sharon's face.

Finally, we pick up the last few things, making room for the plumbers to come in and do their thing, and we close the shop with a

chapter 21: A Shift

collective sigh of relief.

Mama Sharon gives the lead plumber her number and asks him to call when they're done. They estimate it will take about four hours to repair the pipes and get everything back in working order. Then, hopefully, we can open our doors for business as usual tomorrow.

Gabe, Tommy, Mama Sharon, and I walk out to the parking lot together, and I notice the weather for the first time today. It's sunny, and I wish the clouds would come.

"Let's go to lunch," Tommy says. "Does Mexican sound good? I'm starving."

Gabe smiles. "You're always starving, bud. But yeah, sounds good to me."

I do my best to avoid eye contact with Gabe. I shouldn't have snapped at him earlier.

Mama Sharon claps her hands as if the decision is made. "Wonderful idea! My treat. Who's driving?"

Gabe volunteers, and they all head toward his truck.

"Dani?" Tommy asks.

"I'm going to pass," I say, not looking at him, "but enjoy!"

"Are you sure, sugar?" Mama Sharon calls out. "We'd love for you to come."

I'm already walking fast toward my car. "No thanks. I have some things to take care of. Have fun!"

I hear footsteps behind me, and I know it's Tommy. He catches up quickly. "Hey, why aren't you coming?" I can hear the disappointment in his voice.

I keep my eyes to the ground and fumble with my keys. "Sorry I can't. I have plans."

"What plans?" he asks, as if it's unheard of for me to have plans of my own.

Anger rises in my chest, and I have to fight the urge to slap him across the face.

YOU'VE REHEARSED THIS. IT'S FINE. JUST SAY THE WORDS.

I stop fumbling and look directly at him. "I have an appointment. Just let it go, please. I don't want to talk about it." I'm surprised by the steadiness in my voice.

"What kind of appointment?" Tommy asks, as I expected he would.

I lie right to his face. "It's with a therapist, okay? I'm trying to work out my stuff, but don't tell the others. I'm not ready to talk about it."

Tommy's features soften, and he leans in close. "I'm so proud of you. Call me after, I want to hear everything. This is good."

He joins the others, and I hear him say, "She's fine. Let's go!"

I can feel them staring as I drive off, but I don't look back. I stay focused on the road ahead and do my best to ignore the guilt that's slowly expanding in the pit of my stomach. When I was little and got caught lying, my mother would beat me, but even worse was the shame that would linger for days after my punishment. Typically, lying is hard for me, but not today. Today it feels far too easy.

I check the navigation system for my estimated arrival time. Traffic is light, so I should get there by 2:00, which means I'll be able to get back on the road and make it home before dark, which is good. I want this day to be over.

As I'm driving, I notice the landscape. The rolling hills are sun-bleached from a long, dry summer. In a few weeks, as the seasons change from fall to winter, the sun will disappear, branches will be bare, and the sky will turn into a dismal blanket of gray. I've grown fond of gray days. I *feel* gray.

Halfway there, the voices start their assault, but they're not screaming cruelly. Instead, they hum words of truth that settle into my bones like a welcome ache, pulling me closer to the end.

I arrive at my destination, park my car, and decide against wearing the ridiculous bulky coat, ball cap, and sunglasses I brought with me. Instead, I choose to walk in just as I am. I'm too tired to look over my shoulder today.

chapter 21: A Shift

As if announcing my entrance, a set of bells attached to the door chimes loudly. I scan the room. It's empty of people except for a woman standing behind the service counter.

I approach. "Hi, are you Liz? I'm Danielle. I called earlier this week."

There are dark circles under her eyes, and I wonder if she struggles with sleep. She looks as tired as I feel.

"Oh, yes," she says. "I remember. Glad you made it. Take a seat over there and get started on the paperwork." She points to a small section of chairs arranged neatly around a scratched-up metal table.

She hands me a clipboard full of papers and a pen. "While you're filling these out, I'll pull your item from the back. But first, I'll need the forms we talked about and a copy of your driver's license. Were you able to complete all the requirements?" Her voice is commanding, and it makes me nervous.

"Yes," I say, hoping she doesn't notice that my hands are shaking. "Here's the certificate, proof of residency, and my license."

She takes the documents, gives them a quick look, and leaves.

The hard chair and cold metal table offer no comfort as I settle in to read through the papers. I check the appropriate boxes and answer each question honestly. When I'm done, I review each page, making sure it's correct and complete. Then I pick at my cuticles and wait.

A tall, thin woman wearing a ball cap and dressed in a black jogging suit walks by. She must have already been here, because I didn't hear the clanging of the door chimes. She walks so quietly, I never would have noticed her if I hadn't glanced up. Our eyes meet, and we both smile casually, as if we're at the supermarket picking out apples from the produce department.

Liz returns and carefully places my order on a thin white cloth on the counter in front of me. She's smiling now, and it softens her face. "This is the one you asked about when we talked on the phone. She's a beauty," she says, holding the shiny black revolver in her hands, admiring it as if she made it herself.

I stare at it blankly. This moment feels insane to me, and I'm not sure how to act.

It seems natural that I would want to hold it, so I ask her if I'm allowed to.

"Of course you can!" she says, excited for me. "I have the same one at home. I keep it locked in my nightstand. It gives me peace of mind and helps me sleep better, just knowing it's there."

I get the feeling Liz wouldn't hesitate to use it.

"Exactly," I say as if we're on the same page. "I live alone, so I think having it will make me feel safer too. It's a crazy world out there, you know?"

The gun is heavier than I expected, but it fits in my hand as if it was custom made for me. I fight the urge to point it up under my chin to see how it feels. My hands shake, and I'm sure Liz notices, so I put it down quickly and suck in my breath.

Her eyes lock on mine for just a second too long, and I'm sure she senses something isn't right. I continue holding my breath.

"Indeed it is a crazy world," she says. "Give me a minute to look over your paperwork."

As she thumbs through the pages, I exhale quietly, trying to regain control.

The door chimes again, and it rattles me.

Who just walked in?

What will I say if it's someone I know?

Should I run?

Fear constricts my throat, but I swallow it down.

"Not today," I whisper to myself.

I am *not* doing that today.

To my surprise, my heartrate slows, and my breathing steadies. I don't look to see who walked in, because it really doesn't matter.

"Okay," Liz says, "everything looks great. Here's your license back and I have your phone number. Like I said, there's a standard

chapter 21: A Shift

ten-day waiting period, and it usually takes about two weeks for your background check to process. Once I get notified that you've cleared, I'll text you when it's ready to pick up. You'll have a safety demonstration when you get here, and then you'll be all set!"

"Okay."

Liz puts the revolver back in its box. "She's a treasure, and she'll keep you safe," she says, as if the gun is my new trusted friend.

I nod and do my best to smile, even though I feel like I might vomit. "Great! I feel safer already!" I say for no reason at all, then quickly turn and walk out the door, jangling the relentless chimes for the last time today.

My body feels heavy, like I'm trudging through mud on my way to the parking lot, but there's something else. It took guts for me to walk into that place and do what I just did. For once in my life, I took charge and did something I'd normally be too scared to do.

I pretend it means something, even though I know it doesn't.

I'm halfway through the drive home when my phone rings. It's Tommy.

"Hey," I answer.

"Hey! We missed you at lunch. I lost count of how many tacos I ate. So good! We have to go there sometime soon. You'll love it. Also, I have to tell you something. I spilled the beans and told Gabe and Mama Sharon you were seeing a therapist. I'm sorry. You know I can't keep secrets. They were both proud of you if that helps. Please don't be mad."

"I can't believe you told them," I say, but I can believe it. I knew he would tell them. I wanted him to. It will make things easier in the days to come.

"I know," he says. "I'm an idiot. I'm sorry. For real." His voice sounds small, and I know he's genuinely sorry.

"It's fine. I forgive you. The therapist was nice—we had a good connection. She recommends weekly sessions, so I need to make sure my insurance will cover it. I think it will be good. I feel better already. Yes to the restaurant. Tacos sound fantastic. Hey, can I call you tomorrow? I'm driving."

"No problem. You sound good, Dani. Tell me more later. Drive safe. Love you."

"Love you too," I say, relieved to end the conversation.

It surprises me how quickly my lies are building. This time was easier than the last, and I'm not sure why. Maybe it's because I have no choice but to lie. Or maybe it's getting easier simply because I don't care anymore.

My thoughts simmer into silence as I make my way home. I barely remember the drive. I don't bother brushing my teeth or washing my face. I just strip off my clothes and crawl into bed. As I drift in and out of sleep, I can feel the darkness pulling, trying to bury me alive. My throat closes up as the deep roots snake around me, tightening their grip. I try to move, to breathe, but the darkness presses in from all sides. The air is thick, like soil filling my lungs. I'm trapped—and no one is coming to save me.

22
Seven More Days

Lately, my world has gotten smaller, and honestly, it feels okay. It's freeing to not care about the future or worry about things to come. Everything feels lighter and easier because I have a plan, and something to prepare for. There is fear, for sure, but mostly the relief of knowing that I don't have to live this way forever, because in just seven more days, it will be over.

I have no idea what happens in the afterlife, or if there even is one, but if there is, I hope Henry and Grandma Vee are there waiting for me. Whether there's something after death or nothing at all, I'm okay with it, because *anything* is better than living like this.

It's been difficult to distance myself from Tommy because we're so close, but I know he's going to be okay. He's doing well these days. *Really* well. He's become active in his church and is making good, healthy choices. I've always thought he wouldn't be able to make it without me, but that's not true at all. He has found his way. He doesn't need me anymore. Life will be better for him once I'm gone. I'm certain of it.

As far as my belongings go, when I moved into my apartment it was fully furnished, so I don't have to deal with furniture. I've sorted through everything I own and managed to organize it into three piles: one for the donation center, one to give to friends, and one for trash. Preparing for the end has been a straightforward process and easier than I expected.

I'm leaving my car to Tommy. He can use it, sell it, or donate it to the church. It's paid off and only has 65,000 miles on it, so I'm sure he'll make good use of it. I'll leave my bike to him, too, so he and Vanessa can go on rides together. He really cares for her, and I have a feeling it may turn into a serious relationship. I hope it works out for them. Tommy deserves to be loved and cherished—I want that for him.

I have zero debt and a decent amount of money in my savings, thanks to Grandma Vee. I'm going to split the majority of it three ways between Tommy, Mama Sharon, and a college fund for Sammie, and then donate whatever is left to a Christian non-profit called Alive and Awake. They specifically serve high-risk youth who have trauma from abuse. I did my research and checked reviews—everything about them sounds extraordinary. It's a program that would have helped me and Tommy when we were younger, and I know it will mean a lot to him.

I've been avoiding Gabe. I stopped responding, but he still sends me encouraging messages and scripture. Tommy says he asks about me often and is confused why I've ended contact. Gabe is wonderful, but there's no future for us because I have no future. My days are literally numbered.

I haven't officially resigned from Thrive, but I think Mama Sharon knows it's coming. Since the incident there with my mother, I've been working a lot less, and they have plenty of knowledgeable staff to cover every shift. I miss taking care of the plants and seeing our customers, but it's better to cut ties now instead of waiting until the end. I hope they'll remember me with fondness.

It's strange to think that 32 years of living can be organized and boxed up in just two weeks. It's an odd feeling, but it settles my mind knowing everything will be in order when the time comes.

With a sudden burst of energy, I haul the trash pile down to the dumpster, load up my car with the bags of items to be donated, then grab my grandfather's gold cross necklace. I've kept it tucked away in a box on the top shelf of my closet for years, and I actually forgot about chapter 22: Seven More Days

it until I saw it today. It's a family heirloom that has been passed down through my family for generations, and because there are no living grandsons in mine, Grandma Vee left it to me. I want Tommy to have it. I know he'll treasure it, so I decided to give it to him today. I mean, why wait?

Since it's Sunday afternoon, I'm guessing Tommy is at church, so I drive straight there. Sure enough, his truck is in the parking lot. I look around for Gabe's truck, but there's no sign of it, which is a relief. I don't want to see him—there's no point.

Before going in, I check myself in the mirror, brush on some lip gloss, and run my fingers through my hair. I don't hate my reflection today—I don't care about that anymore. Excited, I check to make sure the necklace is in my purse, grab the matcha I bought for Tommy, and head through the front double doors of the church.

Tommy is sitting at a table next to the stage, looking down at paperwork. I sneak up behind him, cover his eyes with my hands, and whisper, "Guess who?"

He spins around and jumps to his feet. "Woah! Dani! What are you doing here? Man, I'm so happy to see you!" He hugs me tightly.

I squeeze him back. "I just wanted to swing by and say hello. I've missed you!"

"You're in a bouncy mood today," he says with a huge smile on his face. "What has you so excited?"

"It's just a good day! Here, I brought you an iced matcha." I hand him the drink and study him. Tommy's eyes are shining bright, he's dressed in a white collared shirt with blue jeans and boots, and his hair is pulled back into a neat ponytail. He looks like he may have put on a few pounds, and he wears them well. He looks handsome, and healthier than ever.

"Thanks for the matcha," he says. "Can you stay for a while? I'm leading a Bible study in ten minutes, and it will take around an hour. If you hang out, we can grab some food afterwards. My treat. I'll take you to the Mexican place down the street. I've actually been thinking about their tacos all day."

Tommy has not changed one bit. I hope he never does!

I smile. "You're always thinking about food! And thanks, but no, I've got things to do. Can you walk out with me for a second? I have a surprise for you."

Tommy raises his eyebrows. "A surprise for me? I LOVE SURPRISES! Come on, let's go!"

We walk out to the parking lot together, our arms linked.

I tell him, "You look great, Tommy. I'm so happy to see you doing well. You've got a wonderful life ahead of you, do you know that?"

"Thanks, Dani," he whispers. "I'm happy."

We get to my car, and I give him instructions. "Okay, stand right here, close your eyes, and hold your hand out."

He obliges, standing perfectly still with his eyes closed while I retrieve the cross necklace and drop it in his palm. I'm surprised by the weight of it. It's a beautiful piece of jewelry. I remember admiring it when my grandpa wore it around his neck.

"Okay!" I say, giggling with anticipation.

Tommy opens his eyes expectantly, then frowns at the tissue in his hand. "What is this?" he asks.

"Unwrap it!" I say, my excitement building. "The surprise is inside!"

He removes the paper and gasps. "Wait a minute. What is this? Oh my gosh! Is this your grandfather's necklace?"

"It sure is!"

"But this is important to you. It's from your Grandma Vee. Why are you giving it to me?"

I press it into his palm. "Stop... It's special to me, and that's why I want you to have it. Every time you wear it, I want you to think of me!"

I take it and loop it over his head, thrilled with my decision to give it to him today.

Tommy just stares at it, silent.

chapter 22: Seven More Days

"Don't you love it?" I ask.

"Of *course* I love it. It's gorgeous, and I appreciate it so much, but… "—his voice is suddenly heavy—"why now? I already think of you all the time. You're my best friend. I don't need a reminder." He pauses and looks at me with concern. "I'm getting a weird vibe. Are you moving away or something? Are you leaving me?"

My heart hurts seeing his worry, but I think of how much better his life will be without me dragging him down. I shake my head at his questions. "No, Tommy. I'm not moving away. I just wanted you to have it, okay? That's all."

Tommy looks as if he might cry. "Okay. If you're sure. I'll treasure this and think of you even more than I do now. This is so special. Really. Thank you so much."

We hug, and when I let go, he pulls me back in and hangs on tighter.

"I love you," he says, choking up with emotion. "I hope you know that."

I whisper, "Yeah, I know." I'll miss him, but this is for the best.

He releases me and presses the cross to his chest. "Thank you."

I smile and open my car door. "I'm so glad you love it. You deserve it. Okay, I gotta run!"

"What's with all the bags?" Tommy asks, pointing to the back seat.

"I cleaned out my closet. I'm donating some things. I've been busy," I say, honestly. It's true. I *have* been busy.

"Wow, you sure have. That's a lot of stuff! You should come over and help me clean out *my* closet next. It's an absolute disaster. I have way too many shoes and clothes. Probably more than you. It's actually embarrassing. Oh, one last thing, we're planning a community retreat this summer in the Santa Cruz mountains at Redwood Christian Park. It's going to be AMAZING! We've booked guest speakers and a great worship team. I want you to come. I'll text you the information so you can mark it down."

"Oh, sounds fun," I say cheerfully, starting the engine. "I'm sure you'll enjoy it!"

Tommy looks confused. "No, I meant I want you to come *too*. It's a weekend event, Friday through Sunday. I promise you'll enjoy it."

I shift into gear. "I'm sorry, I can't make it, but I know you'll have a great time. I really have to go. Love you!"

I drive off, feeling fantastic. As I'm pulling out of the church parking lot, I glance in my rearview mirror at Tommy, who is still standing in the same spot with his arms crossed over his chest. He has a confused look on his face, but it's okay. He'll be fine.

I drive to the donation center and drop off the bags—one more item completed. This is exhilarating! I had no idea this was going to feel so good. It's strange, but I keep forgetting the point of it all. I've thought about it so much that in some ways I've minimized what I'm actually preparing to do. Sometimes I forget that I have a really hard thing coming up, but for today, I feel productive and accomplished. I know the stigma that's associated with what I'm going to do, but for me, it's a way out from a lifetime of agony—nobody should blame me for that. It feels good to get my things in order. It feels like relief. It feels like freedom!

My phone dings with a text message. I'm sure it's from Tommy. He's probably thanking me again for the necklace.

I see who it's from, and my heart leaps in my chest. It's not from Tommy.

I open the message, hoping it's good:

"Hi Danielle, this is Liz from San Jose. I've received your clearance, and your item is ready for pick up. We're closed today, but I thought I would let you know. Our hours are Monday through Saturday, 10:00 to 7:00. See you soon."

I text back quickly, "Great! I'll see you tomorrow. Thanks, Liz!"

My body freezes, my mind scrambling to process the news. A mix of excitement, fear, and adrenaline washes over me.

I think about when I almost overdosed on pills and how dreadful it was. The only thing that could be worse than people finding out I took

chapter 22: Seven More Days

my own life would be if I tried and was unsuccessful. The questions and judgment would be more than I could handle. I couldn't bear it. I would never be able to face anyone again. Just thinking about it makes me feel nauseous.

I tell myself to calm down. "This is not the time to fall apart, Danielle. This is what you wanted. This is good. This is necessary. You have a plan, and you're sticking to it."

I shake off the bad thoughts and turn the music up, roll my windows down, drive straight to the flower shop, park, and rush in the door. I have to hurry because they close in ten minutes.

I walk right up to the woman behind the counter who reminds me of my Grandma Vee. "Do you have any fresh yellow roses in the back?"

She smiles warmly. "Funny you should ask! I just received a new shipment. One dozen, dear?"

"Make it two!" I say, feeling brave.

Seven more days.

Just seven more days!

check on your **happy** friends

23
The Weight of Sadness

The surge of energy and elation I've been feeling has worn off. Now I just feel numb. I keep trying to fathom what's happening to me—in my mind and body. I don't feel anything anymore. I don't care if I sleep or stay up all night, if I eat or skip meals, or what others think about me. None of it matters. My heart doesn't race like it used to. I sometimes wonder if it's still beating at all. I feel lonely. A cold kind of lonely that makes my bones ache.

Images have been flashing like a movie in my head. I see myself drowning in the ocean. I see people crying at my funeral. I imagine being dead.

As I'm washing my face, I notice my reflection. I'm bland. Blank. I'm nothing at all.

Today is going to be a busy day, so I'm doing my best to muster the energy for it. We're having our annual barbecue at Thrive, and we expect a big turnout. Nobody knows it yet, but today will be my final day there. I'm not sure how I'm going to handle it, but I can't keep showing up in this condition. I need to put some distance between me and the shop before my day comes. Besides, business is growing, and I've already trained the new employees. The time is right for me to leave.

The shop is buzzing with excitement when I walk in. Daisy has a new, bright orange bandanna tied around her neck, and Mama

Sharon is stirring two crockpots; one full of her famous Jamaican Stew Chicken, and the other with her spicy homemade chili. It smells so good it makes my mouth water, which surprises me.

I guess I am still human.

Bright colored bowls are filled with hardo bread, cornbread, hot salsa, shredded cheese, and diced onions. Mama Sharon and Papa Reg have been working hard.

I greet Mama Sharon. "Good morning. It sure smells good in here!" I'm surprised that my sense of smell still works. I'm surprised my body is still functioning at all.

Mama Sharon looks up and smiles. "There she is! How are you, sugar?"

Her voice instantly soothes my soul—I'm going to miss her.

"I'm fine, Mama Sharon. What do we have going, and how can I help?"

"I think we're in good shape! We have about an hour before everyone gets here, and there's not much left to do. My sister, Shanice, will cover the shop until noon, then I'll hang a sign directing customers to join us out back. I'm not worried about sales today, I just want folks to eat and enjoy themselves, including you!"

"Sounds good! What's on the menu?"

"Papa Reg is in the back barbecuing Jerk Chicken and tri-tip, and racks of ribs are in the smoker. There's coleslaw, rice and peas, macaroni and potato salads in the refrigerator, and baskets full of bread on each table. At Tommy's request, I made his favorite oatmeal raisin cookies, and my sister made lemon, banana cream, and berry pies. The apples are washed, but the pears and grapes still need to be. Would you be a dear, and do that for me?"

I'm in awe of how Mama Sharon and Papa Reg take care of people. No one will leave this place hungry, that's for sure. They have a way of making everyone feel like family, especially me.

"Yep, I'm on it!" I say, feeling better. This shop and these people

chapter 23: The Weight of Sadness

have helped me through many tough days. My loneliness is less here, and the weight of my sadness seems to lighten as soon as I walk in the door.

I pull my hair up in a bun, tie an apron around my waist, and start washing the fruit. Mama Sharon and I work together in silence, but it's too quiet for me, so I ask her for a favor.

"Mama Sharon, would you sing while we're working? Before anyone gets here?"

She starts humming. The warmth of her voice wraps around me and calms my mind. I tilt my head back, take a deep breath, and close my eyes, letting her rich, soulful voice seep into the dark chambers of my heart.

Papa Reg walks in, gives me a playful nudge, then hums in tune with Mama Sharon. I stop what I'm doing and watch as he inches his way toward her, pulls her in close to him, and gently kisses her on the forehead, all the while humming and swaying to the sound.

I'm in awe of the love they share. What a beautiful thing to give and receive love so freely. It makes me wonder if Gabe and I could have built a happy life together. I like to think we could have.

Once the food is prepared, we walk around to make sure everything is ready.

It's a beautiful October day—not too warm with a light breeze—so we opt to forgo the popup canopies and set everything up in the sunshine.

Red and white checkered tablecloths run the length of four long picnic tables with benches on both sides for plenty of seating. Yellow and white daisies are arranged loosely in dozens of small, clear vases down the middle of each table. At the back of the building, we have all the food arranged in the shade. One table holds the meat that's covered in big aluminum pans to keep everything nice and warm, another is full of enough side dishes and desserts to feed a massive army, and the last one holds drinks, utensils, and everything you need for a feast. Not a detail was missed. It looks amazing.

Mama Sharon and Papa Reg are generous, loving people. Not only did they invite their employees, volunteers, friends, and staff from neighborhood businesses, but they encouraged them to bring their families as well. Last year there was a huge turnout. I remember sitting with Henry and talking to him for the first time at this luncheon. The memory stings. So much has changed since then.

Mama Sharon's smile is as warm and bright as the morning sun. "Okay, Reg and Dani, I think we're ready. It all looks and smells so good! Why don't you two take five, drink some water, and let's get ready for the crowd."

At 11:30 I begin greeting people as they walk in. Lyle and his lovely wife, Megan, from the nursery in Half Moon Bay are the first to arrive. We hug, and I start to walk them back to the tables, but Lyle stops me.

"Dani, Megan and I wanted to let you know how much we enjoy working with you. We talked about you on the way over here today, and we both think you're amazing. You spread light wherever you go, and you've made doing business fun. It's not very often we come across someone as kind and friendly as you, and we wanted to be sure and tell you how much we appreciate you."

I'm stunned.

"Oh, my goodness," I say, feeling overwhelmed with gratitude. "Thank you for your kind words! You two have been wonderful to me and the shop. Truly! I'm so glad you're here. Please find yourselves a seat, get some food, and I'll be by to chat with you later."

Our rockstar volunteer, Trish, and her three little ones arrive, followed by Tommy and Vanessa. I hug them both and marvel at how happy they seem.

I spot Mama Sharon and Papa Reg's bonus son, Michael, and his wife, Mandy, walking toward me. Little Sammie is riding high on his daddy's shoulders. He squirms until Michael sets him down, and then he runs to me, his arms outstretched, his face beaming. I scoop him

chapter 23: The Weight of Sadness

up, and he squeezes my neck in a hug.

"Titi? Can you play with me? Can I sit by you?" Sammie asks, his voice bouncing and bubbly.

"Yes!" I say to this perfect little human who makes my heart sing. "Let me finish here. Then we'll play, okay?"

I set him back down next to his parents. "I love you, Sammie."

"You love me every day, all the time, everywhere!" he shrieks as he runs in circles.

Michael and Mandy smile and wave to me. I wave back, quickly wiping away the unexpected tears.

Thank you, Sammie bear. I love you, I love you, I love you.

Jay from the pizza parlor down the street shows up, along with Loni and her husband from the hardware store. Then Veronica, who used to work with Henry at The Café. I haven't seen her since his funeral.

We meet eyes. Veronica does her best to smile, but I can see her pain. Thinking of Henry still hurts.

She hugs me tightly and whispers, "I love you."

"I love you too," I tell her. What else is there to say?

Next in line is Officer Matteo, accompanied by his lovely wife and their two sons—both the spitting image of their father.

I shake his hand, touched that he came. "Hello, Officer Teo. You made it!"

"Hey, Danielle, good to see you. Of *course* I made it. I would never pass up free food!" He laughs, then introduces me to his sweet family. Mama Sharon will be thrilled to see them here.

Folks keep coming, and by 12:20, the place is packed.

My face feels tight from smiling so much and my arms are growing tired of hugging people, but I'm not complaining. It's beautiful—I needed this.

Mama Sharon puts a sign on the front door directing people to the back, grabs her sister's hand, and leads her to sit with us. Shanice is tall and stunning and has a strong presence about her, just like Mama Sharon.

Papa Reg claps loudly to get everyone's attention. "I have something to say, but first I want to make sure everyone has a full plate in front of them. Everybody good?" He scans the crowd.

Tommy raises his hand like a kid in a classroom. "I need more cornbread, Papa Reg. Can I grab some real quick before you start?"

Papa Reg laughs his big, hearty laugh. "Tommy, son, you get all the cornbread you want. I'll wait."

Tommy dashes to the table, grabs three cornbread muffins, two of his favorite cookies, and a handful of grapes, then rushes back to his seat next to Vanessa. "Thank you, sir. Ready now!" he yells as he's crumbling the cornbread into his huge bowl of chili.

Papa Reg clears his throat and everyone stops talking—all eyes are on him.

"My brothers and sisters," he says, "we are so glad you're here. Today, as we gather at Thrive's third annual barbecue, I want to take a moment to acknowledge and honor you all—our customers, colleagues, friends, neighbors, vendors, family, and volunteers. We started small. It was just me, Mama Sharon, and Dani, but we've grown recently and are adding three more positions, which is a huge blessing. Ya'll are the heart and soul of our little plant shop, and we appreciate the support you've shown us. Enjoy your food, get seconds and thirds, eat as much as you want, there's plenty! We love y'all and we thank you. God bless you each and every one. Now, if you'll give us just a minute more, my beautiful wife—who you know as Mama Sharon—will pray and bless our food."

Mama Sharon stands, folds her hands, closes her eyes, and bows her head. "Gracious heavenly Father, as we gather here today, let us remember that it is You, Lord, who made this all possible. Father, we thank You for this beautiful day, for the breath in our lungs, for these wonderful people here with us, for our shop, and for this meal to nourish our bodies. Father, if there is someone here today who is struggling, would You comfort them? Would You reveal yourself to them in ways only You can? Let them know that they are loved, they matter, and they belong. Bring us peace, Lord. We love you, in Jesus's name, Amen!"

The group responds with a collective "Amen!" and the party gets started. We eat and laugh, there are smiles and hugs, and for a moment it feels as if this is my goodbye celebration. I hadn't thought of it when I came here today, but this is the last time I'll see all these people. I hope they know how much they've helped me, and I hope, in some small way, that I've helped them too.

Sammie runs up and pats me on my leg. "Titi you play with me now?" His voice is so pure and sweet I can barely take it.

"Yes! Let's do it!"

He grabs my hand and leads me to the bean bag toss. He throws the first bag and lands it right in the hole! He shrieks with delight, runs, grabs the bag, and brings it back to me.

"Your turn!" he squeals.

We play and play, share a piece of pie, sing a song, and end our fun with an arm-wrestling match on the corner of the picnic table. Sammie and I go three rounds—I always let him win twice.

He smiles triumphantly, puffs out his chest, and shows me how big his muscles are. "Me win! Keep practicing, Titi, and you will be big and strong just like me."

My heart fills to the very brim. Sammie yawns and reaches for me, so I take him in my arms, hug him tightly, and whisper in his perfect little ear, "I love you every day, all the time, everywhere."

"You love me, Titi," he whispers back, and nestles his sweet little face in my neck.

Holding Sammie close, I walk back toward his parents and keep whispering to him, "I do love you, Sammie bear. So, so much. You always remember that. I love you, I love you, I love you."

Michael reaches for Sammie, takes him into his arms, smiles, and gives me a hug. "Thanks, Dani. This kid talks about you nonstop. He adores you!"

I smile back, trying my best not to cry. Sammie's love for me and mine for him caught me off guard. It's pure in a way that's hard to explain. It's special because it's an honest love—not earned, just freely given. It's as if someone handed me a piece of light and said, "Here. This is just for you." That's what Sammie is for me—light, joy, and boundless love. I smile at him one last time and walk away, tucking his love into my heart and carrying it with me.

Holding back tears, I do my best to stay busy. I check on guests, refill waters, and as I'm passing around a tray of cookies, Shanice approaches me. "Honey, there's two people here to see you. They're standing over by the door and asked for you specifically."

My stomach drops. Who could it be?

I spot them by the door and rush over to say hello. "Oh, my goodness. Beth! Gracie! What a nice surprise!" I'm thrilled to see them.

"Wow!" Beth says. "I can't believe you remembered our names!" Both her and Gracie are smiling, and they look genuinely happy to see me.

I'm awestruck by Gracie. She's standing tall, looking directly at me. The change in her is astounding.

I ask her, "How's your Venus flytrap?"

"You mean Miss Jaws? She's awesome!"

"Cool," I say, smiling. "You look different, and I'm loving the hair."

"Right? I love it too. I tossed all the Goth culture stuff—I'm over it."

I'm amazed. Gracie is responding to me playfully. She looks like a completely different young woman. She's wearing a bright orange t-shirt, fitted jeans, and white high-top tennis shoes. Her hair looks darling pulled up in a high ponytail with fun pink streaks framing her radiant, youthful face.

I search her eyes and ask, "How *are* you?" I remember when she finally looked up at me that day we met at the shop. I was shocked by

chapter 23: The Weight of Sadness

how striking her blue eyes were, but they looked empty and terribly sad. Today they're clear and bright—I can't get over the change.

"I'm good," she says casually. "I don't want to disappear anymore."

My throat tightens and my mouth is suddenly dry.

Disappear? Gracie? Noooooooooo. Not you. Never!

She holds her arms out, palms up. They're crisscrossed with scars, but none are recent. "I ditched the so-called friends I was hanging out with because they were cruel, and they made me feel horrible about myself. Just because I care about plants, animals, art, and the environment more than I care about dating guys and taking selfies, does *not* make me a weirdo—I would never want to be like them! I've made some new friends who have similar interests, and it's been great. I'm healing and growing and focusing on myself now, and it feels amazing. I'm choosing happiness!"

She smiles, her chin lifted confidently, and I'm speechless. How did she become so wise?

"Wow, Gracie. That's something. That's powerful. I'm so, um, well, I'm just so proud of you!" I'm stumbling over my words, and I'm not sure what else to say, so I turn my attention to Beth. "And how are you?" I ask, noticing how happy and content she looks.

She smiles. "I'm wonderful. Thank you for asking. We came to thank you, Dani. That crazy plant, Miss Jaws, was like a bridge that helped us stay connected. We cared for it together, and it gave us both something to focus on other than our problems. The tension between us eased, and as the weeks went by, things slowly got better. Gracie is in counseling, off social media, and spending more time doing things she loves, like art therapy. Anyway, we wanted to stop by and say hi, and Gracie has something for you." She looks at Gracie and nods.

Gracie hands me a manilla folder. "Here, I painted this for you."

I open it and find an absolutely stunning painting of a Venus flytrap. I gasp. "Oh wow. This is gorgeous!!! You painted this? For ME?" I'm completely shocked.

"Yep," Gracie says, looking slightly embarrassed.

I stare at her masterpiece. "The colors and detail are incredible! You really captured the intricacy of the plant in such a cool and unexpected way. I'm so impressed! Oh my gosh, is that a mealy worm in its trap?"

"Yep, it sure is," she says with a huge smile.

Why did she do this for me? I don't understand. It's so incredibly thoughtful.

She points at the sign for the barbecue. "Hey, are we allowed to eat? It smells good and I'm starving."

I laugh. She sounds like a typical hungry, healthy teenager. "Yes! Please! Eat all you want. And thank you so much for this, Gracie. I will treasure it always."

She gives me a quick hug and heads for the food line.

I say to Beth, "I think your daughter is going to kick down doors and move mountains in this world."

"I think you're right," she says, then takes my hand and squeezes it. "Dani, you really made a difference for me that day. When you assured me that everything was going to be okay, I believed you, and I know that sounds silly because we'd just met, but what you said made me realize that of all the scenarios I played out in my head, her being okay was not one of them. I thought of her being miserable forever, and never having friends or living a happy life. I kept thinking of obstacles in her future, but not once did I actually think of her getting through it and being okay. I wish there was some way I could lift you up, like you lifted my spirits that day."

I look at her, tears streaming down my face. "You just did, Beth. You just did."

Gracie has had her share of food and is ready to go. We chat about plants a few minutes more, and then it's time to say goodbye.

I walk them to the door. "Thank you, ladies. You have no idea how you've encouraged me. It was so good to see you again. And Gracie,

chapter 23: The Weight of Sadness

thank you for the beautiful painting." I manage to get the words out, choking down the lump in my throat.

She smiles. "We'll be back soon for another plant. I think Miss Jaws needs a friend."

I just smile in response.

Please please please don't ever come back. I won't be here! I'm not brave like you, Gracie.

Beth takes my hand. "We will see you again, Dani. I'm certain of it. Oh, and later, when you have quiet time, be sure to look at the details in your painting. I think you'll be surprised at what you find."

I watch as Beth and Gracie walk to their car; my worn out heart pumping in my chest as if I'm running out of time.

Daisy runs up, sits at my feet, and paws at my leg. I crouch and hug her tightly, breathing in her scent one last time, and whisper, "I love you, Daisy girl. Take care of everyone, okay?"

I hold her a moment longer, then guide her back to the others.

I take a deep breath and return to the festivities where my friends are enjoying themselves. This is how I want to remember them—just like this. I soak in their images as long as I can, whisper my unspoken goodbyes, then sneak out while no one is looking. Leaving others to clean up is something I never would have done before, but today is different. It's time for me to go.

As I'm leaving the parking lot, I see Gabe pulling in. Sadness floods my chest. I hesitate, wanting to stop and talk to him, but reality nudges me to keep driving. There really is nothing to say.

I'm so sorry, Gabe, but you deserve better than me. Find someone who is actually beautiful—who's not broken—and love her.

As soon as I get to my place, I text Mama Sharon: "I'm sorry I had to leave. I'm sure Tommy can stay and help clean up. I want to thank you for today. It was wonderful! Everyone had the best time, and the food was AMAZING! I'm so grateful for you and Papa Reg, and all you've done for me. Please give Sammie my love. Thank you for everything.

I love you all very much."

After pressing send, I toss my phone on the couch. I won't be looking at it anymore tonight. It's early, but I decide to change into my pajamas and crawl into bed. I hold Gracie's folder to my chest, take a few deep breaths, and then open it. My finger traces the lines of the Venus flytrap, swirling over Gracie's brushstrokes, admiring the details and beauty of her work.

And then I see it.

Small text is scribed along the border of every curve and angle of the stems and traps of the plant. The words are tiny, so I have to hold the painting up close...

I am known. I am loved. I am enough. I am seen. I am valued. I am okay. I am becoming. I am breathing. I am living. I am worthy. I am brave. I am me.

I squint to read a final phrase written even smaller along the edge of the mealworm...

I am still here!

Tears fall down my cheeks, blurring my vision, but I keep reading the words over and over. I sob until my whole body feels wrung out, as if every ounce of life has been sucked away.

I replay Beth's words in my mind and picture Gracie's face, her smile, and the change in her, and it makes my heart soar. But soon, the darkness presses in. I am not okay, I never will be, but Gracie *is*, and that's all that matters right now.

I don't know if Mama Sharon was directing part of her prayer toward me today, but it felt like she was. And I don't know if it was God, the universe, or my imagination, but I felt loved today. As if I belonged, and people really do care about me. I was not expecting that.

Maybe my life was not a complete waste.

I turn off the light, nestle deep into the warmth of my blankets, and try my best to remember the sound of Sammie's giggles as I close my eyes and attempt to sleep.

chapter 23: The Weight of Sadness

Alone in the darkness, I sense something. I don't know if it's actual peace I feel inside, but there's something about knowing I'm almost to the end that brings me comfort. I jump out of bed, go to my closet, open my safe, and for what seems like the hundredth time, I check to make sure it's still there.

It is.

Of *course* it is.

I run my hand over the barrel, feeling relief in the cold, merciful steel.

It's ready when I am, and I'm getting there.

check on your **happy** friends

24
Every Detail

I'm afraid just one mistake could lead to someone finding out my plan, and that is my biggest fear—one I've played out in my head hundreds of times. I know it's not likely to happen, but the what-ifs have been bouncing back and forth in my mind like a ping pong ball. Back and forth, back and forth, back and forth—crazy scenarios of someone finding out and trying to stop me. Even this morning, when I called and made my hotel reservation, I got the feeling that the woman I talked to, Hope, suspected something. I had a hard time answering her questions, and I hesitated when I shouldn't have. I'm worried that she knows, and she'll have the police waiting for me when I arrive tomorrow. Is that logical? Did she really sense my intentions?

My phone rings and scares the living hell out of me.

It's Tommy.

Again.

I add up the number of calls and text messages I've ignored from him in the last week. Five phone calls, nine texts, and climbing. Tommy is relentless.

My phone beeps with another message from him: "Helloooooo? Okay, you're either ghosting me or you've been kidnapped. If it's ghosting, text me back #1. If you've been kidnapped, I know you can't respond, so I'll jump in my truck and come find you."

The last thing I need is for Tommy to come over and see my almost empty apartment, so I text him back immediately: "I'm not kidnapped. Hurray! And I'm not ghosting you. I've been busy. What's up?"

"Excuse meeeee? I've messaged you 20 times, and I've called, and this is how you respond?"

Oh boy, he is clearly not happy with me.

"Nine," I reply, trying to keep it light.

"Nine what? You're not making any sense. I'm calling you right now so pick up your phone!"

Tommy exhausts me, but I have to get this over with, so I answer on the first ring.

"Hi," I say.

"Hi???? That's all you have to say? First of all, where have you been? Second, why did you say nine?" He sounds wound up.

"I was kidding!" I say, trying my best. "You said you messaged me 20 times, and I was correcting you. It was only 9. Look, I'm sorry. I've just been busy."

"Busy doing *what*?"

"Oh my gosh, Tommy, calm down!" I say, my frustration building. "I'm just taking some time and distancing myself, that's all. What do you need?" I do *not* want to deal with this—I don't have the energy for it.

"I have things to talk to you about, and what do you mean you're distancing yourself? From what? From *me*?" Tommy's voice is getting louder. He sounds confused and I don't blame him. I'm confused too.

I hate this. I hate this so much.

"We're talking *now*, Tommy. What do you need?"

"I need *you*! Geez, Dani. Since when do I have to have a reason to call you? What's going on? And please, answer the question. Is it me you need distance from?" He sounds as if he's on the verge of tears.

"Yes. I need a break from everything, including you. Just for a little while. I'm sorting some things out. It's nothing personal." I say it, regretting every word.

chapter 24: Every Detail

"Okay, I'll let you go then," Tommy says, sounding crushed.

"Okay, bye." I end the call feeling like the biggest jerk on the planet.

I hope he doesn't, but knowing Tommy, he'll probably call right back.

Three little dots blink on my phone screen indicating he's typing a message.

No message comes, and the dots disappear.

Dots are back—he's typing again.

They disappear again.

I wait, fully expecting my phone to ring or more texts to start pouring in, but they don't.

He hates me and I don't blame him. I hate me too.

Shaking off my guilt, I try my best to focus on my tasks. I can't afford to miss a single detail.

My mind starts ping-ponging again. Two nights... I should have reserved the room for two nights instead of one. The least I can do is pay for two nights, because it's a five-star hotel, and they will have a big mess to clean up. I picture the day-after scene, and fear blisters the back of my throat. Will I traumatize whoever finds me?

I stop myself from spiraling and take a deep breath. I can't control everything. The hotel is not my problem. Tommy is not my problem. I have to let it go.

My palms are sweaty as I put my one remaining credit card back inside my wallet. I struggled when I gave my account number and expiration date to Hope. Normal things like blinking, swallowing, and reciting numbers are taking all of my effort and concentration. But I can't fall apart now. I can't!

My stomach growls, and I can't remember when I ate last. I didn't expect to be hungry, but I am. The only food left in the kitchen is a box of stale crackers—it will have to do. I grab a handful and wash them down with water.

Grabbing my notebook from underneath my mattress, I scan my checklist and feel accomplished. Most everything is done. I'm in good shape.

My bank accounts are closed out, my lease is paid until the end of the month, my belongings have been sorted through and disbursed, and everything is done. Every box is checked. All the details are covered. The only thing left is to write out cards, organize a few more things, then waste time until tomorrow afternoon when I'll pack my bag, leave my keys on the table, and head for the hotel. And the first thing I'm going to do when I get there is sit on the balcony and drink the champagne Hope promised me. She thinks I'm celebrating something, which is ironic because in some ways I am. I feel like I've been planning this day in my head all my life, and it's finally almost here.

On to the next task.

The cards I selected are simple and elegant. They're cream colored, with a picture of a bouquet of yellow roses sitting on a table in front of a large window. The window's view is slightly blurred, bringing your attention to the roses that look just like the ones I have on my counter right now. They're just opening up into a full bloom. Yellow roses were Grandma Vee's favorite, which made them my favorite too. I think the cards are perfect.

I address the envelopes first because I can't figure out what to write on the inside. I didn't think this was going to be so difficult. I'm starting to understand why Henry didn't leave any notes. I mean, what do you say to help people understand? How can a few sentences express my gratitude for those who made my life tolerable? I grapple with words for an hour, and finally decide on just three short sentences:

Please forgive me. It's better this way. Forever my love, Dani.

It's the best I can do for them, but Tommy is different. Just thinking of him fills me with dread.

Don't do that! He'll be better off without you. Tommy is not your responsibility.

I decide to write him a letter instead of a card. It's the least I can do.

I still have lemon and ginger tea, so I boil some water, drop in two

chapter 24: Every Detail

bags, and let them steep while I fire up my laptop and prepare to write.

The first thing I do is open a Word document and save it as "Tommy's Letter" in a folder named "Confidential." I'll write a draft tonight, read it and edit in the morning, print it out, and then delete the file before I leave. I've already deleted most everything off my computer, so this will make it easy for me.

I run through my checklist one more time. Everything that I can take care of today is done. All that's left is getting through the next 24 hours. Then I'll pack up the last of my things and drive to the hotel.

Shifting my thoughts to Tommy's letter, I rack my brain for what to say to him. I wish I could just write, "I'm sorry" ten thousand times, but even that would not be enough.

I settle onto the couch with my laptop and do my best to draft the most important letter I've ever written—the one in which I say goodbye to my best friend who has stood by me through it all.

check on your **happy** friends

25
Black Out

With everything finished, all I have left is to survive one more night in my apartment. It's been days since I've slept, and I feel like I'm on the brink of insanity—or maybe I've already crossed over. I close my eyes and try to relax, but the air suddenly turns thick. My throat feels restricted, as if it's closing up, and it's difficult to breathe. My heart gallops in my chest so violently that I think I might have an actual heart attack, and that would be good, wouldn't it? It would save me the trouble.

I attempt to open the safe but can't remember the combination.

Think! Think!

I try again, still nothing. Third try, nothing. Finally, on the fourth try the safe door clicks, releases, and opens. The room spins as I reach for the revolver and small box of bullets. Holding my breath, I carefully extract one bullet and slide it into the chamber, then rotate the cylinder and swing it into place.

Click.

It's ready.

I'm ready, and my hands are shaking. This is my answer. This is what I've been waiting for. One pull of the trigger and all my pain will end.

The shaking turns violent as I press the tip of the barrel under my chin. It's heavy, so I have to tighten my grip and use both hands to steady myself.

Am I doing this now?

IT WOULD BE EASIER, WOULDN'T IT? NO DRIVE. NO HOPE AT THE HOTEL. NO DELAY. NO DISTRACTIONS.

I pull the hammer back and press the muzzle harder into my throat.

Decide!

My finger wraps around the trigger.

The revolver is shaking.

I breathe in.

Decide!

One little pull is all that's between me and nothing.

One little pull.

Inhale.

Exhale.

Calm.

I kneel, steady, eyes closed.

A little pressure.

A little more.

The trigger pushes into the crease of my index finger.

Just a little harder...

A deep moan escapes my throat, and I drop the gun to the floor.

No. Not yet. You have a plan. Stick to it. Every detail matters.

My head pounds, and a wave of nausea rises in my throat. I barely make it to the toilet in time to throw up the crackers I ate hours ago. I don't know why I ate them—it's too late for food. It's too late for *anything.*

I feel trapped, as if there's a force pulling and pushing and pressing in on me. I can't take it anymore—I'm completely freaking out!

Desperate for relief, I rip off my clothes and collapse face down in the middle of the bathroom. My bare breasts press into the cold tiles— the side of my face squished on the floor as I stare at the baseboards, trying to catch my breath. I notice grimy, dark buildup in the grout

chapter 25: Black Out

lines and stray hairs gathered in the corner like tiny tumbleweeds. I can't lift my head or look away. I'm breathing in the germs and filth, and there's nothing I can do to stop it. Too weak to move, I stay in the same position until my hip bones ache from the pressure.

The pain is unbearable.

Everything hurts.

My inner voice is screaming.

ALL THE ATTENTION AND THE REASSURANCE YOU'VE BEEN GETTING LATELY IS BECAUSE PEOPLE FEEL SORRY FOR YOU. THEY PITY YOU. YOU'RE A DESPERATE, PATHETIC BURDEN TO EVERYONE. EVEN TOMMY—YOU'RE HOLDING HIM BACK.

THE ONLY REASON MAMA SHARON LOOKED AT YOU WHEN SHE WAS PRAYING IS BECAUSE SHE FEELS OBLIGATED. SHE'S PROBABLY THE ONE WHO TOLD LYLE AND HIS WIFE TO SAY SOMETHING KIND. YOU'RE A PEST. A BURDEN. NO ONE WANTS YOU AROUND. THEY'RE JUST PRETENDING.

AND GABE? DID YOU REALLY BELIEVE HE WAS INTERESTED IN YOU? NO! TOMMY ASKED HIM TO PAY ATTENTION TO YOU BECAUSE YOU'RE SO PATHETIC. THEY SEE YOU AS A CHARITY CASE. NOTHING MORE. YOU DON'T BELONG. YOU'RE NOTHING. NO ONE CARES ABOUT YOU. NO ONE WANTS YOU. YOU'RE FILTHY. YOU'RE BROKEN. YOU'RE WORTHLESS.

The words stab and rip into my skin like poisoned arrows. I shake my head, hard, trying to free my mind, but it doesn't work. Every organ in my body is pulsing and pounding, my heart ricocheting in my chest. In a panic, I sit up and grab the trash can liner, pull it over my head, and hold it tight around my neck.

Short, shallow breaths suck the bag in and out of my mouth. I keep my eyes open, focusing on the thin plastic barrier that blurs and distorts my view. My breath comes in bursts as I try to suffocate myself.

Inhale.

Exhale.

HOLD IT TIGHTER.

Inhale.
Exhale.
My arms weaken.
In.
Out.
There's no air.
TWIST THE BAG MORE. END IT.
In. Out. In. Out.
Nothing.
Gasping.
Spots in my vision.
HOLD IT TIGHTER.
HOLD IT TIGHTER.
WORTHLESS.
WORTHLESS.
WORTHLESS!
I let go. I can't hold the bag any longer. It loosens from my neck and my lungs fill with air.

No!

Crazed, I fling it off me, stand, and nearly pass out. I rush to the wall and consider pounding my head against it until my skull cracks open, but I don't do it. Instead I run into my bedroom, crouch in the corner, and sob.

I want to die.

I am so tired.

Out of the darkness, the moonlight shines through my bedroom window, casting a cool glow on the carpet, and it feels wrong. I don't deserve light. I scramble to rip the covers off my bed and hang them over the window until all the light disappears and my room is completely blacked out.

My desperation sickens me. I have no right taking up space in this world. If there really is a God, and if He's merciful like everyone says He is, then I hope He'll show mercy on me tomorrow and not let me fail.

I cannot fail.

An unsuccessful suicide attempt would be the worst possible thing that could ever happen. Worse than life. Worse than death. Worse than *anything*.

Before I can shake the thought, another disturbing image pops in my head. I see myself pulling the trigger, the shot entering my skull, but I don't die. I survive. There's blood and brain matter splattered all around me. My face is disfigured. I'm still breathing. I'm still aware. I still feel *everything*. The idea twists me up into knots, and I know this is the end for me. I'm alone. More alone than I've ever felt before.

Through the remainder of the night I lie on my bedroom floor, naked and worn thin, staring at the ceiling, waiting for morning to come.

check on your **happy** friends

26
The Day

I didn't sleep a wink. I haven't moved. I haven't closed my eyes. My stomach is twisting in knots—empty. There's no more food in my apartment, but even if there was, I don't need it now.

The taste of stale vomit burns my throat.

I'm exhausted.

Starving.

Thirsty.

Unrelenting pain pounding in my head.

Too tired to breathe.

Just staring at the ceiling in my darkened room.

Air in. Air out. My chest rises and falls against my will.

It's Friday, October 17th, 6:00 in the morning. Today is the day. In just five hours I'll load the last of my belongings, drive to the hotel, and end my life.

I ask myself if I can live for just one more day.

No, I can't.

Can I live for Tommy?

No.

Mama Sharon?

No.

Can I live for Sammie? Sweet, sweet Sammie bear?

No, I can't. Not even for Sammie. Thinking of him hurts and makes me feel hollow.

I'm so tired.

I'm so, so desperately tired.

A loud knock on the door startles me.

My dead heart slams in my chest. I hold my breath, lying completely still. If I'm quiet, hopefully whoever is at the door will leave.

They knock again. Who could it be? Who would show up at my apartment at this hour?

Three more loud knocks rattle the walls.

Could it be the police? Did someone find out?

Trying not to panic, I drape a blanket around my shoulders, put my ear to the door, and whisper, "Yes? Who is it?"

They knock again—even louder this time.

My stomach is churning into knots.

"Please go away!" I yell, but the knocking continues.

"Open the door, Dani! It's me!"

All the air is sucked from the room, and I'm frozen in place.

I'm in complete shock.

This is my worst nightmare.

It's Tommy.

What is he doing here?

My heart is pounding so hard in my chest I can feel it throughout my entire body. I scan the room frantically, looking for anything I don't want him to see.

Why is he here?

I'm so confused.

Trying to stay calm, I speak through the door. "It's six in the morning! What do you need?"

"Just open the door, Dani, PLEASE! It's an emergency!"

I don't want to, but I know he won't leave until I open it. It takes all my energy just to unlock the bolt and turn the knob.

Tommy looks crazed, but I can see the relief on his face as he

chapter 26: The Day

pulls me in and hugs me tightly. It catches me off guard. I just stand there wrapped in my blanket with my arms dangling to my sides. I feel detached. This cannot be happening right now.

I am so tired.

Everything hurts.

I feel sick.

My head is in splitting agony.

"Dani," he says softly, still holding me.

I cough. "What?"

He hugs me tighter. He's crying.

I shut my eyes against the pounding in my brain.

This *can't* be happening.

Tommy finally releases me from his grip and looks me in the eyes. "Listen, Dani, I will never ask you for anything again, I promise, but I need you to get dressed and come with me. You don't even need your purse or phone, just come with me. Right now! PLEASE!"

Something about the desperateness in his voice gets to me. He's literally pleading. I try to think this through—I was not expecting this, but he's my best friend, and it's the least I can do, because he doesn't know it yet, but this will be the last time we see each other.

My voice shakes. "Give me a minute. I'll meet you downstairs."

He hesitates, as if he doesn't believe me.

"Tommy, I'll be right there. I promise! Now go!"

I don't wait for a response before closing the door, but just as quickly as I try to shut it, he sticks his foot out, propping it open.

"What the hell, Tommy? I said I need a minute!"

"Sorry, it can't wait. I need you to come with me right now."

I stare at him, my mind spinning.

Why is he doing this? Why???

I hate him!

I try to think.

Focus.

Do something!

Ok. Tommy just complicated my day, but I can still make it back in time. It's okay. Nothing needs to change. I'll just go do whatever this is and get right back.

"I need to use the bathroom," I say, gathering some clothes.

He nods. "Okay, but please be quick and do not lock the door."

I don't bother responding. What is he doing? Why shouldn't I lock the door? Nothing makes sense!

I close the door and lean on the vanity, still squinting against the brightness and my throbbing headache.

I'm shocked at my reflection.

My skin is pale, my hair is a greasy mess, and I haven't showered or brushed my teeth in days. The bags under my eyes are as deep and dark as gutters. I look worse than awful, but I don't have the energy to care anymore.

I drink from the faucet, get dressed, slide my feet into tennis shoes, and open the door. Tommy is right there waiting with my black hoodie draped over his shoulder. He hugs me tight, then takes my hand and leads me out the door.

This isn't like him. I ask, "Where are we going? Why are you acting this way?"

"Just because. You'll see." He leads me out to the parking lot, opens the passenger door of his truck, helps me inside and buckles me in as if I'm a child.

A moment later, he jumps in the driver's side, slams his door shut, and takes off like we just robbed a bank. My eyes stay glued on him, trying to figure out what's happening, and what in the world he could need me for.

"Where are we going, Tommy? What is it? What's happened?" My words come out loud and frantic, because I AM frantic!

Tommy keeps his eyes on the road. I've never seen him like this, and I don't know what to make of it.

chapter 26: The Day

"I just need you. That's all. Just be with me and stop asking questions."

"Tommy! It's six in the morning and I have plans today! I need to know what's going on!" I'm screaming at this point, and I don't mean to, but I feel out of control—everything feels out of control.

Tommy keeps driving and doesn't say a word.

I swallow my anger and let it sit in the pit of my stomach for the rest of the drive.

Thirty long minutes later, he pulls off the highway and parks on a dirt road. Glad to get whatever this is over with, I open the door, pull my body out of his truck, and look around. We're out of the city limits, standing at the bottom of a mountain full of pine trees. It's still dark, but I can see a glimmer of light shining through the branches. The air is crisp and smells fresh and woodsy. I love the smell, and wonder why I haven't spent more time in nature. Why haven't I spent more time in the mountains? Regret falls on top of the anger and simmers inside me.

Tommy is scrambling, trying to unload things out of the back of his truck. He has two backpacks and an ice chest. Has he lost his mind?

"Okay," I say, "I've been quiet for most of the drive, and I'm sorry for screaming at you, but I don't understand what you're doing or where we're going, and your timing is *not* good, Tommy. This is not a good day for this. Now, tell me what's happening!"

He turns to me, calm, and holds out a headlamp. "Dani, you're stuck with me now, so for once in your life, can you please just follow along and trust me?"

I put it on. I don't have the strength to fight him, so when he starts hiking up the trail, I fall in line behind him. I don't speak a word, but tears are streaming down my face. I don't understand. *I hate him for this!*

Tommy leads me up a trail that curves around the side of a mountain. It's steep, and still dark out, so I have to concentrate on my steps—my world contained to the small circle of lamplight. I am *not* in any shape to be doing this. I can feel my legs growing more and more tired, and my breathing is labored. Other than mine and Tommy's footsteps, it's completely quiet.

As if sensing my discomfort, Tommy looks back. "We're almost there, stay with me."

Just when I think my legs might give out completely, we reach a clearing, and I realize we're almost at the top of the mountain. We step close to the edge, and I gasp at the view. Soft patches of grass, wildflowers, and moss-covered boulders of every shape and size cover the ground. It feels secret, as if we just stumbled on a hidden oasis in the middle of the woods.

"Come on, Dani," Tommy says. "We're almost there, but we've got to hurry!"

I take his outstretched hand and try to keep up as he climbs to the highest boulder. He throws the backpacks up to the top, one by one, then asks me to help with the ice chest. We struggle, but we make it to the top. Tommy points for me to sit down. I sit, and I cry. Whatever this is, I want it to be over.

"Dani, look!" Tommy shouts.

I follow his gaze. Dawn is breaking, and with it an explosion of color paints the sky in shades of red, pink, and orange. It's breathtaking. I've never seen anything like it before.

We sit in silence, gazing up at the brilliant colors surrounding us. Within minutes, the vibrant shades fade into blues and purples, and then, like a grand finale, the sun breaks through the clouds, and the sky turns into a soft, hazy blue. It all happened within minutes.

We watch for what seems like forever until I clear my throat to break the silence and glance over at Tommy. "You kidnapped me to watch the sunrise?"

"Yes," he says, still looking up.

"Okay..." I'm confused. "I just don't understand what's going on.

chapter 26: The Day

Please, tell me!" My voice sounds desperate, and I can't stop the tears.

We sit quietly for a few minutes until the clouds disappear completely and the sky turns a beautiful grayish blue.

Finally, Tommy turns to face me. "Dani, please be still and just listen, okay?"

I'm bracing myself for something big, but I have no idea what it could be. Whatever it is, he'll have to figure it out on his own. I'm not involved in anything anymore.

He kneels in front of me and takes my hands, his eyes pleading with me in a way that scares me.

"Danielle Vivian Lee," he says, "I want you to know that I see you. I *know* you."

His voice is filled with emotion, and I wonder where this is going. I'm so tired and confused.

"You are my best friend. You say you're five foot seven, but I think you're closer to five six. Your birthday is June tenth. I know that purple is your favorite color, that you love reality tv shows, and sometimes you eat cupcakes for dinner. Your favorite flower is a yellow rose, you detest mayo and make your tuna with mustard, and you're basically addicted to coffee. You're a pescatarian, but occasionally you'll eat a real burger with me, and I love that about you. All the guys adore you, but you won't give anyone a chance and I don't understand why. You know more about plants than anyone in the world, and your face lights up when you talk about them. And even though I know you went through hell as a kid, up until early this morning, I thought you were one of the happiest, most confident people I have ever known."

He takes a breath. "But then I read my letter. And before you get upset with me, I read it by accident. It was in our shared computer file and my name was on the subject line, so of *course* I read it, and as I did, I realized I wasn't supposed to see it until tomorrow."

He pauses, and I stare at him, the blood slowly draining from my face.

"And today, when I came to your apartment, I saw it for the first time. The darkness you've been hiding—it was there, covering your face, and I need you to know there's still hope, and you don't have to live this way." He squeezes my hands. "Listen to me. If you ended it today, I would be crushed, and for the rest of my life I would beat myself up for not doing more. I love you so much, Dani, but you don't feel my love, because if you did, I think it would be enough for you to keep trying. And there's someone who loves you even more than I do. I've told you over and over, and it's true. Jesus loves you—He really does. I didn't know what to do after I read your letter, so I prayed about it, then jumped in my truck and raced over to get you, and I just praise God that I was in time, because I don't know what I would have done if it was too late."

He's looking in my eyes like he can see to my soul. "You've been through some things you never talk about, and I know you suffered terribly as a child. I'm just so sorry you felt you couldn't talk to me about it. I want you to know that *everyone* who meets you loves you. *I* love you. You are so precious to me! I need you. The world needs you. And I thought if I could convince you to come up here with me and watch something as beautiful as the sunrise, that maybe, just maybe, you would stay with me today and cancel your suicide plans, because I want you to live."

We sit, staring at each other, his last sentence hanging in the air with the weight of a grenade ready to explode.

27
There's Still Time

Tommy stops talking. He's out of breath, and tears are streaming down his face. I just sit and stare at him, speechless.

Now I understand what this is all about. He's trying to save me.

I feel weighted down, as if I can't move, so I sit and try to absorb what's happening. I have no idea what to say or do, so I do nothing at all. Soon, the tears start falling, and within seconds, I'm sobbing—my body limp and helpless. Tommy takes me in his arms, and I let myself go. I lean into his chest and weep. I weep until I have nothing left, and he just holds me close—so close I can hear his heartbeat. Finally, I blow my nose on the tissue he hands me, and I try to compose myself. I stare at the tissue, keeping my focus fixed on it, terrified to look up. I fold it in half, over and over, until it's a soggy little square. I don't have any words to respond to him. I mean, what do you say to someone who read your suicide note a *day early*?

He was supposed to read his letter tomorrow, after I was already gone.

We sit in silence until Tommy jumps to his feet as if he knows what should happen next. He grabs everything off the boulder, takes it to the clearing, spreads out the blanket, and bundles my sweatshirt into a makeshift pillow. He opens the ice chest, then gestures for me to come over.

I don't know if I have the energy to move, but somehow, I make it to the blanket and plop down. Tommy has a plate ready for me with strawberries, blueberries, a banana, and the top of a blueberry muffin.

I feel like I'm in some sort of alternate world where everything is happening in slow motion.

I look at the plate, and back at Tommy. "You brought my favorites? Why would you do that? And where's the bottom of the muffin?"

Tommy's eyes are red and puffy like mine, but he manages a smile. "I brought you food because you need to eat. I skipped dinner last night, and my stomach was growling on the way to pick you up this morning, so I ate the bottom half of the muffin. I know you like the tops best anyway. Now eat."

It feels weird to be talking about food at a time like this, and it strikes me as funny, but when I laugh it comes out high-pitched and hysterical, so I just cover my face with my hands and cry some more. I blow my nose again and pop a few berries into my mouth. The fresh tartness wakes me up. I devour the muffin and banana, chug down the water and orange juice he gives me, then close my eyes and take another deep breath. This isn't what I had in mind for my last meal, but it will do.

Tommy takes my empty water bottle. "Dani, you look exhausted. Why don't you lie down on the blanket for a little bit? Let's just take a breather, okay?"

I do as he says, lying on my back with my head resting on my sweatshirt, until a sudden wave of panic runs through me and I bolt upright. "What time is it?"

Tommy looks at his watch. "It's only 9:00," he says calmly. "You're fine."

I relax a bit, knowing I still have time. I settle onto the blanket, close my eyes for just a second, and let the sun warm my skin.

28
Too Late

I wake slowly, breathing steadily. My eyes flicker at the sun and I close them again, trying to adjust to the light. I stretch and roll over to my side, allowing myself time to wake completely. I rest for a bit longer, then squint to see blades of grass and wildflowers swaying in the breeze. Disoriented, I sit up and look around until I spot Tommy, who is pacing like a madman.

He sees me stirring, hurries over, and kneels next to me. "How are you feeling?" he asks, his voice gentle, like he's speaking to a child.

I yawn and stretch again. "I don't know. Was I asleep?"

He laughs. "Dani, you've been asleep for four hours."

My eyes widen as I look at his watch.

He follows my gaze. "I know it's later than you want it to be, but we have more to talk about, and I think if there's ever a time that you should change your plans, it's right now."

I lie back down, pulling my knees up to my chest, and cry, quietly this time. I feel so empty. I can't believe I missed it. How could this have happened? I was so careful with all my plans, down to every last detail, and then Tommy showed up and ruined everything. I feel defeated, like a total failure.

"Tommy, you don't understand what it's like for me. I can't live this way anymore."

He sighs. "You're right, I don't understand completely, but I do

chapter 28: Too Late

know you can't go on like this. Nobody could. There's a way, Dani. There is more for you. There's so much more for you. There's hope for a better way to live, and you deserve something better. I love you, Dani, and Jesus loves you too."

Tommy is desperate to save me, but I don't need saving. It's too late for that. His intentions are pure, but I didn't ask for any of this, and now my plans are ruined.

If I could, I would sit in the sun and eat berries with the sweet smell of pine trees, wildflowers, and happiness, but we can't stay this way forever. Yes, the sunrise *was* beautiful, but eventually the sun sets, night falls, and darkness comes.

I cannot handle the dark.

Tommy is still talking, but I can't hear him anymore. I close my eyes and take deep breaths, trying to drown out the voices screaming in my head.

The day is not over yet.

I'll figure it out.

I still have time.

One Year Later ...

29
Me and Tizzy

The alarm blares like a trumpet, jolting me awake from a deep and peaceful night's sleep. With eyes still closed, I fumble around until I find the snooze button and tap it. Tizzy is purring softly in my ear as I roll over, giving myself just a few more minutes under the covers. Tizzy is my sweet kitty—an orange tabby that I rescued from the local animal shelter. She was scheduled to be euthanized, but I saved her just in time, and in some ways, she saved me too. Now we're inseparable. She would love for me to stay cozied up with her in bed, but I can't today. I have plans.

Still sleepy, I shuffle into the kitchen and stumble over one of Sammie's toys. I've been picking him up once a week so we can spend time together, and now my place is full of his things. I don't worry about the mess; I welcome it. I treasure the sweet chaos he brings into my life. Days with Sammie are some of my favorites.

My home isn't perfect, but it doesn't need to be. Once I surrendered my need for order and control, I began to notice things—Sammie's tiny handprints on the sliding glass door, crumbs on the kitchen counter, coffee rings on my new dining room table—these aren't messes to clean up; they're signs of life. Evidence of love and moments shared. Sweet reminders that I'm alive. I'm still here. I belong.

While the kettle warms, I stretch and sip on lemon water, easing into the quiet rhythm of the morning. Tizzy purrs and weaves herself around my ankles, her tail flicking against my legs.

"Okay, Tizzy Tiz, let me get you some fresh water and breakfast."

Tizzy meows her approval and trots over to her bowl, happy to be eating earlier than usual. As she nibbles her food, I sip on my tea, then head to the bathroom for a quick shower.

Just as I'm drying off, I hear a loud knock on my front door. I freeze. You've got to be kidding me. It cannot be him already!

Before I can even tie my robe, the persistent knocking gets louder, and it doesn't stop until I open the door, and there he is. It's Tommy, grinning from ear to ear, holding a ridiculously huge bouquet of bright yellow roses.

"Good morning, daughter of the King, who loves yellow roses, blueberry muffin tops, and sunrises. Are you ready for a beautiful day?"

I laugh. "Good morning to you, weirdo best friend who has zero patience. These are gorgeous. Thank you! You're early!" I take the flowers and hold them to my nose.

"Sunrise is at 7:14, so we need to get on the road. We do *not* want to miss this! Everyone is waiting. You've got three minutes. Hurry!"

As Tommy jogs across the street, I glance out the door and see Gabe standing next to his truck, with Vanessa sitting in the back seat—she spots me and waves. I wave back, both of us smiling. Daisy and Gabe's dog, Rex, are sitting happily together safe and secured in the bed of his truck—they've become the best of friends. Parked right behind them is Papa Reg in his big SUV with Mama Sharon sitting in the passenger seat.

My heart flutters at the sweet surprise.

I didn't expect everyone to be here.

By the time I'm dressed and ready to go, they're lined up to greet me with warm smiles and hugs. I can tell they're happy to be here. I'm happy to be here too.

Tommy, who's acting as if we've got a plane to catch, yells for us to load up so we can get going. I love how important this is for him. I

chapter 29: Me and Tizzy

wouldn't have planned it, but I'm suddenly glad he did.

We're all heading to hike up the mountain and watch the sunrise, just like Tommy and I did a year ago today.

I don't remember much about that day. I remember the sky, the field of wildflowers, and the feeling of the sun on my skin, but the rest is a blur. I hadn't slept for three days, and I felt like a total zombie. Tommy has since shared that he prayed over me while I was laying there—out of it. He pleaded with God, read scripture, and tried everything he could. He was desperate for me to keep trying, but I was not in a place to hear any of it.

In my head, I had already given up, but I didn't have the strength to deal with Tommy, so I postponed my plans to end my life—or so I thought. Then Tommy did something clever. He asked, or I should say, he begged me for just one thing, and I couldn't say no. He asked me to meet him for just one more sunrise, and I agreed to give him that. He didn't know that I was still planning on ending it at that point, but because my original plans fell apart, I didn't see the harm in just one more day.

But when the next day came, he asked me for one more sunrise.

When that day ended, he asked me for another one.

Tommy took time off work, and for ten days straight, he slept on the couch in my apartment and took care of me. He made sure I ate, reminded me to shower, prayed for me, and kept my cup filled with hot lemon ginger tea. He lit candles, played soft music, read to me, and did everything he could to make sure I was comfortable. If I had a nightmare, he would console me until I fell back asleep, and each morning we went and watched the sunrise together. Some days I walked to his truck, on harder days he carried me, but we always managed to get there in time.

Tommy talked my head off the first two days, but after that he just sat with me in the quiet. Each morning, we watched the sky in complete silence, and before I knew it, my breathing was a bit easier, and I no longer dreaded going.

On the sixth day, Tommy said something that got my attention. He may have said it before, but on this particular day, I was listening. He told me I was not a burden. He said that he wanted me to live—that we would figure it out together. His words felt like a life raft. My heart shifted just a fragment, but it was enough for me to stop planning my death.

By the seventh day, I agreed to talk to someone. I don't know how Tommy pulled it off, but he connected me to a wonderful woman who was an intervention specialist. We had an online appointment, so I didn't have to leave my place. She asked questions that were uncomfortable for me to answer, but she was kind about it, and I was honest with her. Even though Tommy hadn't let me out of his sight even once, we agreed on a safety plan if I had thoughts of suicide again—who I would call, and what to do if I started feeling out of control. It was around that time that I realized I wasn't planning it anymore, but the idea was still safely tucked away in my mind as an option if I needed it. Tommy exhausted me and I was distracted, but looking back, I think that hope and a little strength were stirring inside. Tommy's prayers were working. I didn't think I really wanted to end it; I just knew I couldn't continue living the way I was living. Something had to change, and I was willing to try.

So much has changed in the past year…

My apartment held bad memories, so when I got Tizzy, we moved into a new place, and we love it. It's bright, with lots of windows and natural light. There's a small yard and a patio with two comfy chairs, a small round table, and beautiful potted plants I bought from Thrive. This home has become my sanctuary. I feel safe here.

Each morning, I meditate on God's word, read from the devotional Mama Sharon gifted me, and pray. I've found great comfort in routine and starting my days with Jesus. He is my hope and my strength.

Tommy still calls every night to check on me and make sure I'm okay. I keep telling him it's not necessary, but he insists. It turns out that day changed his life too. He said it deepened his faith and gave him conviction to help others. Now, he travels around to churches, college campuses, prisons, and special events to give his testimony and share his profound love for the Lord. He wants me to join him on stage, but I'm not one for attention like he is. I'm not ready to share my story. I'm just focusing on healing and living one day at a time.

I'm attending church—the same church Tommy and Gabe go to. I haven't been baptized yet, and I'm not sure when I will be, but months ago, on a beautiful Sunday morning after the service, there was an altar call, and I knew it was my time. Tommy walked with me up the very long aisle, and I fell to my knees at the altar. As the pastor guided me through the words, declaring Jesus as my Lord and Savior, strength came and settled softly on my heart like a breath. Afterwards I stood up—not as a victim, but as a chosen child of God. Redeemed. Freed. Made new.

Soon after being saved, I joined a small group for women struggling with trauma and mental health issues. Although it took a while for me to feel comfortable sharing, I eventually opened up, and it helped me tremendously. The power of community is extraordinary.

A young woman named Priya joined us a few months ago. She caught my attention because the dullness in her eyes concerned me. I recognized the haunted look from my own reflection. After a while, she agreed to meet me for coffee outside of the group. Each time we've met, I've asked her to meet again, and she keeps showing up. Lately, I've noticed her eyes look a bit brighter, and I think she's going to be okay. Every day I pray that she'll keep trying. I pray for her healing, and I pray that she'll never feel alone in her struggles.

Gabe and I have been in a relationship for the last four months. From the time we met, he was convinced that God had plans for us, so even when I pushed him away, he stood strong, praying and trusting in something more to come. He's a godly man. He's gentle, kind, protective, patient, funny, and for some reason, he's wild about me. He's all the things I could hope for in a partner.

Tommy adores Gabe, which is helpful, because Tommy is extremely protective over me. So much so that it's become a bit of a problem. If for some reason I don't respond to his calls or text messages right away, he panics, thinking something bad has happened to me. It's complicated—Tommy and I are so close, and we've been through *so* much that our trauma crosses over and gets tangled up together. I can separate it, but sometimes he can't. I hate that my struggle has had such an impact on him, but now that he and Vanessa are serious, I pray he'll ease up a bit and not worry so much. I can't take away his pain, but I can pray and trust that God will work it all out for our good. He always does.

I am forever grateful for everything Tommy has done for me; I don't know many people who would go to such lengths to help a friend in need. He showed up for me that day, thank God, but he didn't save my life. Jesus did. In some ways, Tommy needs me now more than I need him, but I'm here for him. Always.

Therapy has been a painful but necessary journey. I've been going weekly for six months, and I have a wonderful Christian therapist whom I've come to trust and respect. As I shared the fear and shame that have followed me since childhood—the flashes of unsettling images, sensations, and emotions—it painted a picture for her. Through slow, steady, trauma-informed therapy, she worked to connect my emotional and physical responses to neglect, physical and emotional abuse, and childhood sexual abuse. That one was *really* hard to face and accept, but it explains and makes sense of so much. I may never remember exactly what happened to me, but I'm learning that healing doesn't have to wait for answers. I can start from where I am, and maybe that's enough. My therapist assures me that I'm doing important work, sorting through the neglect and abuse I endured, so I'll keep trying my best and trusting the process.

chapter 29: Me and Tizzy

One important thing I've learned is that what happened to me as a little girl wasn't my fault. Logically, I knew I was not to blame, but the process my therapist guided me through brought me to a critical breakthrough in my healing. I needed to hear someone else say that it wasn't my fault—I *needed* to hear the words. I have no reason to feel guilt or shame about those horrible years, because I was an innocent child. I praise God for the freedom that knowledge has given me.

Another huge breakthrough for me was forgiveness. It felt impossible at first—unfair, even. But after many conversations with my therapist, many prayers and meltdowns, finally, little by little, the anger lost its grip until there was no bitterness left—just clarity. I wasn't saying what they did was okay—I know it was horribly wrong—but I was declaring that I trusted God to heal what they broke inside of me, and when I did that, my heart changed. When I finally forgave my parents, the kids who bullied me, the teachers who looked the other way, and all the people who wronged and hurt me, I felt a release, and then peace found me. Forgiveness wasn't a weakness. It was a pathway to healing. Praise be to God.

I haven't heard from my mother since she sent those hateful messages, and my father hasn't reached out once since he left. I'm grateful to have them out of my life, but there's a part of me that's sad—for them—not for me. They don't know that I'm healing, changing, and becoming better. They'll never be proud of me, or know that their daughter is making a life for herself. I can't imagine having a child and not caring about them. It's too much for me to bear, so instead of dwelling on it, I give it to the Lord and let Him carry it for me.

I finally gave it up—the endless cups of coffee and rivers of caffeine that wreaked havoc on my mind and body. I still enjoy coffee, but for the most part I drink lots of water and tea. Usually lemon ginger, but I've added other calming herbal teas to my collection. I'm eating balanced meals and cooking with fresh produce, clean proteins, and whole foods. Nourishment has become an act of care—not just survival—and my body is responding. I have energy, I sleep well, my mind is clear, and I feel healthier than I've ever felt.

I no longer feel the need to hide my hands. I've stopped destroying my cuticles and have taken up knitting instead. It keeps my fingers busy. I'm not good at it, but Tommy happily wears the lopsided scarf I made for him, so I'll keep trying, and who knows, maybe with practice I'll get better.

I began journaling daily. Once I started on the path of healing, my therapist suggested it would be a good idea, and I'm surprised how much I enjoy it. I share my feelings, write positive affirmations, record random thoughts, and copy scripture to battle the darkness when it tries to creep in, but mostly I keep track of adventures. For instance, in the last year, I've watched 87 sunrises and 54 sunsets—some with Tommy, some with Gabe, but mostly just me and Tizzy. I've walked on the sand at three different beaches, hiked at Mammoth Lake, and I've spent a lot of time in nature. I broke out in an awful rash from poison oak, volunteered at an animal shelter, fished once but didn't care for it, built a campfire, fell asleep gazing at the stars, read eight books, and ran a 5k. In other words, I've started living.

I can't believe I would have missed all this.

There are tough days, setbacks, moments of doubt, and triggers that cause me to stumble, but with each struggle comes a deeper understanding, and a new, healthier way of coping. And when dark thoughts swirl around in my mind, I recognize that they are just that—thoughts. They have no power over me. I don't believe the lies anymore.

It's been a grueling battle, but I'll keep fighting. Healing is slow, but it's happening. I can feel it. Small steps. Progress. Getting better. These things take time.

Somehow, Rex, Daisy, and the six of us manage to reach the top of the mountain just in time to watch the sunrise. Papa Reg is out of breath and declaring he would only do this for me. God bless his big, beautiful heart. Vanessa was kind enough to pack coffee, tea, juice,

chapter 29: Me and Tizzy

fruit, and the blueberry muffin tops that I'm sure Tommy insisted on bringing.

We all sit quietly, sip our drinks, nibble on breakfast, and watch as the dawn breaks into a stunning tapestry on the horizon. Each sunrise is beautifully unique, and today's is a doozy.

I would have missed this.

I WOULD HAVE MISSED THIS!

Sitting up here on the mountain, everything seems clear. It occurs to me that it's not by chance that I met these friends. It was God, orchestrating our paths and weaving them together as part of His divine plan. I can't imagine where I would be without them. Gratitude washes over me as I think of God's love. He alone knows the intimate parts of my heart and exactly who and what I need in my life.

Once the sun is up and our bellies are full, we decide it's time to go. As we start back down the trail, Tommy announces that we'll be meeting in this same spot, on this same day, every year from now on. Everyone agrees to come, except for Papa Reg, who is undecided. He grumbles something about being too old to hike up a blasted hill, and it makes us all laugh.

My mood is surprisingly light. I was prepared for a rollercoaster of emotions, but that's not what happened. There were some tears, but mostly it felt like a celebration. The joy catches me by surprise, and a steadiness settles inside of me. It feels like courage.

I truly am so grateful to be alive.

Gabe takes my hand. Our fingers interlace as we walk behind the others, Rex and Daisy trotting beside us. I smile, feeling loved. They didn't have to show up today, but they did. They showed up *for me!*

These are my people. My family. This is where I belong.

check on your **happy** friends

30

Jesus Loves Me

I'm late. Beyond late. It's-almost-over kind of late, but at least I made it.

The heavy doors creak behind me as I step into the auditorium packed full of people. I'm shocked. I didn't expect this big of a turnout. The chairs are filled, and the standing-room-only crowd is leaning on every wall and doorway, taking up all the available space. I squeeze past rows of people as quietly as possible, trying hard not to be noticed as I search for a spot, and then I see him—Gabe is standing in the far corner of the room. Our eyes meet, and he smiles as if I'm his favorite person. I smile back, realizing he's fast becoming one of mine. Mama Sharon's face lights up when she sees me, and Papa Reg smiles affectionately as they wave me over to join them. Gracie, looking beautiful and confident, is standing next to Mama Sharon. She finally got her driver's license and decided to join us today. Gracie has become a strong young lady of faith, and I am so proud of her. How wonderful it is to have loved ones who look for me expectantly. It's a new feeling—one that I find deeply comforting.

There's a tangible buzz of energy in the air, but other than an occasional cough or the cooing of a sweet baby resting in its mother's arms, the room is silent as Tommy delivers his testimony. I watch my lifelong friend pouring his heart out, and I can't help but feel a sense of pride—we've come a long way together.

Thank you, God, for my best friend!

Tommy looks sharp in his dark jeans and tailored, white-collared shirt. I'm surprised he didn't pull his hair back, but it's a nice change to see his brown waves falling loosely to his shoulders. There's an ease and confidence about him on stage—as if he was born for this.

He spots me in the crowd as I'm navigating my way over to Gabe, and immediately stops speaking. He literally stops his presentation! A huge grin spreads wide across his face as he waves to me excitedly, like a little kid in a school play whose parents just walked in.

I'm mortified! What is he doing?

I shake my head and mouth the word, "stop," but he doesn't stop.

"Hey, really quick, that girl right there." Tommy points to me, and every head turns in my direction. "The one with dark curly hair wearing gray sweats who just walked in, do you see her? She's my best friend for life. Her name is Dani. Everybody, wave to Dani and make her feel welcome!"

Heat rises to my face as all eyes are on me. I stop, smile, and wave back in my awkward little parade of one.

After a collective chuckle, Tommy draws them back in and continues. Thank goodness!

Grateful to be out of the spotlight, I make my way across the room to my people. As I scoot past Mama Sharon and Papa Reg, Gabe reaches for my hand and gently guides me in front of him so I have a perfect view of the stage. He wraps his arms protectively around my waist, and it anchors me. I feel safe with Gabe. With him, my heart can rest.

Settled now, I turn all my attention to Tommy, who has captivated the room.

"Friends," he says, "thank you for coming today and listening to my testimony. I pray it blessed you. Before I close, I'd like to share just a few more things."

He takes a deep breath and sets his notes aside, his eyes searching the crowd.

"Listen, if you take anything away from what you've heard today, let it be this: God doesn't love you out of obligation. He doesn't care about your past or the things you've done. He does not wish you were different. He loves you as you are in this very moment, right here, right now."

I'm holding my breath so I don't burst into tears. I am so proud of him!

"Let me tell you something that I want you to remember every single morning before your feet even touch the floor. Our Lord and Savior Jesus Christ, the Prince of Peace, the King of Kings, delights in you." His voice is booming with conviction.

"I'll say it again. *Our Lord and Savior Jesus Christ*"—he pauses, and I can see his eyes sparkling from where I'm standing—"*the Prince of Peace, the King of Kings, DELIGHTS IN YOU!*"

The crowd rustles with energy. Shouts of "Amen," "Praise Jesus," and "Preach!" ring out. I see people wiping their eyes and hugging each other, and I get the feeling that something deep and meaningful is taking root in this very moment.

Tommy pauses, his face flushed, but I can tell he's not done yet.

"Jesus loves you," he says, his voice much quieter. "Please remember that. And finally, I want to remind you to check on your friends who are struggling. Depression, anxiety, trauma, mental illness, and addiction are very real. I've shared a lot about those struggles today—it's a dark and lonely journey no one should walk alone. We need to pray hard and show up for each other as best we can."

He pauses again, scanning the room until he finds me. His eyes lock on mine. "So, yes, be sure to check on those who are struggling, but check on your happy friends too. You know the ones I'm talking about. The folks who are always smiling and positive and going out of their way for others. The peppy, loving, radiant ones who bring sunshine wherever they go. We all know them, right?"

Tommy's voice is light and easy, but I can feel momentum building—

he's going somewhere with this, and I'm not sure I'm prepared to hear it.

"These are the people who breathe life into the world. We don't worry about them. Why should we? It seems as if they have it all figured out!"

He rolls his shoulders and takes a deep breath, as if he's collecting himself.

"I'm not one of those people. I'm an open book. I share my worries and struggles openly—I don't know if that's good or bad, it just is. All my adult life, people have rallied around me, loving and supporting me when I've needed it, and I've accepted their help. Gladly! I didn't care about being vulnerable. I was screaming about my pain as loud as I could, hoping everyone could hear me."

He presses his lips tightly together, and now I'm rooting for him. *It's okay. It's okay! Say it, Tommy. Somebody here needs to hear this!*

He clears his throat, squares his shoulders, and I can almost see the courage rising in his chest.

"But that is not the case for everyone. Many suffer in silence. They wear a mask for the world, and beneath that mask they're slipping. They scream without making a sound. They isolate themselves, live in torment, and continue to show up as if they're perfectly fine, but they're not. It may be just one out of dozens of your friends who seems okay but isn't. We need to check on them. We must pray and let Christ lead us. That one time you follow a nudge and check on a friend might end up being the one thing that gives them enough strength to keep trying. It might change their life, and I promise it will change yours. So please, check on the broken and the needy, but check on your happy friends too, because you never know what they might be going through."

Heads nod all through the audience.

"Thank you for having me here today. I am blessed because of it. Love y'all, and Jesus loves you too!"

chapter 30: Jesus Loves Me

With his hands raised high like he just kicked a game-winning field goal, Tommy jumps off the stage and heads in my direction. Everyone rises from their seats in a thunderous applause, but he's oblivious to the attention. He's becoming somewhat of a big deal around here and is doing all he can to help others. Tommy is a gifted and relatable speaker, and I know this is just the beginning for him.

Tommy moves quickly through the crowd—smiling, shaking hands, and hugging folks—but he keeps his eyes on me. He reaches our group, hugs Gabe and Mama Sharon, vigorously shakes hands with Papa Reg, gives Gracie a high five, and I stand back and watch—taking it all in.

The smiles, joy, laughter, and love in this room flood my heart. I'm so grateful to be alive and a part of this beautiful thing that's happening—whatever it is!

I would have missed this—all of this!

Papa Reg, Mama Sharon, and Gracie all say their goodbyes, and I notice Gabe gathering his things. He leans in close and whispers, "I'm going to head to the parking lot and give you and Tommy a moment. Take your time, I'll be waiting. Love you."

I simply nod, and even though I haven't said the words out loud yet, my heart is shouting them from the highest mountain… *I love you, Gabe. I love you too!*

I wait and watch for Tommy until he finally finds his way to me.

Now it's just the two of us, facing each other.

"Hi," he says, then spins around in front of me. "Like the fit? I thought this was a good choice for today."

"Hi!" I say back. "Yes. I noticed right away. Excellent choice. You did great up there. That was a lot!"

He exhales slowly, scanning the room. "You're telling me. I barely made it through."

"You were magnificent. I am SO proud of you."

"Really?" He looks at me with hope glistening in his eyes.

"Yes. Absolutely. You were incredible."

There's a shift in his expression. "I was worried because you didn't text me back yesterday. You weren't here, and I was stressed that you weren't going to make it. Are you good? Is everything okay?"

I step toward him, lay my hands on his shoulders, and look him directly in the eyes, because I need him to hear this. "I had a bad day yesterday, but it was just that—a bad day. I'm allowed to have those sometimes. Everyone does. We all struggle. But a bad day does not equal a bad life! Do you understand me? I'm better today. I'm really good, actually. I promise."

Relief washes over his face, and his grin is back. "When are you going to join me up there and give *your* testimony?"

"Not any time soon. I'm not ready," I say, honestly, knowing I'm not even close.

Tommy's eyes are shining. "I can't wait for that day! Oh, and listen, I'm totally appreciating this new you, but an hour late, Dani? And you're wearing sweats to my big event? What is even happening?"

I consider his words and look down at my comfy clothes. "Hmmm. It didn't occur to me how I should dress because I was rushing to get here before I missed the whole thing. I was taking a leisurely afternoon nap with Tizzy and lost track of time." I chuckle, amused with myself because it's unheard of that I would be napping lazily on a Saturday afternoon, but it's the absolute wonderful truth.

We burst into laughter like we always do. We've laughed together, like this, for years, but things are different now. I love how much we've changed.

Tommy's expression shifts again, suddenly serious. "Do you think we're going to be okay?"

I'm not surprised by his question. Underneath all the charm and confidence still lurks the scared little boy he once was. The one who sat with me in the treehouse when we were both trying to survive in a world that was scary and hurtful. We were so young and confused, and it was a horrible time, but we had each other,

chapter 30: Jesus Loves Me

and that was enough to get us through.

We will *always* have each other.

I smile, wipe the unexpected tears spilling from my eyes, and answer without hesitation, my heart light and full, "I *know* we are going to be okay. I can feel it. We just need to trust the Lord, and take it one day at a time, okay?"

Tommy nods in agreement and hugs me. "Trust the Lord. One day at a time. That's it! That's the golden nugget I needed from you. Thanks, Dani. I'm so glad you came. Love you."

"Love you too," I say as I watch him walk toward Vanessa, who is all smiles as she's waiting for him. He reaches for her hand, and just before they walk out the door, I call to him, "Hey, Tommy!"

He spins around, his eyes meeting mine.

"Jesus loves you!" I yell as loud as I can, tears streaming down my face as I smile at my best friend who led me to my Savior.

Tommy's smile is bigger than mine. "*Jesus loves YOU, Danielle Vivian Lee!*" he bellows back, and I believe it with all my heart.

Before leaving, I take a few minutes to myself and notice the quiet. Not just the quiet in the almost empty auditorium, but the quiet in my head. My mind is peaceful, and I can't help but wonder what happened to the inner voice that used to scream lies at me for all those years. Once I gave my life to Christ and declared Him as my Lord and Savior, the voice quieted down and eventually disappeared completely. Then a miracle happened, and that's when I knew, without even a flicker of doubt, that Jesus really is real.

Slowly, He washed it all away—the shame, guilt, fear, and torment that held me captive for so long. He washed it away and made me new. Christ has given me the most precious gift—my miracle—a second chance at a new life in Him.

I'm still learning and growing and becoming who God intended me to be, but like Tommy said, Jesus loves me just as I am, and that is enough. Christ has filled the empty places of my heart and mended all the broken parts, and for the first time ever, I feel free.

The door creaks and gets my attention. It's Gabe, with an easy smile on his face.

"I hate to rush you, but we're the last ones here and they're waiting on us to lock up. You ready, sunshine?"

Goodness. I love *it* when he calls me that.

"I'm ready!" I say cheerfully, and I mean it.

I *am* ready.

I'm ready for love, for life, for a future, and for whatever God has planned for me. There will still be hard times and suffering, and days when my faith wears thin, but through it all Christ remains faithful; He will never leave or forsake me.

The love and acceptance I was so desperate for as a child, I have finally found in my heavenly Father. In Him I am loved. I am worthy. I am free to live as the real me, Danielle Vivian Lee, a grown woman who is better, not because the pain is gone, but because I've experienced the rescuing grace of my Savior, and nothing, not even the darkness of my past, can take that from me.

Tommy said it a million times, but I didn't understand the weight of his words back then like I do now. Jesus really does love me...*every day, all the time, everywhere!*

the end

check on your **happy** friends

Also By Kathryn Mae Inman

Counting Spoons: A Memoir of Heroin, Heartache, and Hope

Kathryn Mae Inman exposes her pain and her love for Jesus in her debut book, Counting Spoons, a Memoir of Heroin, Heartache, and Hope. When addiction took hold of her youngest son, she thought it was the end. But it was actually the beginning. She cried out to a God she did not know and He answered. Families struggling in addiction will find hope in this story. Counting Spoons is about lies, crime, addiction, desperate love, and a miraculous rescue. It reveals the power of redeeming grace and the joy of a comeback.

www.kathrynminman.com

About the Author

Kathryn Inman is the author of two published books and a passionate storyteller who writes from the heart. She's excited to see what God has planned next as she continues her mission to shed light on the hidden battles people face. Soon, Kathryn and husband Darwin will be building their forever home in Escalon, California—a peaceful nine acre ranch they will fill with horses, a couple dogs, fruit trees, a vegetable garden, and a spacious porch made for watching sunsets. At its heart will be a cozy mudroom, ready to welcome their six sweet grand-babes, boots, hats, and all.

A Message from Kathryn

Thank you so much for reading *Check on Your Happy Friends*. If you enjoyed it, please consider leaving a review and recommending it to a friend. Visit my website to stay connected, and let me know if I can pray for you—I would be honored.

Email: kathryninmanfaith@gmail.com

Website: www.kathrynminman.com

Before You Go

If you've made it to this page, thank you for walking this journey and reading *Check on Your Happy Friends*. I am so grateful.

While this story was fictional, the struggles and suffering it touches on are tragically real. Trauma, depression, anxiety, and the darkness of suicidal thoughts are struggles many carry in silence. If that's you, or someone you know, you are not alone. You matter. You are fearfully and wonderfully made, and the world is a better place with you in it.

Healing is possible, though it rarely follows a straight line. It takes time, honesty, support, community, professional help, and sometimes crisis intervention. I pray that you will seek Christ and let His light guide you on the path that brings healing, peace, and freedom to your life.

Resources

If you are in crisis or just need someone to talk to, please reach out. There are people who care and are ready to listen:

United States:

- 988 Suicide & Crisis Lifeline:

  Call or text 988 or visit https://988lifeline.org
- Crisis Text Line:

  Text HOME to 741741 for free, 24/7 support

Other Countries:

- Visit https://www.befrienders.org to find support services near you.

What I've Learned Along the Way ...

Beyond the phone numbers and websites, I wanted to share information I gathered as I researched—signs to look for, suggestions, and small ways to help that might make a big difference.

What to Watch For

- Pulling away from loved ones or usual routines.
- Talking or joking about not wanting to be here.
- Won't commit to future plans.
- Unexplained excitement or calm after deep distress.
- Sudden changes in mood, sleep, appetite, or personal hygiene.
- Giving away cherished items or making final arrangements.

Suggestions on What to Say

- "You're not alone. I'm here with you."
- "You matter. Your life matters."
- "I believe in you."
- "Let's walk through this together."
- "It's okay to feel this way—let's find help, together."

Suggestions on What You Should Not Say

- "You just need to pray more." (Faith matters, but pain is real.)
- "It's not that bad."
- "You'll get over it eventually."
- "Just go for a walk. Happiness is a choice. Others have it worse."
- Avoid any statements that dismiss or minimize their struggle.

What Might Help

- Listening without trying to fix everything.
- Showing up consistently—even when words are few.
- Don't assume someone is okay just because they seem happy or busy. "Smiling Depression" is not an official diagnosis, but it's a widely used term for people who appear outwardly happy and functional, but are suffering on the inside.
- Normalize emotional conversations—create space for people to share how they really feel without judgment.
- Encouraging professional help with compassion.
- Praying over them and pointing gently to the hope of Christ.

A Message From the Editor

Do you know someone who is struggling with suicidal thoughts?

Perhaps this is a better question: If someone in your life is struggling, would they come to you for help?

Years ago, God broke my heart for survivors of sexual assault through an unexpected friendship with one. My eyes were opened to a world of trauma and pain that I was largely unaware of. I became an ally, and here's something I've found in the time I've been involved in advocacy: When you share your thoughts, views, and beliefs on issues like trauma or suicide, you may not know who you're reaching, but people are listening. They're evaluating whether it's safe to confide in you. When you speak up with support and encouragement, conversations follow. It rarely goes the other way around.

That person in your life who is barely holding on behind the mask they put on for the world...they're listening to the things you say. They hear the opinions you express. They see what you post on social media. Are you showing them that you care, that you understand, and that you would receive them with empathy and compassion—without the shame and judgement they fear?

Supporting those struggling with suicidal thoughts is a proactive pursuit. I'll share a brief story for an example:

She walks aimlessly toward the railroad tracks. It's the place she's always been drawn to at times like this, but tonight is different. Tonight, she won't stop herself. She won't turn back. She plans to end her life.

If you look at her posts on social media, you'll see an intelligent, accomplished, socially active, compassionate, caring, beautiful young woman with a dazzling smile, and you might assume that she's got it all together.

But those posts don't show her depression. They don't show the anxiety that torments her. They don't show how she's harmed herself.

They don't show the trauma she carries from a violent rape, and they don't show the lack of empathy or interest from her family and friends who should care more than anyone else. "Aren't you over that yet?" is the message they convey when she tries to talk about it.

She checks her phone on the way to the tracks. There's a message. She stops and reads it…

When I met her, I knew none of her struggles. She was advocating for survivors. I didn't know her reasons; I only knew that she cared, and I doubted she would have much interest in talking to me. She seemed popular. She seemed like she had lots of friends. I assumed that she had it all together.

I was so, so wrong.

At the end of this book, Tommy encourages his audience to follow God's leading when they feel Him nudging them to check in on a friend. He says, *"It might change their life, and I promise it will change yours."*

He's right. God often works that way. I've experienced it many times. He put it on my heart to reach out to that woman, and I did. I sent a message along the lines of, "If you know the pain of this trauma, I believe you, and I'm sorry." She responded. She was a survivor. I kept writing to her, and in time, she confided in me, and I became her ally.

I didn't know this until months after that night when she was on her way to the tracks, but the message she read was one I'd sent her, and it made the difference. Jesus deserves all the credit, but my friend tells me that I saved her life. I was the first person to ever say to her, "I want you to live," and I've had the incredible privilege of encouraging her as she finds healing and hope. She's my Dani, Jesus holds her heart, and she is one of the many reasons this book is so important to me.

So, what can we take away from that?

In Matthew 22 (NIV), a religious leader asked, *"Teacher, which is the greatest commandment in the Law?"*

Jesus replied: *"'Love the Lord your God with all your heart and with all your soul and with all your mind.' This is the first and greatest commandment. And the second is like it: 'Love your neighbor as yourself.' All the Law and the Prophets hang on these two commandments."*

In John 13:34, Jesus said, *"A new command I give you: Love one another. As I have loved you, so you must love one another."*

That is our calling as Christians, and when we follow—when we go to the lost and the hurting, making them our priority, and loving them as Jesus loves us, it changes us. Jesus works in us. We feel His heart, and life is never the same.

Dani said, referring to Tommy, *"I don't know many people who would go to such lengths to help a friend in need. He showed up for me that day, thank God, but he didn't save my life. Jesus did."*

Would you go to the lengths Tommy went to? I want you to know, it's worth it! To see a life saved, hope restored, faith found or strengthened, and the healing Jesus can bring to a broken heart... It's an amazing thing to witness, and it's an amazing thing to be a part of.

Jamie Tworkowski, founder of To Write Love on Her Arms, puts it so well: *"We often ask God to show up. We pray prayers of rescue. Perhaps God would ask us to be that rescue, to be His body, to move for things that matter. He is not invisible when we come alive. I might be simple but more and more, I believe God works in love, speaks in love, is revealed in our love. … We were made to be lovers bold in broken places, pouring ourselves out again and again until we're called home."*

What will Jesus say to you when you're called home? I want to live my life and love others in such a way that I'll hear this: *"Then the righteous will answer him, 'Lord, when did we see you hungry and feed you, or thirsty and give you something to drink? When did we see you a stranger and invite you in, or needing clothes and clothe you? When did we see you sick or in prison and go to visit you?' The King will reply, 'Truly I tell you, whatever you did for one of the least of these brothers and sisters of mine, you did for me.'"* Matthew 25:37-40 (NIV)

I urge you to follow Tommy's example. Share your faith boldly, give your heart to the hurting, and if there's a Dani in your life, love them like tomorrow depends on it.

MICHAEL JAMES EMBERGER, EDITOR

www.michaeljamesemberger.com

About the Editor

Michael James Emberger is an author and advocate with a heart for survivors of trauma and abuse. His books include:

BELIEVED
a novel written to encourage survivors of sexual assault and help raise awareness about the crime.

BELIEVE HER: HOW TO BE AN ALLY TO A SURVIVOR OF SEXUAL ASSAULT WHEN YOU DON'T KNOW WHAT TO SAY
A Guidebook for Christian Men.

DEAR SURVIVOR
For my Sisters in Christ who have suffered trauma.

DAUGHTER OF THE KING
a collection of stories, wisdom, warnings, advice, encouragement, and hope from a village of women sharing what they wish their younger selves had been told.

check on your **happy** friends

Bailey & Huhn Publishing, LLC

Breathing life, hope, & freedom into the hearts of readers.

Visit us online:
www.baileyhuhnpublishing.com

Connect with us:
@BaileyHuhnPublishing

f ◎ in

Bailey & Huhn Publishing is dedicated to helping authors share stories that inspire, encourage, and bring hope.

The Spirit of the Sovereign Lord is upon me, for the Lord has anointed me to bring good news to the poor. He has sent me to comfort the brokenhearted and to proclaim that captives will be released and prisoners will be freed.

ISAIAH 61:1 (NLT)

Bailey & Huhn Publishing, LLC
Spring, Texas 77380
info@baileyhuhnpublishing.com